HIVE

'Compelling'
Emma Darwin

'Wonderfully pacy'
Broo Doherty

HIVE
APRIL DOYLE

Shortlisted for the Exeter Novel Prize 2019

The Book Guild Ltd

First published in Great Britain in 2022 by
The Book Guild Ltd
9 Priory Business Park
Wistow Road, Kibworth
Leicestershire, LE8 0RX
Freephone: 0800 999 2982
www.bookguild.co.uk
Email: info@bookguild.co.uk
Twitter: @bookguild

Grateful acknowledgement is made to Broo Doherty at DHH Literary Agency for
permission to quote from her judge's report on Hive (Exeter Novel Prize 2019)

This work is entirely fictitious and bears no resemblance to any persons living or dead.

Typeset in 11pt Baskerville

Printed and bound by CPI Group (UK) Ltd, Croydon, CR0 4YY

ISBN 978 1913913 779

British Library Cataloguing in Publication Data.
A catalogue record for this book is available from the British Library.

For the bees, and all who are working to save them

1

It was a cold March evening. Victor loaded up his lorry for an early start the next day. He would need to be on the road well before the sunrise. The hives, stacked like bricks, were covered loosely with netting. He made sure they were all safely strapped down, then went round to check again, stooping slightly, bending towards the wooden boxes, talking to them as he went along as he always did. *You can tell them anything*, his mother said, when he was little. *I do. Whisper it. They're listening.*

It was dark now. Lights were on in some of the houses, a comforting glow from behind the curtains. The housing estate had never been finished. Victor's home was at the end of a cul-de-sac where only one side of the street had been built. He rented the adjoining plot for his hives. The undeveloped land had been left to weeds and brambles – ideal for the bees – and no one could ever complain that his lorry was blocking the traffic since the road came to an abrupt end just beyond the house. Victor made one final circuit around the lorry, then he bid them goodnight and went back into the house where his wife was waiting with their two little girls. They sat together, comfortably curled on the sofa under a big blanket, his daughters' eyes wide with the importance of being allowed to stay up late. Iris stroked their hair. 'This is the last night you'll see Daddy for a while,' she said.

'There's plenty of firewood,' said Victor. 'It's all stacked inside the back gate. If the power goes off again you can bring the mattresses down to the living room, heat things over the fire…' He frowned. 'Perhaps I should bring the wood inside the house.' He half stood up to go but she held his arm.

'You fret too much,' Iris told him. 'It'll be fun, won't it, girls? Like camping.' There were deep shadows under her eyes.

Victor sat back down on the sofa and put his arms around her, around them all. He hated to leave them, but at the same time he fizzed with excitement about the days ahead, the wonder of seeing the bees at work, being a part of it. It was easier to go than to stay. Maria and Sophie quietly watched the fire dance in the grate. Victor stole glances at them, their eyelids beginning to droop in the warmth of the little living room. Their cheeks were rosy with tiredness, and their mouths were stained with the tomato sauce Iris had cooked for their evening meal. She'd made them a feast, flitting round the kitchen, using some of their precious store of pasta and tinned tomatoes. She deftly sliced the remaining stub of chorizo thinly over the top of each bowl. 'No point in saving it indefinitely,' she said. There would probably be no more. Things they had once taken for granted had disappeared from the shelves. No more tea, no more chocolate, no more bananas.

'Don't worry, Daddy,' said five-year-old Sophie, her eyes half-closed. 'The bees will look after you.' Her breath wheezed in and out.

Iris squeezed her eyes tight shut.

'They always do, sweetheart,' he said, taking Iris's hand.

Maria, two years older than her sister, looked up at him. 'Don't they ever get lost?' Her brow furrowed. 'How do they remember their way home?'

'It's in their nature,' said Victor. He smoothed Sophie's hair from her warm forehead. 'Just like I always know how to get back here, to you.'

Iris had turned her head away – Victor bent to kiss her neck.

In the morning he was awake well before the alarm went off. He would leave without waking Iris. They'd said their goodbyes the night before. But as he slid across the mattress, away from the warmth of her, she reached for him, catching hold of his T-shirt. 'Victor,' she said, her voice blurry with sleep. 'Please don't go.'

'We need the money, love.' They were scraping by as it was. Iris made a little with her web design, but without the pay his bees brought in they would be in trouble. How could they afford Sophie's medicines if he lost his job?

'What if something happens, and you're not here?'

'I'll phone you every day,' he promised.

The streetlamps outside their house had not been switched on for months, and the darkness of the early hours was complete, the moon and stars obscured by cloud. The pre-dawn air was cool, but it was not as cold as it had been. The scent of the grass rose up to meet him: the wet earth, and things growing in it. He greeted the hives before climbing into the cab and, as he always did, pressed a kiss to the photograph of his wife and daughters which was permanently tucked into the corner of the dashboard. Two and a half hours until sunrise. He checked his Satnav – there was plenty of time. The engine purred quietly into life and he pulled away from the house and headed away from the town. Driving east, towards the sunrise and the coast, towards the first of the farms. There was very little on the roads. A few lorries, heading to the ferry terminals, perhaps. A handful of private cars. People cocooned in their own little worlds.

Victor's routine was the same each year. During the quiet winter months he tended his hives and plotted his route through the farms of Kent. Then, from March, he lived like a nomad for six months, travelling from farm to farm. He moved his bees across the orchards of the High Weald and the North Downs, then to the soft fruit farms which thrived near the coast, sweeping south towards Romney Marsh and back across the Weald for fields of peas, beans, potatoes and squash. He set out his five hundred or so hives, ate with the farmhands, slept in his cab. Some years, when things were running to schedule, he was able to sneak home occasionally to see his girls and swap his dirty clothes for clean, but this year was different. He'd noticed differences in the trees – compared to the same time the previous year the blossoms on all the fruit trees were more advanced, meaning there would be less time for his bees to do their work. He would need to stay on the road until pollination was completed. He had to stay with the hives, would not leave them for even one night. He was their shepherd and their guardian. They were more than his livelihood. They were his charges, and without them – the possibility of failing crops was too difficult to think about.

Other bee farmers were in operation across the country: from Northumberland to Cornwall, from Herefordshire to Suffolk. The drop in wild insect pollinators had become so marked that the only way to ensure a decent harvest was to call on Victor or one of his colleagues. In the winter they met online to compare the conditions of the fields, the harvests, their bees. Sometimes they spoke about the decline in their own hives. Serious diseases. The possibility of colony collapse. To talk about it made it real. These conversations were stiff with tension. Victor skirted the subject warily, afraid to engage in the online discussions in case it brought bad luck. Silly to be superstitious, thought Victor, crossing his fingers just the same.

Flipping through the radio stations, searching for a distraction, he settled on a song from years ago – from the time when he'd just met Iris. A nervous evening at a cocktail bar in town. Absolutely not his thing, but he was desperate to impress her. He needn't have worried, she told him later (much later), because the very first time she saw him she'd decided he was the one. He glanced again at the photo: Iris sat with her tanned arms around Maria and Sophie, holding them tightly, defiantly, as though she could protect them from whatever was coming.

There was a barely perceptible difference in the sky now; the impenetrable darkness had softened somehow. He could just make out the cutout edges of the trees which lined the road. The line on the illuminated map on its little screen led on towards the first of the farms. The Satnav would guide him in.

Victor moved with the rhythm of the bees, and the weeks of pollination drew on. He travelled eastwards on his route towards the orchards around Tenterden and then onwards. Despite having done his rounds so many times, each year had its differences. The temperature affected the bees, and it only took a few days of bad weather to slow their progress. On those days Victor watched the rain from under the shelter of the trees and tried not to worry about getting to the next place on time.

After two or three days on a farm, depending on its size and the weather conditions, the bees had time to visit each blossom several times, ensuring pollination would be a success. Then, once all of the bees had returned to their hives for the night, Victor covered the hives with netting and loaded them back on to his lorry, leaving the farm with heartfelt thank-yous from the farmer, and promises that the payment would be transferred to his bank account.

He longed for Iris and his girls. 'You could travel with us,' he always said, every New Year, when the Christmas decorations had been packed away and they were planning for Victor's next journey. Iris always had a reason not to. She was pregnant and unwilling to spend all that time sitting in the cab. It would be uncomfortable. Maria was too little, only a baby. When Maria started toddling it would have been unreasonable to expect her to put up with the strange routine of the road. Then Iris was pregnant again. Sophie arrived early and Iris wouldn't stray too far from the hospital. Soon after that, Maria started preschool. They had their own friends. They had their little routines in place. Life was already difficult enough. It wouldn't be fair on the girls. Time on the road, no real space of their own, imposing on strangers for their meals.

'They're not strangers,' Victor often said. They were like family, some of them. And the food was the best they could manage. And when the bees were at work there was plenty of room for the girls to run and play (he thought of their own small back garden with most of the space given over to the hives). 'Farms are dangerous places,' said Iris, her face clouding with anxiety. And he kissed her and told her she mustn't worry, and that he would miss her while he was gone.

The Walker orchards were his favourite on his annual route, and he deliberately left it to last. Apple trees, pears, plums and cherries, acres and acres, set in the generous rise of the Downs in the hills beyond Hattenden. He set off for the farm in anticipation of Caitlin's warm welcome. In his mind's eye he could see the long, tree-lined driveway up to the familiar red-brick house, his lorry shepherded by Caitlin's two rangy collie dogs who always met him at the gate. As he turned off the main road and along the lanes to the farm, his headlights lit up the fence which bordered her land – and he read the signs which, he was sure, had not been there before. *Trespassers Are Always Prosecuted. PRIVATE PROPERTY*, said another. *STRICTLY NO ADMITTANCE. This Farm Monitored by CCTV AT ALL TIMES*. When Victor turned off to the farm driveway, the wooden gates were shut. He hopped down from the cab and slid the bolt from its catch, leaning against the gates, pushing them open and securing them until he could drive through. There were no dogs to greet him, not even the distant sounds of barking from the farmhouse.

Caitlin Walker stood in the yard in the near darkness, a cup of coffee in one hand. Though she'd eked out her last packet for a couple of months by using smaller and smaller amounts in the machine, this was her very last cup. She'd topped it up with hot milk and, if truth be told, the flavour was hardly there at all, but she could taste it like a memory: the bitterness, a dark smoky shadow of the beans. She'd heard that coffee was still available if you knew who to ask and had enough money to pay. But with the farm barely bringing in enough to cover her costs Caitlin was not one of those people – she would have to make do with artificial coffee substitute like everyone else. It was even better than the real thing, if you believed the advertisers. According to the man in the village shop it was okay – well, it was hot and brown, anyway – and you had to try not to think about real coffee while you were drinking it. This might be the last cup of real coffee she ever had. Tears pricked behind her eyes as she took the last few sips, embarrassed that she was feeling so sorry for herself – but it didn't matter; there was no one else there to see. She stood with her hands around the empty mug, the last of its heat fading away, trying not to think about the future, her ears straining for the sound of the lorry. Where the hell was Victor?

Out on the lane a vehicle came to a stop, then after a long pause there it was, his lorry coming up the driveway, the headlights sweeping over her. She waved her free hand. There was still hope. As long as the bee farmers kept going there was hope.

*

Victor grinned when he saw Caitlin waiting. She always had a smile and something to eat when he arrived. He wondered what it would be this time. Some bacon? Or eggs, maybe, or a slice of hot toast, the butter melting in… His stomach growled. He stopped the lorry in a hiss of brakes and jumped down from the cab.

Caitlin was thinner since last year. Her face was pinched. It looked like she'd been crying. Instead of their usual handshake he held out his arms to her and bent to give her a brief, awkward hug.

'Good to see you.' Caitlin wiped her eyes on her sleeve. 'Come on, the sun won't wait.'

Now for the best bit, thought Victor. Months from now there would be fruit on the trees and all because of the bees. He unlocked the catches, slid the bolts from their housing, pulled the straps over the hives so that they were free. He greeted the bees as he always did, with secret words he whispered into the hives. He asked for their help. He asked them to do their miracle, to make apples, cherries, pears and plums appear on the trees. He begged them, in a way he'd never done in the past. Then he turned to Caitlin with a smile. 'Here goes.' He removed the netting, pulling it away in swathes, gathering it in his arms and dropping it to the ground – they could fold it later. The sun would be up soon and the bees would wake. There was no time to waste. He hefted the first crate into his arms and passed it down to Caitlin. She rested it on the tarmac for a moment before transferring it to the trailer she'd hitched to the back of her quad bike. It was the best way to distribute the hives throughout the orchards. The hives were designed to be easily moved, squat squarish wooden crates with box joints at the corners, and a flat lid so that they could be safely stacked on top of one another. They were sturdy and solid – painted and patched every year in shades of yellow and blue, and at this point in the season were beginning to look a bit tatty.

Caitlin and Victor worked quickly, loading up the trailer with hives, Victor securing them while Caitlin climbed onto the quad bike and revved the engine. 'Hurry.' The light was seeping into the sky now; they had to get moving. Victor clambered onto the back of the bike and gave her a thumbs-up. They drove on a dirt track between the ranks of apple trees until they reached the last rows by the field's edge, then they hefted the hives from the trailer, setting one at the end of each row. Caitlin turned the bike and they headed back for more, racing against the sunrise.

2

It is a constant source of wonder to me that every day we are surrounded by the most interesting and complex creatures. I am not talking about human beings – interesting and complex though we most certainly are. Every day we wake into a world of insects. Vast populations who live and work all around us in the most fascinating ways. And, whether we are conscious of it or not, we depend on these tiny creatures for our current way of life.

Perhaps on your holidays you have been plagued by midges or mosquitoes – clouds of seemingly useless insects which unapologetically ruin our picnics and nature rambles. Wasps and hornets which seem to have only one purpose: causing us pain.

You might have wished them away, and considered how much better life would be without the bugs which annoy us in our hard-earned leisure time. But, how often have you stopped to wonder what might happen without the insects around us?

Come with me as I journey to investigate the brief

yet fascinating lives of the tiny creatures with whom we share our planet. We will journey from the plains of North America to the forests of Madagascar, not forgetting the rich habitats of our own back gardens, in our search for insect life.

J.C. Ravensworth, *Insect Life*
(Associated University Press, 1995)

3

Victor and Caitlin hurried to unload the hives from the trailer, distributing them amongst the blossoming fruit trees. Caitlin was constantly in motion, not meeting Victor's eye, helping to lug the hives about, turning away from him to twitch stray weeds out of the ground, or snip at errant twigs with the secateurs she kept in her jacket pocket. He'd never known her so quiet. The sun had risen now, and the bees would be warming up and beginning to stir. They waited quietly until they saw the first of the insects venture out into the morning. 'Best let them get on,' said Victor. Caitlin nodded.

With the hives all in place, they returned to the lorry to fold the protective netting and to wind and stow the straps. There was nothing left to do. Caitlin stopped moving. She stood before Victor with her hands by her sides and exhaled – the breath leaving her in a long, slow, controlled sigh. He imagined her lungs squeezed out, completely emptied of air.

Silence.

He couldn't bear it, would always rather have music than quiet, voices to fill an empty space. He dived into the soundless place between them. 'How are you?'

She drew a shuddering in-breath. 'Breakfast?' she asked. She turned and walked towards the farmhouse, staying slightly ahead of him on the driveway. 'Things aren't so good,' she began. 'I expect you saw the signs out there?' Had he not come across them on the other farms, she asked him? Surely hers could not have been the only place to have seen trouble? A few farms back they'd told him of a break-in, but he hadn't thought anything more of it, he said; farms had always been a target for theft.

'It's different this time,' said Caitlin, opening the front door, slipping off her falling-apart boots and padding down the hall towards the kitchen. 'This time they don't just want to take stuff. They want to do us damage.'

Caitlin had resorted to signs and warnings about CCTV because she couldn't afford security staff. She checked that the frying pan was hot enough then cracked three eggs into it. The smell of cooking reminded Victor of how long it had been since his dinner. The night before, at the Stevens farm, there had been very little to eat. They were down on their luck: falling crop yields, low prices from the supermarkets for what little they'd managed to produce. Mrs Stevens apologised to Victor as she set the bowl of soup in front of him. He knew it was all they had and felt guilty for taking it from them.

'There's not many that can pay for guards,' said Caitlin, and Victor nodded. 'Fewer still who have the money for security fencing.' She set a teapot in front of him. 'It's dried mint,' she told him. 'Tea ran out months ago.' She turned back to the cupboard for a mug.

Victor couldn't remember the last time he'd had a cup of real tea. He poured the pale green water into his mug. The scent rose with the steam, something like fresh-mown grass.

'It happened last August,' said Caitlin, her back turned to Victor, checking the eggs. 'We'd just finished the fruit harvest. Cherries were long gone, of course, but the apples and pears were in crates ready for the lorry to collect the next day. That night there was a break-in. First thing I knew, Nell and Hettie started barking, raced round to the yard. By the time I got there...' Caitlin's voice shook; she hung her head.

Victor said nothing. She was about to tell him something unimaginable.

'They shot both of 'em,' said Caitlin. 'Both of my beauties. Took some of the fruit, smashed up the rest. Painted filthy words over the barn.'

'I'm so sorry.' Victor had never felt more inadequate. He sat and stared at his hands while Caitlin served up the eggs, then she excused herself and hurried from the kitchen.

He should have followed her to see that she was okay. But Victor's hunger overcame him. He ate his breakfast, scraping the plate with his knife to make sure he'd left nothing. Then he lifted the plate to his mouth and licked at the last traces of golden yolk. It would not do to waste food.

'Forgive me,' said Caitlin, a little later. Victor had washed up the dishes and the pan. He'd dried them on a tea towel and was standing awkwardly in the kitchen wondering again whether he should go and find her. 'I shouldn't have just disappeared. Needed to pull myself together.'

'Did the police find the people who did it?' asked Victor.

'Police?' She snorted. 'They came and took pictures, filled out a form. I never heard anything more.' She set the dishes back in the cupboard. 'I keep thinking, one day I'll be over it,' she said, 'but it's always there when I close my eyes at night. If Thomas was still here...' She shook her head. 'Let's go and see how your bees are getting on, shall we?'

They walked back towards the orchard, Caitlin easily matching his long stride. She apologised for not taking the quad bike. Electricity was so expensive now. Victor waved her explanation away – it was far better to walk, he told her. Exercise. Fresh air. He spent so much time cooped up in his cab. They fell into silence – this time Victor let it sit between them. It felt comfortable now, the not speaking. A blackbird hopped along the ground in front of them with its pinking cry. A lark called from a neighbouring field, its tiny body invisible as it rose into the sky. Victor stopped walking and looked up, shielding his eyes with his hand.

'There he is,' said Caitlin, pointing. 'Not so many as last year, I think.'

Now that Victor had the bird in his sights he could follow it as it climbed. The sun was warm on his jacket and he slipped it from his shoulders, laying it over his arm as they walked on. They were coming towards the first rows of apple trees now, the blossoms thick and creamy-pink on the branches. He breathed in – a tender sweetness. On a day like today it was hard to believe there were horrors in the world – but they were there, waiting in the shadows, in the anxiety on Caitlin's face, in the empty dog baskets still sitting by the back door of the farmhouse.

Caitlin and Victor walked on along the wide grassy path in between the hives at the ends of the rows. There was very little evidence of the bees. By this time of the morning on such a warm day he would have expected to see more of them going in and out of the hives, a cloud of bees around each hive entrance, and setting out between the branches, busy in the blossoms.

'What's wrong?' asked Caitlin.

'I don't know.' Victor frowned. He knelt in the dew-damp grass in front of one of the hives, the water soaking his jeans. Caitlin pulled on her hat, making sure the veil was down over her face. She slipped on her gloves. Victor's fingers fumbled on the catches and it took him several attempts before he was able to lift the lid.

All that preparation, the protective clothing – it had all been unnecessary. Inside the hive the little bodies were sluggish and slow. Some were dying or already dead. A few were not quite gone, their legs moved slowly in the morning air. But even as Victor and Caitlin watched, their movements became slower. Without saying a word he replaced the lid and knelt by the next hive, while Caitlin crossed the track to inspect the hives on the other side. They worked silently, until they had reached the end of the first field, then they walked through to the next. But they already knew what they would find. It was only to confirm what they both had already somehow known after that first lid was lifted: it was too late. Victor lowered himself shakily to the ground next to the last of the hives, trying to find his breath.

Caitlin came quickly to his side. 'Put your head between

your knees,' she told him. He leaned forward, bending his head over his legs, looping his arms around his knees. She rested her hand on his shoulder for the tiniest moment. 'What could have happened here?'

'Disease, most likely.' Victor's voice was muffled. 'Plus they're exhausted already and we're not even halfway through the season.' He lifted his head. 'I've got to try to get some sugar into them, see if that helps. 'Have you got any?'

'Not for months now,' she said.

'In the lorry,' said Victor, getting shakily to his feet. He checked his pocket for the keys. 'There's a bottle of sugar water in the cab.'

4

When Annie was five she learned how to do something which felt like magic. A large bumblebee, fluffy as a kitten, its buzz a low thrum against the window, had exhausted itself looking for a way out of her bedroom. It crawled along the windowsill, heaving itself along the white glosswork, coming to rest by one of Annie's plastic horses.

Annie ran into her parents' room. Her mother was folding laundry still warm from the washing line. Annie's mother always knew what to do – she would know what to do now.

Her mother followed Annie back to her room and looked at the bee for a moment. 'I think she's hungry,' she said. 'Go and fetch the honey,' she told Annie. 'And a little spoon.'

Annie's mother always trusted her to do things. She trotted down the stairs, the carpet rough under her bare feet, her hand smoothing along the high bannister, just within reach of her hand. The plastic squeezy bottle of honey was kept next to the marmalade and strawberry jam which her mother made every year, the sweetness filling every corner of the house. The honey bottle was sticky to the touch. Annie licked her fingers as she padded to the cutlery drawer. On tiptoes she selected the most elaborate teaspoon, her favourite – a rose twined along the handle, the leaves and thorns part of its raised design. Annie hurried back up the stairs. Her mother was in silhouette at the window. The afternoon sun lit up her long wavy hair, lighting it from the back so that she had a halo. She turned to Annie as she came back into the room. 'Good girl,' she said, in her careful way. 'Now. Put a very little honey into the spoon. Here, set it on the windowsill, so you won't drop it.'

Annie did as she was told, her tongue poking between her teeth in concentration. She flipped the top of the bottle open, turning it slowly upside down so that the liquid gold oozed down towards the little hole. 'One drop,' Annie said, softly. 'Two.'

'Perfect,' said her mother. 'Now. Move it closer, so the bee can drink. That's right.'

Millimetre by millimetre – she didn't want to hurt the bee – Annie pushed the spoon closer until it was nearly touching the bee's head.

'Good girl. Tip the spoon a very little, so that she can smell the honey.'

And that did the trick. Annie watched in fascination as the bee turned to face the spoon and unfurled her filament of tongue, sinking it into the golden honey. 'She's drinking,' said Annie, turning her face up towards her mother.

'You saved her, I think,' said Annie's mother. 'Clever girl.'

Annie leaned on the windowsill, resting her head on her

folded arms, and she watched the bee for what seemed like hours. Her mother went back to the laundry but popped her head around the door every so often for an update. 'When she's full, she'll feel much better, and then she'll want to fly away,' said Annie's mother. 'Watch for the moment – you'll have to open the window so that she can go.'

It happened just as her mother said. After a long while the bee had eaten enough. She coiled her amazing tongue back in towards herself and the droning buzz began again. It was time, thought Annie. She opened the catch on the window and pushed it open, letting in a breath of hot summer air. 'Go on, little bee,' Annie told her. 'Off you go home.' The bee lifted off, her wings a blur, and flew heavily, unevenly, towards the garden.

5

Victor and Caitlin sat at the kitchen table, a pot of chamomile tea between them. The sun had long set; the surviving bees were back in their hives for the night. The sugar water had revived some of the bees temporarily, but there were a great many unresponsive little bodies.

'I should have noticed there was something wrong.' Victor drained his mug and set it down in front of him.

'Like what?'

'I don't know.' He pressed his fingers to his temples.

'What will you do now?' she asked him.

'Two more days here, then on to the soft fruit farms, just like I'd planned,' he told her. 'Got to stick to the schedule.'

Caitlin sipped from her own chipped mug. 'I suppose.'

He looked at her, blurry in the low light of the candles on the dresser. Another power cut. 'Maybe your trees will be okay.' But the soft fruit harvest would take a hit. And the vegetables. If they were lucky there would still be enough wild pollinators to make a difference. He rubbed his eyes.

'Didn't you think,' said Caitlin, clasping her hands

together and stretching her arms above her head, 'for a while there, that things were going to get better?'

Victor nodded. Time was, not so many years ago, that public concern for wildlife had grown into something tangible. Beekeeping had a moment. People started to plant more flowers, and farmers looked for alternatives to the pesticides which were causing such harm to insects. But then – the first World Crash hit and the economy nosedived. 'We can't blame people for trying to put food on the table, Caitlin,' he said. 'More important to find work than plant flowers.'

'True enough.'

The second Crash was still sending out shockwaves. International trade deals collapsing, governments struggling to keep up. And, now that there were food shortages, crop yields mattered more than concerns over pesticides and fertilisers.

Victor said goodnight to Caitlin and wearily climbed the stairs to his bedroom. He took his phone out of his back pocket and plugged it in to charge, then he lay on the bed, exhausted. Things were slipping. The seasons, the wildlife, the bees… Victor closed his eyes, but sleep wouldn't come.

6

Two years later

January. With no more than seven weeks before the start of pollination season, Victor had only twenty-one viable hives remaining. The rest of his bees had perished and he hadn't been able to establish new colonies. It was the same all over the country. His online group could talk about nothing else. Now that death and disease were all around them it seemed pointless to avoid talking about it. That and the break-ins. Desperate people stealing bees. It would do them no good, thought Victor. It would take more than one hive to pollinate an entire crop. Alex in Wiltshire had installed closed-circuit television cameras around his hives, the feed coming through to his living room where he and his wife ate and slept, taking it in turns to watch the screens. In Devon, Sara was employing her friends as round-the-clock security guards.

Victor had bought a padlock and motion sensor for the back gate and fixed razor wire along the top of the fences. Iris didn't like it. Iris didn't have a choice. 'Bees are like gold dust,' Victor tried to explain, but she shook her head. It was like living in a prison camp, she told him – but she was even more upset that, despite having so few bees, he was still talking about leaving for the whole of spring and summer, leaving her with the girls and the horrible wire looped all the way around their home. She crashed around in the kitchen, the saucepans taking the brunt of her anger.

Maria and Sophie sat on the living room floor with their Collection – Iris's name for the cardboard box of random stuff they carted about with them all over the house and garden. Dolls with arms and legs missing, odd socks, bent teaspoons, broken crayons, a balsa plane with the propeller missing. A chipped enamel mug, hairclips, an old mobile phone, buttons and badges, and a rubber band ball. Anything unloved or unwanted went into the Collection, and they curated it with a great deal of seriousness. To Maria and Sophie it was a museum, a series of characters, the beginning of countless stories. No matter how much they begged their parents they weren't always allowed to watch their screens, and it was then that they turned to the Collection. They had tipped the box out onto the floor near Victor's feet and were sorting through it quietly. He couldn't help but smile when he watched them playing together. For a brief moment, the clouds lifted. Then he checked his watch. 'Time for your medicine, Soph.' She rose and fetched her inhalers and the nebuliser from the cupboard, then sat next to him on the sofa and went through her routine, perfectly capable of doing it unsupervised, but from her regular glances in his direction he could tell she was relishing his attention.

'All done,' she said, packing the nebuliser back into its

box, taking it back to the cupboard and putting it all away.

Victor turned back to the figures on his screen. Twenty-one hives were not enough to travel with. Was it even worth setting out? He'd been procrastinating for days, reluctant to contact the farmers, trying to think of an alternative, wondering what they would do now for money if he didn't go. And – the bigger question which he could not ignore – what would everybody eat when the crops failed? He would test the water with Caitlin. She was easier to talk to – and she would not be afraid to tell him what she really thought. Before he could change his mind he quickly wrote her an email and hit send.

Less than a minute later his mobile phone rang. It was Caitlin. 'What the hell, Victor?' Something of the old strength had returned to her voice.

'Let me ask you this,' he said. 'What would you do with only a handful of viable hives?'

A pause.

'I tell you what I'd do,' she said. 'I'd keep going. A few hives is better than nothing. That's still thousands and thousands of bees. That's still a harvest of some kind. Don't tell me you're giving up.'

Victor watched his girls, their heads bent over their treasures. Maria, with her perennially messy hair, pushed it repeatedly out of her eyes. Iris had coaxed Sophie's unruly mane into plaits and finished them with pink butterfly clips. Sophie, as far as he knew, had never seen a wild butterfly.

'I can hear you thinking,' said Caitlin, at the other end of the line. 'Victor?'

Victor sighed. He had to try to make this work.

But, what if it didn't work? What then?

7

Annie sat cross-legged in the simfields, her notebook in one hand, her pen in the other. She'd been at work since four am, carrying out regular systems checks. Around her, the bees rose and fell in the warmth generated by the ground heat pump. Even with the unpredictable temperature of a British spring, an unexpected sharp frost would have no effect on her hives. Here under the Dome they were protected – Annie had programmed the seasons to correspond with the sort of temperatures they had experienced before the changing climate brought uncomfortably hot, dry summers and long, wild winters. The white wooden hives stood in short towers at specific locations around the simfields, each one painted with a black serial number on its side. The bees thrived under the artificial sky, gathering nectar from the carefully chosen range of trees and wildflowers Annie grew in the simfields and pollinating the plants while Annie gathered her data.

In the last two years, bee numbers had collapsed. Whether privately owned or wild, they were now at an all-time low. Annie's research facility was one of the few places in the country engaged in efforts to preserve the various native species and her colonies of Western Honeybees – *Apis mellifera* – had been protected from the fall in populations. They were little things, so much smaller than the bumblebees. She watched them now, as they busied around the entrance to one of the hives, crawling out onto the bottom board and taking off into the simfields. She followed the path of one of them, its furry thorax narrowing to a smooth-looking abdomen, gold and dark brown, shiny iridescent wings a blur. Approaching a buttercup, the bee hovered into position, back legs hanging down, its wings working up and back to keep it steady, before it made contact with the flower, unfurling its long tongue for the nectar. On a nearby plant, a bee that was dusted with bright yellow pollen preened and wiped itself down until the pollen was cleaned from its body and safely stored in the pollen sacs on its legs, like bright golden saddlebags. There was no sense of competition or strife between them; the bees came and went, working together. They never seemed to be still. Always flying, hovering, crawling, preening, vibrating, shimmering, shivering. Always busy.

Meanwhile, outside the Dome lay the real countryside, the heart of rural Kent where animals and insects should have been enjoying their lives in the wild, finding food and shelter, reproducing, thriving. When Annie had first set up the project on the back of completing her PhD she'd had to battle for funding, justifying her reasons for setting up the artificial environment. Yes, there were fewer bees, but surely there was still a sufficient richness of plant species for the bees to thrive in the open air, to contribute to the pollination of fruits and crops in the locality? But Annie had long been monitoring the changing climate, the fluctuation in temperatures, the drop-off in species variety. She pushed for the funds to build simfields under a vast glass dome. It was lucky for her that, at the moment of submitting bids for a grant, she had won the support of a government minister who had taken an interest in the trend for species decline. He'd negotiated with the Ministry of Agriculture to secure ten years' funding for Annie and two assistants. Those ten years would be up in eighteen months.

Annie stared out at the world beyond the Dome. To one side, the buildings of Hattenden Agricultural College: the ornate Victorian façade of the main building, its clock tower and spires. The grounds swept grandly round the building, beautifully landscaped with banks of rhododendrons and artfully positioned trees which led the eye out onto the woods and fields beyond. The Dome and the rest of its facilities had been built close to the boundary wall of the college, and on the other side of the wall lay the village of Hattenden. In the college's heyday the village had been a hub for all of the surrounding villages and farms. It had resisted change and the centre of the village still looked much as it always had, with a handful of little shops and a great stone church clustered round the village green. On the village outskirts a council estate had been built, and beyond that some newer houses, on what had turned out to be a flood plain. Some villagers left their sandbags outside their houses year round; it hardly seemed worth tidying them away, and so they became part of the landscape.

The village was big enough to feel like a thriving community on market days, but small enough that people recognised all of their neighbours. A friendly place, where new arrivals were by and large welcomed, but if they wanted to keep to themselves most people understood, and after a few friendly forays would leave their new neighbours alone.

When the Dome was built there had been a flurry of interest in the village. Within the college the project was cause for celebration; it brought their little institution up to date and put them firmly back on the academic map. In the village, although a small Parish welcome committee had done their best, some of the old guard were not so sure. It hadn't mattered to Annie either way – she was there to work, after all, and apart from trips to the grocery shop and occasional visits to the baker's at the weekend, she rarely spent any time outside of the Dome and her little house just beyond the green. She delegated the invitations from various clubs and committees to her research assistants or politely turned them down. After a while people stopped trying to get to know her, which was just what Annie had hoped. She loved her quiet, studious life, and the fact that her place of work was so close to the open countryside, the very environment in which one day her research might be of use.

There had been a time when the trees around the college were alive with birds, and the sky was criss-crossed with them. Now all she saw were drones and, very occasionally, an airplane, high in the atmosphere, leaving its trail. In the surrounding countryside, hedgehogs became first endangered and then near extinct, the rabbits and hares stopped breeding, and the wild pollinators had all but disappeared... no more butterflies. A few ground-nesting bee species. Her research was more vital than ever. If pollinators ceased to make their homes in the Weald, crops would go unfertilised and the population would go hungry. Hungri*er*, she corrected herself.

She had collected her new ration card from the District Warden's Office the previous day. She'd stood outside the office, turning it over in her hand, disbelieving. Limits on cereals, meat and dairy. Fruits and vegetables presented in tins. Sugar was a distant memory – though artificial sweeteners would be freely available. When she was little, Annie's grandfather had told her all about rationing during the Second World War. How strange it had seemed to her, growing up. How alien, in a world where the supermarket shelves were always stocked and nothing was ever out of season. And now, they had come full circle.

The world outside looked more or less the same as it always had – if you didn't know about the shortages. If you ignored the army presence stationed at the corporate farms. Around Hattenden the small independent farms had been left to fend for themselves, and one of the Warden's responsibilities was to organise security rotas made up of residents. There were those who protested that they had no interest in guarding the fields, to which the Warden replied that everyone had to eat, therefore everyone would take their turn.

Outside, it was another warm, sunny day. Annie made a note to herself to check the water tanks to ensure they had sufficient reserves. The project was more or less self-sustaining for energy and water, though the increasingly dry seasons were putting a strain on their resources. She'd search online later to see if there was anything more they could be doing to recycle their water onsite. She would just lie down for a few moments in the long meadow grass to rest. Buttercups nodded their golden heads over her. The sun was bright through the Dome. She closed her eyes.

'Dr Abrams? Dr Abrams?'

A shadow fell across her. Annie opened one eye. One of her research assistants, Matt, was standing over her with an amused expression.

'I wasn't sleeping,' she said.

'Okay then.' He covered his smile with the back of his hand.

'Was there something…?' she asked.

'Somebody to see you,' he said. 'It's the Warden.'

'Attica?' Annie sat up too quickly – spots danced in front of her eyes. 'I'll be there in a minute. Go, tell her. Don't keep her waiting.'

Attica Blake, Warden of Hattenden district, was the most senior member of their community. Since policy decisions at regional level had been devolved to small local groups, Attica was effectively their Chief. Local Wardens left Westminster free to concentrate solely on matters of national importance, meaning that the Government's valuable resources were no longer taken up by the time-consuming day-to-day concerns of the electorate. What did Attica want with her? Whatever it was, she would have to play nicely. A good relationship with Attica was vital if Annie wanted to smooth the way for more funding.

The first thing people always noticed about Attica was her hair. Long and grey and plentiful, falling well past her shoulders in waves. She wore it down like a young girl. Her face was youthful too. She stood at the double doors to the simfields – Matt had managed to keep her on the other side, at least, where there was no risk of her carrying contaminants into the protected environment. Attica raised her hand in greeting and smiled her effortless smile. It was impossible to guess at what she wanted. Perhaps she had come in search of a jar of honey. Although it was against the Dome's code of practice to take from the bees, Annie would be prepared to offer Attica a very small amount if it would keep her on side.

'I'll come straight to the point,' said Attica, following Annie into her office. Her gaze swept Annie from top to toe. 'The orchards are coming into blossom,' said Attica, 'and I'm informed that the bee farmers are in trouble. The Walker farm, for one, uses Victor Martin's bees as pollinators, and according to Mrs Walker he has very few viable hives after the last season, with little chance of full recovery in the next year.' She looked Annie straight in the eye. 'Dr Abrams, we must use all of the resources available to us to avert a crisis. In short, I am required to requisition your bees in order to assist with this year's pollination effort.'

The ground tilted under Annie's feet. Had she heard correctly? No. It was not possible. She must have misunderstood. She felt herself swaying and reached out for the edge of her desk.

'Dr Abrams.' Attica swooped in and took Annie's arm, guiding her into a chair with her sinewy strength. 'You are very pale. When was the last time you ate something?'

Annie looked away, reluctant to have Attica's assistance. 'Last night,' she said. 'Some soup.'

Attica went to the door of Annie's office and called for Matt. 'Is there anything to eat?' she asked him. 'Dr Abrams is in need.'

A moment later he appeared at the door with an open box of protein bars. 'There's a couple left,' he said. Then, seeing Annie's face, he disappeared and came back again with a glass of water.

'I felt dizzy earlier,' said Annie, accepting the glass. 'Should've known better than to skip breakfast.' She sat up a little straighter and faced Attica, trying to compose herself. 'Could you repeat what you said before?'

'I think you heard me,' said Attica, with a lopsided smile. 'And you know I wouldn't ask you unless it was absolutely necessary.'

'I'm afraid it won't be possible,' said Annie. There was steel in her voice. 'As you know, I've spent almost ten years building up the research. Our ultimate aim is to reintroduce our bees back into the wild – but not now, and not this way.' She forced herself to bite back the words she really wanted to say, giving Attica precisely one minute to leave the premises, to take her idea with her – it was never going to happen; it would destroy all of her research. Annie took another bite of the protein bar. 'The bees aren't ready. To send them out now would put all of my colonies at risk of diseases which they are not yet capable of resisting. In a few years' time, perhaps.' Another bite. Annie could feel herself rallying. She was on familiar ground now, talking about the project. 'Once we have bred several generations of resistant bees and proved them hardy enough to survive in the new climate we can release them in controlled numbers, with the appropriate levels of observation and readjustment where required.'

'We don't have a couple of years,' said Attica. Her smile had faded into a thin line. 'I'm very sorry to put you in this position, but we have no alternative. If this year's crops fail, rations will have to be tightened yet again.'

Annie was torn. If she was going to apply for more funding to consolidate their work, the District Warden's backing would be key to a successful bid. She had to keep Attica on side. 'What about artificial foods?' said Annie. 'Lab-grown meat.'

'Not enough to feed us all,' said Attica, gently.

'But, the corporate farms are doing well, aren't they?' said Annie. 'They promised us.'

'They're working at full capacity,' Attica assured her. 'High-yield crops, intensive farming, hydroponics – but it still won't be enough.'

'Provisions will have been made,' said Annie. Surely the authorities would have plans for every eventuality, no matter how unprecedented or terrifying.

Attica shook her head. 'There are no provisions,' she said. 'No plan B – if you'll pardon the terrible pun. We must look to our own efforts. We must do what we can.' She put her hand lightly on Annie's arm – Annie tried not to flinch away. 'Nobody is coming to save us,' said Attica. 'We must try to save ourselves.'

8

As every child knows, bees make honey. As every child also knows, bees have a vital part to play in helping to produce many other foods through pollinating our crops. It is estimated that we are dependent on pollinators, primarily bees, for a staggering one third of our food. In recent years, bee populations have fallen worldwide at an alarming rate. We have been watching, and measuring, their decline. Numerous studies pinpoint the rapid fall in numbers over the past ten years in response to a variety of factors, including changes in land use and the development of single-crop agriculture. These have radically altered bee habitats, changing them out of all previous recognition, permanently altering their landscapes.

In addition, our increasing use of pesticides and artificial fertilisers has threatened the health of our bees. Surely we are all aware of the devastating effects of neonicotinoids – perhaps the most widely used insecticide in the world, which kills not only those insect species which threaten our crops but also affects the insect pollinators we wish to encourage.

The effects of these toxic insecticides don't stop there; they continue their inexorable march up the food chain to birds and small mammals. Add to this parlous state of affairs the effect of climate change. Temperature fluctuations beyond the established norm have affected insect habitats.

As if all this wasn't enough to contend with, bee species must battle against pests, parasites, invasive species and diseases such as mites, hive beetles, foulbrood and Nosema disease. Is it any wonder, therefore, that bee species have suffered such a decline?

A recent report showed that four out of five invertebrate pollinators are extinct or near extinction, which illustrates a continuing trend first highlighted by the United Nations.

For how much longer will we continue to ignore these staggering statistics? We can already measure the devastation to our crop yields. This is observable not only in wild colonies. The decline in commercial bee populations is now under threat. And yet we continue to look the other way, insist this is a problem for somebody else to address. Ladies and gentlemen, fellow human beings. We can no longer pretend. It is time for us to do something. It is time for us to act.

J.C. Ravensworth,
'Report to National Conservation Convention' (2016)

9

Annie and Matt stood at the door to the facility, watching for the return of Annie's other research assistant, Emily. The Dome and its adjacent administration rooms were situated at the very edge of the campus – from where they were standing the rest of the Agricultural College was spread out in front of them, the red brick of the main buildings illuminated by the afternoon sun. The rumble of traffic from the distant main road, the whisper of wind in the surrounding trees. A couple of volunteer gardeners tended the beds around the main block. Annie had very little to do with the college, but she knew there were very few official students, these days. Not many could afford to study. Parts of the college had been thrown open to anyone who wanted to teach in return for whatever people could afford. Sometimes a dozen eggs in exchange for an Accountancy class, or the offer to mend a boiler or cut hair in return for a course in Animal Husbandry or American Literature. Payments were arranged between the tutors and their students, and the college provided the rooms in return for a donation for heating oil and a commitment from everyone involved to keep the classrooms clean and tidy. As Annie watched, a gaggle of students left the main building, heads down, deep in conversation.

'We should keep some of the hives back, as insurance,' said Matt.

'Not a chance,' said Annie. 'She's taking all of them.'

A pause. 'Not if she can't find them all,' said Matt. He looked out towards the woods beyond the college.

Annie turned on him. 'Don't you get it?' she said. 'This isn't some kind of college prank. They need every single bee they can get their hands on for the farms. This is serious.'

'Okay,' said Matt. He held up his hands in surrender.

'I don't like to think of the bees working for us,' said Annie. 'We got ourselves into this mess, didn't we? We should be letting them repopulate, not using them.'

Matt opened his mouth and closed it again.

'Have you got something else to say?' she asked. 'Go on, then. Spit it out.'

'Perhaps it might be time to take another look at mechanical pollination methods,' he began cautiously.

'Not this again,' said Annie. When was he going to get it into his head that she wasn't interested? If she'd wanted to research mechanical methods, why would she have devoted the best years of her life to bees? She tried to keep her voice steady. 'How many times, Matt? That's not what we do here.'

Matt didn't know when to drop it. 'But, when Mr Martin takes the bees, we could use the time to—'

'Don't. Just… don't.' She couldn't look at him any more.

'Only trying to help,' said Matt.

It took all of Annie's resolve to bite back a petty retort.

Rise above it. Be the bigger person. As she stared furiously ahead – Matt standing awkwardly by her side – an ancient Land Rover rounded the main building and came to a stop.

'Thank God,' said Matt under his breath, though not quietly enough that Annie didn't hear.

Emily's head was only just visible over the steering wheel, her short black bob sleek as a seal. She pulled on the handbrake and hopped down from the driver's seat, starting to talk almost before she'd opened the door. 'I got all of the seed for the meadow repair,' she said. 'But they were out of beech saplings, didn't know when they'd have any more.' She went round to the back, opened up the boot, so that she was obscured by the door. 'Are you two going to help me?' she asked. 'Not going to lie, these weigh a ton. Oh, and I managed to find some flaxseed too, Matt, just like you wanted. How much do you love me right now? Matt?' Her head appeared around the side of the door and she took in their expressions. 'What's happened?'

10

'I still can't believe it.' Emily paced the floor in Annie's office. 'We can appeal the decision, can't we? Write to our MP, take it to the press?'

Annie sat on the floor, legs crossed, leaning her head back against the wall. 'And tell them what?' she said. 'That we're not prepared to help with the food effort? Can't imagine we'd get much sympathy.' She closed her eyes, trying to calm her agitation. Her mind churned with rage, sorrow, fear… There must be something she could do. Think. *Think.*

'It's short-sighted,' said Emily, outraged. 'It's foolish. It's—'

'It's not something we can say no to,' said Annie. And yet she couldn't just let the bees go, along with all they'd worked so hard for. Then it came to her. She opened her eyes. 'But I tell you what. If they're taking the bees then I'm going with them.' Satisfied, she held out her mug for a refill.

Emily topped it up with sloe gin. She poured the remains of the bottle into her own mug, then slid down the wall so that she was sitting opposite Annie.

'That way,' said Annie, 'I can make sure they're being looked after properly. Heaven knows what sort of person this Victor Martin is. I'm not letting them go to a complete stranger.'

Emily nodded.

'Our bees have never been outside. They'll be susceptible to all kinds of disease, predation, they might be thrown by the open spaces – you know they've never had that much freedom before.' There were tears on her face. She dashed them away with her fingers, furious with herself for crying in front of Emily.

Seeing her mentor like this scared Emily. It made her stomach clench like it had in those bad old days when she'd lived with her mum and a series of loathsome stepdads. *Don't look at me like that. Where the fuck is my beer? Get out of my chair. You look like a slut.* She'd lost count of the number of times she saw her mother sobbing. Now, sitting across from Annie, watching the tears slide, she saw her mother and longed again to make everything right. 'Annie, I think it will be okay.'

Annie laughed. 'How can you possibly know that?'

A long pause. Emily's thoughts flitted, desperately searching for an answer. 'Let me come with you,' she said.

Annie looked up from her drink. It wasn't a bad idea. With two of them to watch over the bees she could make sure they got their usual routine – as far as possible. They would see the faces they were used to, hear familiar voices.

'We'll monitor their progress, said Annie. 'It can form part of our research.' She fumbled for her phone. 'I'll call Victor now.' The words slurred.

'You've had quite a bit to drink,' said Emily, cautiously.

'Tomorrow morning, then,' said Annie. She drained her mug and held it out unsteadily. 'Any gin left?'

Emily shook her head. It was late, and she was desperate to sleep, but she was reluctant to leave Annie by herself. 'Are you okay to get home?' she asked.

Annie shook her head. 'I think I'll just stay here. Got my sleeping bag.' There was a small sofa in her office, and she sometimes concertinaed herself onto it to rest if she had a late finish or early start.

'Come back with me,' said Emily. 'Matt's making dinner. You can have the spare bed.'

The second bedroom had once belonged to Matt. The accommodation the research assistants shared on the outskirts of the college campus was part of the funding deal – two bedrooms for two assistants. Annie's first researcher, Tara, had been called back home to care for her elderly father, and then Matt had joined the team. He'd been working there for a couple of years now, and at some point he and Emily had become a couple. Annie didn't know the details; she didn't want to. As long as it didn't affect their work it was none of her concern. Ordinarily she liked to maintain a professional distance with her researchers – but tonight? Tonight her world was collapsing. If she went home she wouldn't sleep – her mind would keep circling the terrible upheaval that was coming. She saw Attica's face again as she delivered the news. Resolute, not prepared to discuss alternatives, her firm politician's smile – it has been decided. This was happening, whether Annie liked it or not. At least at Matt and Emily's house there would be sympathy, and friendly faces. And besides, their house was so much closer than hers. Annie smiled blurrily. 'Yes please,' she said.

11

Emily slipped quietly into her bedroom. She crossed the floor in the darkness and lifted the covers to climb into bed.

'How's the boss?' asked Matt, reaching across, gathering her in. There had been no dinner. It was so late when they finally returned, Matt was already in bed and the kitchen was tidied. Too tired to eat, Emily had helped Annie up the stairs, hoisted her into the spare bed, removed her shoes, pulled the blankets over her and left a glass of water on the bedside table and a bucket on the floor.

'She'll be okay,' said Emily. 'Listen. She's decided to travel with the bees. I said I'd go with her.'

Matt made a questioning sort of noise.

'You know what she's like,' said Emily. 'Always so single-minded, keeping everyone at arm's length. She needs someone with her.'

'You're right,' said Matt. He breathed her in. 'I'll miss you.'

Emily closed her eyes tightly, squeezed them shut. 'Me too.'

Matt pulled her closer. They lay for a while, not speaking, then he gave a sigh.

'What is it?' said Emily.

'I was just remembering.' His voice was soft in her ear. 'All those marches, all those protests, and still it came to this.'

Emily nodded in the dark. Along with teenagers all over the country, all over the world, she and her classmates had walked out of school to join the Children's Marches. And somewhere in the crowds, Matt had been marching too. 'Didn't everything seem possible back then?' she said.

He murmured his agreement. 'Wish I'd known you then,' he said.

She laughed. 'You wouldn't have looked twice.'

'Don't be so sure.' He slid his hand down over the curve of her hip. 'Imagine it. Maybe we would have been married by now.' He paused for a moment. 'With kids.'

Emily took his hand in hers, lacing her fingers with his. 'This isn't a world for children,' she said, her voice little more than a whisper.

'We must have hope.' Matt's voice was subdued.

'I want to,' said Emily. She relaxed into his arms. How was it possible that two people could fit so perfectly together?

'There's no reason why we can't continue the project when things get better,' said Matt.

Emily said nothing for a long while. 'There might be lots of reasons why we can't,' she said. 'But I'd like to try anyway.'

'I've had an idea,' said Matt.

She turned towards him, asking him to explain, but he

wouldn't say more, no matter how much she begged him, and then he kissed her, and as they began to move together she let the question go.

*

12

Despite her throbbing head, Annie came down to the kitchen with a brave face. Matt and Emily were already seated at the table, hands cupped around their mugs. They looked good together, thought Annie.

'Chicory?' asked Emily. 'It's better than that synthetic stuff.'

Annie nodded.

'Eggs?' said Matt. 'I swapped a bag of kindling for half a dozen.'

'Yes please.' Annie pulled out a chair and sat down. 'I just phoned Attica,' she told Emily. 'She's going to ask the bee farmer if it's okay for the two of us to come along.' She caught the look which passed between Matt and Emily. 'She thinks the farmers would put us up for a small fee.' She turned to Matt.

'It's okay,' said Matt. 'Emily told me everything last night.'

Annie blushed. She couldn't even remember how she'd got to bed.

All morning they worked to get the bees ready. Attica called back to let them know Victor could take two people in his cab, and Emily phoned round to the first of the farms to ask if they could arrange beds. Then, while Annie worked on ways of collecting data while they were out on the road, Matt and Emily went out to the simfields.

They walked through the long grass towards the first stand of hives; the artificial lights warmed them like the sun even though outside the Dome a layer of cloud had covered the sky.

Emily took Matt's hand. 'You were about to tell me something last night,' she said.

'Hmm?' he teased. He stopped walking and pulled Emily close.

Emily softened into him for a moment, then leaned back. 'No you don't.' She smiled. 'You said you had an idea.'

His expression became serious. 'If I tell you…' he said.

'What is it?' said Emily. He was infuriating sometimes.

'Annie can't know,' said Matt. 'You have to promise.'

Emily nodded.

Matt planned to hide some of the colonies before Victor arrived. Not the established ones – if they were missing Annie would notice straight away. But if he took them from the nursery rooms, where young colonies of bees were established and nurtured, it would be less obvious, said Matt. They did not yet have standard hives and were kept instead in starter dwellings.

'We could use hives from the workshop,' interrupted Emily.

'Exactly,' said Matt. There was a shed of sorts outside the Dome, a late addition to the project, where they repaired and reconstructed the hives – Annie left this side of things to her assistants and rarely went in – as a result it had become a bit of a dumping ground, with exterior panels stacked up against the walls along with other odds and ends of wood. There were even some decommissioned hives at the very back of the building which would do in an emergency. And – they both agreed – it *was* an emergency. Annie would be furious if she found out, said Matt, and Emily began to doubt that they were doing the right thing, feeling the first stirrings of reluctance at going behind Annie's back. Were they about to make a terrible mistake?

'She can't bear to lose them,' said Matt. 'You heard her.'

Emily paused for a moment. There was still a chance that Annie might spot the missing colonies, but... they would risk it. They would choose their moment carefully – and then act fast.

It was time to get back to their work. Most of the hives in the simfields were in excellent condition, which wasn't a surprise with Annie in charge. They were all suitable for transportation; Annie had seen to it when she set up the project that they would be able to move them around the fields when necessary. Matt and Emily checked the structure of each one to make sure they were sturdy enough for travel and made a small list of repairs they would need to make.

When they got back to Annie's office just after noon, they found a note stuck to her door – they should take a break. She'd gone back to her cottage to get something to eat and pack her bag.

They looked at each other.

'Let's get started,' said Matt.

*

Annie looked around her little kitchen. It was unsettling, the thought that she would soon be gone from this place, the carefully ordered world she'd created. There was a sachet of powdered soup in the cupboard, and while she waited for the kettle to boil she fetched the last of the cream crackers from the biscuit tin and ate them standing by the kitchen sink, looking out of the window across her small garden to the fields beyond. She packed her bag then walked around the cottage, emptying the shelves. There had been stories of burglaries. She did not want to leave anything on display, and so she took down her books and keepsakes, and family photographs. She lingered over the framed image of her mother standing next to her father – Annie's grandfather – in his orchard. He wore a battered straw hat that Annie couldn't remember. Her mother looked young. The photo had been taken long before Annie came. One hand rested on her hip; the other sheltered her eyes from the glare of the sun. There was dust on the glass. Annie wiped it with the edge of her sleeve then she put it into the cupboard with the rest.

When she returned to the Dome mid-afternoon Emily was alone in the office. 'Where's Matt gone to?' asked Annie.

'He said he needed some fresh air,' said Emily. 'I don't think he'll be long.'

Annie nodded. She had planned to work in her office but it had come to her that this might be the last time she would be alone for weeks – possibly months. The very thought of it was draining. She would take advantage of the few hours of stillness left to her. 'When he comes back, could you help him to finish getting the hives ready?' Annie unplugged her laptop. 'I think I'll take this back home and deal with my emails there. I'll be back this evening in good time for Victor.'

'Of course,' said Emily. She fiddled with a stack of papers. 'Take all the time you need.'

13

In Annie's memories of visits to her grandfather's house in Herefordshire, it was always summer. He had a small orchard behind his house in Bosbury where she would occupy herself happily for hours, leaving the grownups to their low voices and uninteresting conversations, preferring the open air and the long grass, the wide sky glimpsed in patches through a lattice of branches. Under the trees in the dark earth around the base of the trunks, the grass appeared to be a deeper green, and teeming with life. Not that anyone would notice who walked quickly through to check on the progress of the fruit. But to those who cared to stop – only me, thought Annie, stroking the grass as though it was the fur of a great animal, digging her bitten-down fingernails into the loamy soil to see the earthworms loop and squirm, watching a procession of ants cross a woody tree root which rose just proud of the ground, following a beetle as it waddled in front of her, its cumbersome body an inflexible metallic gleam. Her whole focus telescoped in on the small patch in front of her, the parade of tiny lives under her gaze, until it became too much for her to take in and she would flop onto her back to contemplate instead the shimmering leaves and pale pink blossoms, the growing fruits, the hum of flying insects.

The grownups were happy for Annie to stay out all day if she wanted to, as long as she promised to stay away from the shed. It was an easy promise to keep. She had been in there once with her grandfather and it scared her. The smell of the old petrol lawnmower which squatted in the gloom, the tools and blades which hung from nails, the shelves of bottles and cans with the yellow labels; the skulls and crossbones. The bamboo canes neatly stacked, and the mousetraps in the corners, set with cheese rinds.

No, Annie was content to stay in the garden. Sometimes she was aware of her grandfather watching from the back porch with his sad eyes and the smallest twist of a smile. He would ask her, on her return to the house, how the apples were coming.

14

Annie's emails took longer than she'd expected. When she looked up from the screen the light was fading from the room. She stuffed her laptop into her bag, pulled the front door shut behind her, locking it and testing the handle once, twice. She took one last look at her home, then hurried along the road to the college. One of her neighbours was out in his front garden with a watering can. He raised his hand in greeting as she passed. She smiled briefly and rushed on. The lorry was already parked in the driveway in front of the simfields. They had gone ahead without her and loaded the hives onto the back.

Emily saw her coming and ran to meet her.

'I'm sorry, I...' Annie tried to catch her breath. 'Why didn't anyone phone me?'

'We knew how busy you were,' said Emily. 'It's fine, Victor knows what he's doing.'

Annie fought a rush of resentment. It should have been her.

Matt appeared on the back of the lorry, followed by a

wide, tall bear of a man. He grinned at Annie and jumped down, walking towards her with a long, easy stride. Square shoulders, shaggy hair, washed-out jeans and old walking boots. An open smile. If anything it made Annie more guarded. He should have been on the back foot, not her. Her patch, her bees. She stood up straight, put her shoulders back. 'You must be Victor,' she said, forcing a smile, shaking his hand. His skin was rough and dry. She folded her arms.

'Strange situation, isn't it?' Victor's voice was a low rumble. 'I hope you don't mind,' he continued, gesturing to the hives, 'I've already introduced myself, told them where we're going.'

'Not at all,' said Annie. There was dirt under his fingernails. He needed to take a scrubbing brush to them.

Victor continued, 'I brought the rest of my bees too – let's hope they all get on.' He chuckled to himself.

He seemed very relaxed, for someone who had practically lost his business. Too relaxed. Annie pulled her coat around her. 'I need to inspect the hives before it gets dark.' She put one foot on the metal step at the back of the lorry and hauled herself up. To her relief, Victor stayed where he was. She walked round the stacks, testing the straps, making sure the netting was closely wrapped around the hives so that none of the bees could fly away while they were in transit. She put her ear to her immaculate hives and spoke to her bees in what she hoped was a reassuring voice, letting them know she and Emily were going with them. Goodness only knew what Victor had told them – they didn't even know his voice. She wished again that she'd been there sooner to oversee the operation. At the end of the flatbed closest to the cab were a small number of rough and ready hives, built more like crates. They must be Victor's. 'I'm Annie,' she told them, and dropped her voice even further in case Victor was listening. 'I'll keep you safe.' But perhaps she shouldn't make those kinds of assurances. What happened if you lied to bees? Was she making things worse, making promises she might not be able to keep? 'I'll try my best,' she whispered, and placed the flat of her hand on the side of the nearest hive, one of her own. Beneath her palm, beneath the wooden slats, was she imagining it or could she feel the vibration of the bees as they moved and shuffled, settling down for the night?

Victor was checking his phone, his head bent towards the glow of the screen. The light was draining from the sky. Annie climbed carefully down from the flatbed and pulled her coat around her. The evening was cooling rapidly. The temperature would probably drop below what the bees had experienced before. She checked the thermometer on her phone.

Victor watched her. 'They'll be fine,' he assured her. 'They're all together, all snug. They'll keep each other warm.'

'I know that, of course.' How peevish she must sound, but… everything she'd worked for was on the back of this stranger's lorry. Her pulse was racing, her heart pattered behind her ribs. She forced herself to take a deep breath.

'I get it,' said Victor. 'I totally get it.' He looked sincere. 'If somebody I'd never met appeared out of nowhere to take my bees…' He shook his head. 'I give you my word,' he said. 'I'll look after them like they are my very own. You can trust me.'

Annie looked at him squarely. 'I'll hold you to that,' she said.

Victor seemed unperturbed.

They had agreed to guard the lorry in shifts that night, its cargo too precious to leave. Matt and Emily would take the first shift. Annie would take over at midnight before their departure at four am. She watched as Matt jumped down from the lorry and gathered Emily in his arms, brushing her hair back from her face with such tenderness – Annie shouldn't be watching. She looked at the ground.

'No way I'll be able to sleep,' said Annie, as casually as she could. 'You two might as well go back and get some rest.'

'I'll be in the cab if anything happens,' Victor reminded her. 'Don't hesitate to wake me if you need to.'

'You sure?' asked Emily, sliding her arm through Matt's, already turning in the direction of home.

'Of course,' said Annie. 'See you in a few hours.' She watched them as they hurried away into the chill darkness.

'Sweet couple,' said Victor. He walked round the perimeter of the lorry, testing the straps. 'Wake me at midnight for the next shift. Or before, if you need to. Just bang on the side of the cab.' He smiled.

How could he be so composed? Annie felt as jittery as if she'd had too much coffee.

Victor stepped up into his cab and disappeared into the back to his bunk. His voice floated down to her. 'You want a blanket out there? I've got spares.'

Annie took one gratefully and draped it around her shoulders. She pulled her hat snugly over her ears and slipped on her thermal gloves, pulling the blanket closer, rough against her cheek. She walked slowly around the lorry, taking note of the number of steps she took, trying to replicate them each time. A bird called. It was the screech of a barn owl, shrill in the darkness, shaking Annie from her counting. She stopped and listened again for the noise – it was so rare that she heard owls these days. It was like a blessing. She continued with her walk, this time counting the steps until she heard it cry again.

The night held no fears for Annie; she had loved it since camping in her back garden overnight when she was a little girl. She promised her parents that she would be fine, and so she was. She could pitch her father's tent almost all by herself; if the ground was hard he helped her with the pegs. Then she would drag the mattress from the old sofa bed in the study, down the stairs and across the garden. It filled the whole base of the tent. She returned to the house for her pillow and duvet, and made one final trip for snacks – her mother always found something delicious to send out with her: sandwiches and an apple, some crisps, a thermos of hot chocolate. They left the back door unlocked in case Annie changed her mind. She never did – not even during the hot August night when she was nine and a storm came, breaking the heatwave. Her mother was very ill by then, though Annie didn't know it. She sat in the little blue chair at Annie's bedroom window; Annie's father stood next to her, his hand on her thin shoulder. They looked out into the rain as it hammered down into the back garden. 'I'll go and bring her in,' said Annie's father. 'Leave her,' said Annie's mother. She was right. Annie would have been inconsolable if he had unzipped the tent door to carry her back to the house. She sat cross-legged in perfect contentment as the rain drummed on the roof. The tent held, and no water came through. She counted the seconds between the lightning and thunder, and made a record of it in her little notebook. She ate her sandwiches and imagined that her tent was pitched in a great forest with soaring trees, and that in the morning she would go exploring for beetles. Eventually the rain became less ferocious and the sound of it lulled her. She lay down in the nest of her duvet and fell asleep, dreaming of butterflies and great flowers which danced in the rain and caught the drops in their upturned petals.

How much time had passed? Annie stopped walking and checked her watch. Midnight. The owl was quiet now, and the silence from her surroundings was complete, pressing on her ears, filling her head. When she resumed walking it was the only sound she could hear – the scrunch of her boots in the gravel. In the early days of the project the night had been full of sounds – much more so than in the town, sometimes. Foxes, tiny rodents of all kinds, rabbits, stoats and polecats. Barn owls, little owls and tawny owls. In the spring, busy colonies of frogs and toads in the ponds around the campus had kept up their choruses for much of the night. The grumbling of badgers. Communities of beasts under cover of darkness. In the early days Annie would often stay late at the simfields – she was so thrilled that everything had worked out as she'd planned. Sometimes she had walked around the Dome at night talking to the bees, telling them how lucky they were, explaining how important it was that everything went well, as she had told everyone it would.

'Do you remember?' she asked them softly, now. Even her quietest voice sounded too loud in the dark. 'You did so well. Now I need you to prove yourselves all over again.' She let her hand brush along the hives as she passed. 'I don't want to let you go. But I know you can do it.'

The weather was changing now – the wind came rushing through the trees, clouds hurried in across the sky, covering the stars, obscuring the sliver of moon. Annie was glad – the clouds would stop the falling temperature. She didn't even mind when it began to rain, tentatively at first, then gradually intensifying. Her bees were used to wind and rain in the simfields, thanks to the technicians who had written the weather programming. She pulled the hood of her coat up over her hat and took shelter beside the lorry. Her hat, her hood, the wind and rain all muffled what it was possible for her to hear. In spite of the cold, underneath all of her layers she felt relatively warm and comfortable, and suddenly very tired. Without intending to stay there for long she leaned against the step on the passenger side of the lorry and before long her eyelids began to droop.

From nowhere, a bang – which shook the lorry and jolted Annie awake. She jerked into a standing position, blinking, adrenaline shooting through her body. Footsteps. Coming round the side of the cab. She faced the direction of noise, hands raised protectively in front of her, knees slightly bent. 'Victor!' she screamed, as loudly as she could, banging hard on the side of the cab.

Victor loomed out of the darkness in front of her. 'What is it?'

'It's you.' She slumped against the lorry, her heart thumping.

'Why didn't you wake me?' he said. It's nearly three.' He rubbed his eyes, his hands balled into fists, like a child. 'Why don't you hop up into the cab and grab some sleep before we go? I'll take my turn out here.'

It had stopped raining. Annie could make out the stars in the spaces between the thinning clouds. Tomorrow night they would be far away from the world she had so carefully maintained for the past ten years. Since the start of the project she had never spent even one night away from Hattenden. She hesitated, thinking of her own bed, only ten minutes' walk away. It was, suddenly, too far. She thanked Victor and climbed into the cab, kicking off her boots, lying down on his still-warm bed, pulling the blanket across her body, falling over the edge into sleep.

15

From Hattenden, the lorry followed the base of the steep scarp of the Downs, passing through sleeping villages and fields of livestock, their perimeters picked out by floodlights, patrolled by security guards with dogs. Victor leaned forward, resting his forearms on the steering wheel, peering into the patch of light cast by the headlights.

Annie sat in the passenger seat, staring out of the window at the dark world outside. Behind her, Emily slept in Victor's bunk, and beyond that, on the flatbed, Victor and Annie's bees in their thousands. Be safe, be safe. Please be okay. As soon as they arrived at the farm she could check on them.

'You should get some more sleep,' said Victor, not taking his eyes off the road. 'It's going to be a long day.'

She knew about long days and hard work, aching shoulders from hunching over her laptop, cramped legs from sitting in the simfields, her eyes sore from close observation. 'We're nearly there now. I'll be fine,' she told him.

The road followed the River Stour, passing south of Canterbridge, and as the sky began to lighten, Victor turned off the road onto a rutted lane, which he followed until they came to a closed gate. He braked and unclipped his seatbelt.

'I've got it,' said Annie, and she hopped down from the cab to let the lorry through, closing the gate behind it and following Victor into the yard. A large red-brick farmhouse sat on one side of the yard, flanked by outbuildings.

Muddled with sleep, Emily climbed down from the cab to help Annie and Victor to start unloading the hives onto a trailer that was hitched to a tractor. An elderly man emerged from the farmhouse, greeting Victor like a long-lost friend then clambering up onto the tractor and starting the engine.

'That's Mr Tyler,' said Victor. 'I'll do introductions later.'

'What happens now?' said Annie.

'Just watch,' said Victor. 'Then next time you'll know what to do.' He hopped onto the back of the tractor. 'Try to keep up,' he said as the tractor pulled away. Annie and Emily followed behind as Victor and Mr Tyler distributed the hives up and down the tidy rows of apple trees in the low light of the early morning.

Annie held her breath as the sun broke over the horizon. Once the light had reached the hives the bees, slowly at first, then with gathering confidence, began to leave their shelters and spread like a fine mist into the trees. They were not used to such wide-open spaces. Victor had assured her that they would be fine, it was instinct, but… what if they became disorientated? They might not be able to find the blossoms, and what if they flew too far away and couldn't find their way back? She watched them closely for signs of trauma or confusion, but they showed none – flying from bloom to bloom, landing on the papery petals, unfurling their proboscises to drink the sweet nectar and picking up pollen grains on their fine leg hairs as they did so. They flew on to other blossoms where the pollen would dislodge and fertilise the flower, and fruit would eventually grow. She'd never imagined she would see this – her bred-in-captivity colonies out in the open air. In the breeze, and bright sunlight. No temperature or humidity controls. It wasn't what she'd wanted, but… how wonderful to see them adjusting so seamlessly to the new environment.

The sound of the bees was soothing. She pulled her little notepad from the back pocket of her jeans and fished in her shirt pocket for one of the pens she always carried. 'Try to get an idea of how far they stray from the hives, would you, Emily?' she said. 'See if you can make a note of how long they're staying out.' She bent her head again to her notebook, scrawling notes, thinking again about how they would collect all the data for this extraordinary experiment.

16

When had she stopped noticing the changes in the hedgerows? In her hurry to get to the simfields every day, with all of her focus on her research, Annie had forgotten to stop and look. But she noticed now, walking the lanes around the farms, and felt a pull deep in her guts. Plants unfurled after the long winter, sending up optimistic shoots into the warming air. Ferns unspooled towards the light. Banks of deadnettles, their small ivory flowers peeking from beneath the blush of the leaves. There was still some wild honeysuckle winding through the hedges, flowering early, the flowers heavy with scent, thick with sweetness. But where was the cow parsley? The buttercups and dandelions? In their place, a species of grass she'd never seen before, its edges cruelly sharp. Annie stopped to admire elegantly striped snail shells, a vole whisking through the long grass, a cluster of ladybirds hidden in the hollow of a tree, suspended in hibernation until the sun called them back to life.

All those changing seasons she'd lost: the wax and wane

of the year, the thrill of the turning leaves, or a first frost, the blush of wild bluebells glimpsed through trees. In her eagerness to save the natural world she had somehow lost sight of it, and now some things seemed to have disappeared completely. The chatter of sparrows and finches was gone – she saw only a pair of skinny woodpigeons sheltering on the branch of a tree.

She stopped walking, her eye caught by a flash of colour in the hedge. There on a new leaf sat a species of beetle she didn't recognise, its body armour a shiny copper. As she watched, it began to waddle towards the stem. She put her finger in its way and it took a short-cut up and over, its feet dotting along her skin, a barely discernible patter-pat.

17

The days turned into weeks. They stopped at each farm for three days at the most, then covered the hives with netting and loaded them back onto the lorry. Victor took the lead ('Don't worry, I've done this a million times'), but Annie followed behind, checking and double-checking that everything was secure. 'It's not that I don't trust you, Victor,' she said each time. 'I just need to see for myself.' She wanted to trust him, she told herself, as she pulled on the straps he'd already tested to make sure they were tight. Victor seemed to accept it, saying nothing.

Annie and Emily put their few belongings into small rucksacks and flung them into the back of the cab before Victor drove on to the next place. Annie's most precious possessions, her notebooks, she took with her everywhere. Emily kept a visual diary with videos and photos to document their progress. It was only March and already it felt like summer.

Victor and Emily were good company and didn't require anything of Annie outside of their daily tasks. The farmers were always grateful to see them and made sure they had comfortable rooms and as much food as they could afford to give. And yet – Annie felt herself becoming threadbare. Every waking moment was spent with other people. Victor, Emily, polite conversation with the farmers. Breakfast, lunch and dinner in company. The constant interaction stretched her thin as a shadow. Night patrols were the worst. Hours of watchful pacing, her senses searching the darkness for any signs that things were not as they ought to be, all the while trying to be companionable. Emily, who knew her best, was the easiest to partner with. She understood about being quiet and not having to talk. Best of all were the times when Annie shut herself away with the day's data. Before starting to type up her notes she would sit perfectly still and close her eyes, revelling in the simple fact of being alone.

They were on a small farm south of Crowborough where the money had run out. Annie and Emily were sharing a tiny bedroom at the back of the house which overlooked a collapsing barn where the farmer kept three cows, and the smell made Emily gag if Annie ever tried to open the window. The yard was littered with rusty machinery and the apple trees were rangy and overgrown.

One afternoon Victor, Annie and Emily left the farmer and his family to patrol the fields and watch over the hives so that they could drive to the nearest town to collect their rations. The farmers had very little to spare, and though they were often welcomed with breakfast after setting out the hives, they depended on their week's rations for food.

While Victor drove, Emily sat behind them on the bunk to phone Matt. Annie turned up the radio to give Emily some privacy. It was uncomfortably warm in the cab, and Annie lowered the passenger-side window, leaning her head against the frame to catch the breeze. 'I'm worried about the bees in this heat,' she said.

'They'll adjust,' said Victor.

How could he be so sure? He was always so infuriatingly calm. Where Annie relied on data, Victor seemed to run on intuition. One thing he'd been right about: it had turned out that her bees knew exactly what to do and weren't at all fazed by being in the wide open. Annie told them how proud she was, walking around the orchards during the day, or at night when it was her turn to guard the hives.

Annie leaned back against the seat and watched the fields flick by. Was it too late to reverse the damage? There was still life. There was still growth. If there was a harvest of some kind at the end of the season, could they build on it next year? The wild pollinator colonies just needed a chance to recover – perhaps with the support of her bees they might. Things could get better. More insects would support more plant fertilisation. More insects would also mean more birds, and the birds in turn would help with seed distribution. The quiet woods and gardens would once more be loud with birdsong. People might begin to grow more flowering plants in their gardens, and this in turn would encourage more insects – in her mind's eye Annie saw abundant growth: plants twining over fences and sheds and concrete patios. People had seen what they could lose; now surely they would take more of an interest in looking after the natural environment, using fewer weedkillers and artificial fertilisers, growing their own fruit and vegetables, even. Returning to the outdoors, depending less on the things which had taken them away from it in the first place – the tablets and screens and computers which had moved people indoors and glued them to their sofas. They could turn this terrible thing around, make it into something positive, rediscovering how good it was to live outside and work with the land… It could work, maybe.

They came to the outskirts of the town, its streets too narrow to comfortably get through with the lorry, but Victor took it carefully, slowing to a crawl to get past the cars parked along the roadside. Lots of the houses were for sale – just like everywhere.

'People don't want to stay in small, out-of-the-way places, not when the future is unsure,' said Victor. They wanted to go where there were people to look after them – the police and army presence was concentrated in larger towns and cities, along with the hospitals and the doctors.

Life in the countryside made you vulnerable. All the same, having lived in the village for so long, Annie would never choose to go back again to built-up streets and crowds.

18

Matt looked briefly his mobile phone to see who was calling. It was Dr Abrams, again. He set the phone back down, letting it go to voicemail. Annie phoned several times each day – he'd pick up once or twice, but he'd taken to leaving his phone on silent so he wouldn't be disturbed. The messages she left were brief.

'It is… just wonderful, to see them at work in the open air.'

'It feels like we're doing something important, Matt.'

'We won't know how successful it's been for a while yet – start investigating how we can get harvest reports back from the farmers, would you?'

'Heading to the next farm tomorrow.'

'We think about ninety per cent of them returned today, we can't afford to lose any more.'

'Matt, this is very unprofessional. Pick up, would you?'

'Matt.'

'Matt? For God's sake.'

'It's hard to tell how many came back today. Seventy-five per cent, maybe?'

She was beginning to sound weary. Matt felt guilty, but if he picked up every time the phone rang he wouldn't have time for anything else. He spent most of his days in the simulated meadows. There was an area down by the lake which needed repair; the liner had leaked, saturating the surrounding area, drowning many of the plants. He'd drained the lake and patched the liner, but sourcing replacement plants was increasingly difficult; many of their old suppliers had folded. He spent several days exploring the wild areas beyond the campus perimeter, where the fields ended and the woods began – taking his spade and digging plant saplings, taking them back to quarantine them in one of the empty nursery rooms before he planted them in the simulated meadows. Dr Abrams would have something to say about it when she found out, and rightly so. But it seemed to him more important to maintain the meadows, restoring for when the bees came back. He made careful note of where he planted each new specimen; that way he could keep an eye on them in their new habitat, monitoring them for any signs of disease. With the last of their special grasses mix he sowed seed over the damaged areas and watered them in.

Last thing every day he checked his emails, replying to any that needed a response and sending a brief daily report to Annie. Then he locked up and walked across the campus to the disused greenhouses to check on what he'd hidden there.

19

The hives had come almost full circle now; the lorry was nearing Sarre Farm on the edge of the North Downs. Then they would turn back towards Hattenden and the last of the orchards at the Walker farm. After that, they would move the bees on to the soft fruit and vegetable farms. The days blurred together.

The best thing about their nomadic life had been leaving the news behind. Since the horror of the Pandemic and the World Crashes which followed, Annie kept one eye on the news so she wouldn't be knocked sideways when the next terrible thing happened. In Hattenden she'd kept a scrolling news banner at the bottom of her screen – the constant news feed formed the background hum to all of her days. It did her no good, and she knew it. But now she didn't have such easy access to the news channel; her phone was old and incapable of keeping up with her apps, and she didn't like to ask to use the farmer's WiFi unless it was for work. Victor avoided the news as assiduously as she had once searched for it. He listened only to music stations in the cab, and if an item of news came on he would click through the channels until he found something else.

They arrived at Sarre Farm. It was large and well-kept, a vast Georgian farmhouse. By this time, they all knew their parts so well that they almost didn't need to speak. After weeks of watching Victor's calm way with the bees, his lack of protective gear, the absence of a smoker, first Emily and then Annie, newly confident, had cast off their veils and gloves. The day ran smoothly in light-filled orchards which glowed with new greens, and Annie felt herself beginning to relax. At the end of the day she sat on the edge of her bed and slipped off her trainers. For once, she and Emily didn't have to share a room. Alone. It was bliss. The bedroom was high-ceilinged and airy, and Annie had pushed the sash windows high to catch the evening breezes. Out in the yard the farmer called to his brother as they began the first watch. She should take a shower, type up her notes. In a few minutes. She lay back, exhausted, breathing in the smell of the fresh sheets, and trying to ignore the growling of her empty stomach.

Something had changed. Despite Annie's many misgivings at the start, she had to admit she was enjoying this new way of life. She had become closer to the bees – perhaps because it wasn't just about data-gathering any more. She felt herself opening up – her perspectives had shifted, recalibrated, as she lifted her eyes from the research. Her world at the Dome had been so small by comparison – now she saw the vastness of the countryside with fresh eyes – the sweep of steep chalky hills which rose from the marshes, the rolling Weald, the wide skies above her, impossibly blue. She was in her right place. A tiny cog in an immense machine. An ant crawling over the landscape, small, small.

There was a knock at the bedroom door and Emily came straight in. Her face was pale, her eyes wide.

'What's happened?' asked Annie, already halfway off the bed. 'Is it the bees?'

'No, no.' Emily shook her head. 'Matt says there are riots in London and Birmingham. They're looting the supermarkets.'

It was what Annie had feared since the start of rationing. 'Go down and ask if we can watch the television for a minute,' said Annie. 'I'll be there in a second.' Rumours of severe food shortages were rife, and not helped by the presence of security guards outside every shop. She'd never seen anyone lose their temper while she was queuing, but it was in the air – the sense that they were all standing on the very edge of what constituted civilised behaviour, the feeling that it would only take something very small to tip them over into madness. 'This is it,' she murmured to herself as she hurried down the stairs, into the little sitting room where Emily had turned on the screen on the wall. 'This is where it begins.'

Although perhaps, thought Annie, this hadn't been the moment at all. Perhaps it had begun on the day when the very first hive of bees was wiped out by colony collapse. The day when the first of the icebergs began to melt. The day when somebody somewhere had decided it would be a good idea to grow green beans on a far-off continent so that supermarkets could fly them in and stock them all year round. It had begun long, long ago, but nobody had cared to notice. Whatever it was that was happening, it was serious, and there would be worse to come. The newsreader's face was pale under her makeup as she spoke to the reporter on the scene. There was a look of naked fear in her eyes that no amount of professional training could cover.

20

Caitlin was waiting for them in her farmyard as they drove in, and Annie liked her immediately. A tall wiry figure, short grey hair curling around a gentle face, the sleeves of her checked shirt rolled up to the elbows, hands on hips, a coiled spring of energy. As Victor stepped down from the cab she bounded forward and embraced him. 'You're a sight for sore eyes,' she told him. She turned to Annie. 'Make yourself at home,' she said. 'I mean it. Only reason I'm still going is because of this lovely man.' She held Victor's face in her hands and squeezed his cheeks as though he was her own child.

'You look well,' he said.

Caitlin laughed. 'Today is a good day.'

They hurried to set out the hives in the orchards and went about their daily routine. Annie stationed herself outside one of the hives in the top orchard, from where she could see the whole farm. Of all the places they had so far stayed at, this one was special. It was well-loved, and though the paintwork needed attention and the tractors were the first generation of electric machinery, the yard was clean and the fields were well-tended.

After the day's work, Annie went to the kitchen to make a hot drink. Caitlin had gone out walking. Annie filled the kettle at the cracked butler's sink and set it on the stove to heat, then she looked at the carefully labelled jars of herbs lined up on the dresser. Dried peppermint, chamomile, comfrey, nettle, lavender. Jars of chicory and liquorice root. She chose lavender, opening the jar and breathing deeply. High summer. Drowsy heat. She dropped a pinch of it into her mug, then stood at the window to wait for the kettle to boil.

The kitchen windows were open to let in the breeze, and it carried Victor's voice in the garden as he talked on the phone.

'You mustn't worry about the news, sweetheart.'

A pause.

'When? When was this?'

Annie knew she shouldn't be listening, but... it wasn't as though she was trying to eavesdrop.

'And... are the girls all right?' Victor's voice sounded strained. 'Best to keep them inside after school.'

A long pause, then.

'I'll come and get you. No... no, Iris. My mind is made up. It's not safe for you and the girls. Hold on.'

His voice was getting closer. Annie dropped back from the window as he came towards the house, and when he opened the back door she was standing by the kettle.

'Have you seen Caitlin?' he asked her.

'She's out,' said Annie.

Victor spoke into his phone. 'I'll call you back.' He ended the call and slipped the phone into his back pocket, then ran his fingers through his curly hair.

'Anything I can do?' asked Annie.

'More riots,' said Victor. 'Round the corner from our house. There's a corner shop, it's only small. Last night people smashed their way in with hammers and the owner had to be taken to hospital. By the time the ambulance arrived the shelves were stripped bare.' He picked at a fingernail. 'I have to go.'

'I'll mind the fort here,' said Annie. She and Emily knew exactly what to do. 'Are you going now?'

He nodded. 'I'll stay there tonight, pack up a few things, then I'll bring everyone back here tomorrow.' He stopped, looked at Annie. 'Tell Caitlin – I'll call her from the road to explain.'

'As soon as she gets back,' said Annie. 'Go, go.'

'Thank you,' said Victor.

Annie had never seen him look so worried. 'It'll be okay,' she told him.

She stood at the back door, and watched him climb into the cab and drive away.

21

Each morning, each evening, Caitlin walked the perimeter of her orchards. It was a custom, a compulsion, a pilgrimage, a remembrance. She had walked these fields daily with her husband when he was alive, and in her footsteps were memories. The retracing of paths helped to keep him with her. Out along the driveway to the hedge by the road, and she tucked in to walk along the inside of the hedge. This was where the cider apples were planted: hard and sour. Kingston Black and Brown Snout. Somerset Redstreak and Cortland. Through a gap in the hedge then into the field they'd planted up with Coxes and Galas, Discovery and Braeburn. The eaters. Juicy and sweet, and fragrant as honey when they ripened. It was her habit, when the fruit was on the trees, to pick one of each variety as she walked round, and eat one apple she found on the way, the juice running down her chin, wiped away with the back of her hand. She was close to him there. Thomas. Thirty-four years of marriage. They had not been blessed with children – she was glad of it now, these days, when there was no good to be found anywhere. Long ago she would have liked to leave their farm to the next generation, and there had been years when she mourned. But now? What good would it do to pass on this land, these fields of trees upon trees? Caitlin passed into the next orchard and walked to the end – this marked the farthest corner and her halfway point. The orchard was planted with Bramleys. When the harvest time came she would take all the windfalls for herself. The old chest freezer which nearly blocked the back hallway was filled with apple sauce and sliced Bramleys ready for pies and crumbles.

The next fields were pears, cherries and plums, then she turned back towards the farmhouse, the home stretch, and her favourite field – the smallest – planted with heritage apples, Thomas's little projects which had resulted in a glorious mishmash of colours and shapes – nothing the supermarkets or suppliers were ever interested in, but Caitlin and Thomas turned the field over to Pick Your Own customers, and sold bags at farmers' markets and autumn fairs. She loved this approach to the house, along the rows of trees. The blossoms were alive with Victor and Annie's bees. The petals danced in the air. She worried about the future, but for today all was well and life carried on. She was grateful for the reminder. As always, she felt the loss of Thomas like an ache. She would never stop missing him. After fifteen years the pain hadn't gone. I'll keep going, for you, she promised. She put her fingers to her lips and pressed the kiss against the nearest tree trunk.

As she got closer to the house she saw the back door opening. Victor walked through, head down, shoulders hunched, hands in pockets. He hurried round the side of the house, along the path and out to the yard where his lorry was parked. He climbed up into the cab and without a pause the lorry pulled away, down the drive and towards the road.

22

Iris locked the front door behind her when they left early the following morning. She'd said nothing to the neighbours about their going. She climbed into the cab next to Victor and the girls, and he drove through the empty streets, past the burned-out shell of the corner shop, its windows partially boarded up. For Sale signs had sprung up since Victor left in the spring, a forest of them up and down the street. Iris talked about those of her friends who were moving to London or heading west to Bristol and Exeter. It was safer there, she told him. The smaller towns would be left to fend for themselves. And there were rumours of shortages of even the most basic medicines. Why, she asked him again, did they have to move even further away from safety, out into the countryside where nobody would even notice if they disappeared?

Victor made soothing noises, nodding to her over the heads of their daughters. Not in front of the girls – we'll talk about it later. Before long they were pulling on to the motorway, heading east, the sun in Victor's eyes. He switched on the radio and found a song he knew the girls liked, forcing himself to sing along, hoping his daughters would join in. They did – and then he let his voice fade out, unable to carry on the pretence, concentrating on the road, hunched over the wheel.

When Caitlin came out to welcome them, Maria and Sophie were wide-eyed and silent, and Sophie hid behind Iris's legs when Caitlin bent towards her to say hello. It was the first time they had ever stayed away from home, explained Victor, and they weren't used to being around strangers.

They'd brought very few belongings, just a bag each, and their food rations in a supermarket carrier bag. Iris set it in a corner of the kitchen and insisted that they would not take any other food from Caitlin. 'We must make do,' she seemed fond of saying, and it took gentle persuasion from Caitlin before she could be persuaded to accept eggs or milk, even for the girls, although Caitlin's cow produced more than enough for everyone, and the chickens were laying well. 'The girls have their supplements,' said Iris. 'You're too kind.' She knew Victor was giving Caitlin money for them to stay in one of her bedrooms, but it pained Iris to accept the food.

Caitlin waited for the girls to come to her. She was aware of them watching her, warily, as she went about her chores. When she left the house with Victor she noticed them peeking from behind the curtains in the upstairs windows, following their progress towards the trees.

The next day, to Victor's surprise, it was Sophie who approached Caitlin first, with Maria a few steps behind.

They trailed after her in the orchard, Sophie slipping her hand into Caitlin's as they walked along.

'Did you see that?' said Victor, from his vantage point at the top of the next field.

Iris sat next to him on a blanket, her knees drawn up to her chin like a little girl, her phone abandoned next to her. She raised her head to see where he was pointing, then rested it again on her knees.

Victor was relieved that he'd been able to coax her outside into the sunshine. His girls would be fine when he moved on to the next farm with Annie and Emily. But would Iris?

'Why can't I come with you?' she asked, as though he'd spoken out loud.

'We've been over this, love. There's not enough room in the cab, and it would be too much to expect the farmers to take us all in.' Victor caught Iris's petulant eye-roll but said nothing; she was scared for herself and the girls. She'd been forced to abandon their house, their friends, their lives. 'Caitlin is different,' he pressed on. 'She's like family.'

'Your family,' said Iris, holding her phone aloft, checking again for a signal. 'Nothing,' she said, dropping it back on the blanket.

Iris wanted an argument, but Victor wasn't going to oblige. 'She's more than happy for you to stay,' he said. 'It's safe here. And the girls think they're on holiday. Just look at them.' Sophie and Maria sat in the lower branches of an apple tree, legs swinging, their pretty cardigans folded over Caitlin's arm. She was watching them like a mother hen.

Iris looked again and gave a wry smile. 'Honeymoon

period,' she said. 'They'll get bored with trees soon enough and start asking for their screens.'

Along with the patchy phone signal the broadband at the farmhouse was limited. He'd seen no sign that his daughters were missing their tablets at all – it was Iris who seemed dissatisfied, wandering the rooms of the farmhouse, trailing her fingers over the bookshelves, staring unseeingly at the pieces of a half-finished chess game. But she would get through it. They all would. And while he was here, he would look after her.

Iris sighed and laid her head on his shoulder. She lifted his hand, turned it over and kissed his palm. 'I wish you didn't have to go so soon,' she said quietly. 'I like seeing you at work.' She pressed the back of his hand to her cheek. 'You're a good shepherd.'

He raised his eyebrows at her in mock surprise. She didn't like the bees, and they both knew it. They scared her. 'Nasty, crawling things,' she'd said once. It was the crawling that appalled her; she couldn't explain why.

'I'll just miss you, is all,' she said.

23

On their last morning, just as the sun was rising, Annie went out of the back door of Caitlin's farmhouse. There was a noise from the fields: the clatter of machinery, and the distant thump of something falling, or being dropped. She stood listening for a moment by the old tractor Caitlin had set in a corner of the garden. It had taken on the quality of a sculpture – monumental, paint gradually giving way to the weather, blooms of rust along the wheel arches, freckled with orange and gold and brown on the moulded metal seat. Annie caught the distant hum of a vehicle on the top road. She walked to the end of the garden and let herself through the wooden gate with the missing catch, the grain of the wood silvered with age and repeated winters. She had no shoes and her feet were wet with dew, the hems of her trouser legs damp where they had brushed through the long grass. She walked on through the field, the flinty soil uncomfortable. She would not turn back, stubbornly pressing on to where she thought the noise had come from, and as she reached the place where the rows of apple trees began, she saw that the first hive – one of her own – was tipped over on its side, the rectangular wooden frames spilling into the grass. The combs on each frame, their golden hexagonal cells broken and bleeding honey into the grass, the strong sweet scent of pollen and honey filled the air. There were bees squashed and drowning in honey, their legs moving slowly, beyond saving, their furry bodies trapped in the sticky ooze. The rest of the colony had fled. Looking farther up the field Annie could see more of her hives on their sides, and empty spaces where they'd placed others. Now there was only flattened grass to show where they had been.

'I should have been there,' gasped Annie. She hadn't touched the overturned hives. Not knowing what to do, unable to think, she'd run back to the farmhouse. She stood in the gloomy kitchen trying to catch her breath.

Victor had followed her back. He hung his head. 'It happened on my watch. I was in the far field. My fault.'

'Nobody is to blame,' said Emily, moving to stand next to Annie. 'There's no way we can protect them all. We can't watch every field all of the time.' Emily lifted her arm, as though she was going to put it around Annie's shoulders – then she appeared to change her mind. She drew back. Annie was relieved. She did not want to be hugged.

'We need to increase the patrols,' said Victor.

'How?' asked Annie. 'There are only four of us.' She looked at Victor. Iris hadn't yet offered to help. Why hadn't he insisted that she should do her part?

He was pulling on his boots. 'We have to go set the hives back up,' he said. 'We can only hope that the bees come back at sunset.'

'Annie, you're shaking,' said Emily. 'Why don't you sit down?'

Annie shook her head and followed Victor towards the door. For the first time, she let him take the lead without questioning. He seemed to know exactly what to do, and she followed his instructions, gently setting the hives back into position and checking the frames before slotting them back into the hives. She watched him trying to rescue her bees, carefully taking them onto his fingers to get them out of the sticky honey. Would they survive, then? He talked quietly while he worked. Whether it was to her or to the bees Annie didn't know, but his voice was reassuring, and she understood, at last, that she could trust him.

The bees did not return. The surviving queens would have taken their colonies elsewhere, Victor explained gently to his daughters. The bees were very clever, he said, holding their hands. They would find somewhere safe to live. The girls were not to worry about them. Annie wished she was little again, then she could have believed him too.

That evening, when Emily and Victor loaded up the lorry to move on to the soft fruit farms, they were twelve hives down. Victor had gently suggested to Annie that she might help Caitlin in the kitchen. Annie didn't need convincing. She couldn't bear to see the empty spaces on the lorry.

Caitlin was cooking a feast, while Sophie and Maria watched from the kitchen table. When Annie protested at all the food she was preparing, Caitlin was adamant. 'I've been careful with my stores,' she told Annie. She tipped a plate of chopped-up apple into a bowl of cake mixture. 'There's more than enough to give you a good send-off.' She stirred in the apple then poured the cake mixture into a tin. 'Girls, do you want to lick the bowl?' Sophie was quickly at her side. She carried the bowl carefully back to Maria at the table. Caitlin put the cake tin into the oven.

It had been a long time since Annie had eaten cake. As the smell of baking filled the kitchen her stomach growled in anticipation. When Caitlin laid thick slices of bacon into a hot pan on the stove, Annie felt almost faint with longing. The rashers began to sizzle temptingly on the heat, and Sophie and Maria crept closer to the pan, giggling. Despite everything that had happened that morning – the destruction of the hives, the loss of the bees and the thought of leaving Caitlin's farm – it was impossible not to feel a little cheered by the prospect of the meal ahead.

Caitlin opened the door into the garden. 'Maria, see if you can find me some lettuce, would you please?' she said, and Maria ran out into the sunny evening to look.

It was a long way from that first early spring night and Annie's double shift in the rain before they left the Dome. Annie and Sophie set the table using Caitlin's pretty china while Caitlin stood at the sink draining whey from the soft cheese she'd made. She saved the whey in a mug – it was for her neighbour's pigs, she explained.

'It'll be hard to leave,' said Annie, counting out plates. 'You've spoiled us.'

'It's been my pleasure,' said Caitlin. 'This big old place, it's better with people in it.'

'You've still got us,' said Sophie, setting out teaspoons.

Caitlin turned to her. 'You girls,' she said.

'And Iris?' wondered Annie, dropping her voice. Where was she? Never joining in, never offering to help.

'Don't worry,' said Caitlin quietly. 'She's lost her home, poor thing – been uprooted – and lost a bit of herself along with it. But she'll come round.'

Annie nodded. Hadn't she felt just the same when Attica told her she would have to give up her bees?

Caitlin slipped her arm through Annie's. 'None of this is easy,' she murmured, looking at Sophie, who showed no signs of having heard. 'All of us have to find our own ways to get through. Iris has her daughters to think of too. What kind of world are we leaving those girls?'

It was comforting to be held in the crook of Caitlin's capable arm. Annie allowed herself to stay there for a few moments more before she drew back, wiping her eyes, embarrassed. 'Sorry,' she said to Caitlin. 'I'm not usually—'

'No sorrys.' Caitlin flapped them away with her tea towel.

For a moment Annie wished she could stay there forever. But it was no good wishing. The riots and food shortages were real to her now. She drew herself upright. They had to keep going, despite the loss of the hives. There was no going back. 'Thank you for everything,' said Annie.

'You're always welcome here,' said Caitlin. 'You and your bees.' She set the dish of cheese on the table, then went to check on the bacon.

Annie watched Sophie's face brighten as Maria burst through the back door waving a plump round lettuce.

'Time to eat, I think,' said Caitlin. 'Sophie, would you give them all a shout?'

24

They left before the sunrise for the first of the soft fruit farms, driving down in the direction of the coast. Emily searched the stations until she found some music from the before times – a disco track from long before any of them had been born, but somehow they knew all the words. 'Turn it up,' said Victor. He was downcast after saying goodbye to his family, his eyes fixed on the road, shoulders hunched over the wheel. The bass filled the cab, thumping in their ears, drowning out everything else. Could the bees feel it too, Annie wondered, the vibrations of the bass guitar and drums? Or was it drowned out by the thrum of the wheels against the road and the wind through the netting?

They arrived at the farm in plenty of time to set out the hives. The sky was lightening into shades of palest pink, but they had a short while before the sun appeared over the horizon. The farm was only a few miles from the sea. A small prefab bungalow with a machine shed towering over it, a series of wooden shacks and a cracked concrete yard – but weed-free, and the buildings were patched but tidy. The land was low – large flat fields divided by hedges and trees to stop the wind from raking up the strawberry plants. From a distance the heaped-up soil and thick straw along the rows almost obscured the plants, but as Annie crossed the field behind the farmer's small tractor with its trailer load of hives, the leaves appeared out of the gloom, the small flowers just beginning to glow white in the light of the early morning. Strawberry fields, raspberry canes, gooseberry and currant bushes.

Annie whispered to the bees as she set the hives carefully at the end of the strawberry rows. Looking over at Victor on the other side of the rows she saw that he was doing exactly the same thing. He looked up and caught her staring. She was hit by a sudden wave of fear. They had lost so many bees. Did they have enough left to make it work?

There were more birds over the farm than Annie had been used to. Gulls circled in the skies above the fields. It was because they were near the sea, Victor said. They hung around the fishing boats. It was always difficult to protect the bees here, he said. The soft fruits, once they began to grow, would be screened with netting.

Back at the farmhouse the kitchen table was set for them with a pot of blackcurrant leaf tea and a loaf of bread. 'Sorry it's not more,' said the farmer's son. His face was gaunt. He and his wife hurriedly pulled on their boots before going out to take the first turn guarding the hives. 'There's some berries thawing in that bowl there.' He indicated a china dish covered by a plate. 'Softens up the bread, like.'

'We're very grateful,' said Victor.

Annie and Emily murmured their thanks.

25

The next farm on the route lay just inland, a little way along the coast. Victor drove carefully along the dark lanes. They were narrow – made narrower by grass and overgrown hedges. Nobody said much. They were quiet because they were all hungry, thought Annie, remembering their last meal at Caitlin's with longing. She'd mopped up the bacon fat with a slice of bread until there was nothing left on the plate at all. She'd eaten two thick slices of cake heaped with soft cheese, and that night, for the first time in months, she'd gone to bed feeling full. At the last place, after their breakfast of bread and fruit, the farmer had had nothing at all to give them, so they'd fallen back on what remained of their rations: protein bars and packet soups. It wasn't enough to keep them going during the long days and nights in the fields. She hoped the next farmer might have something for them. She had a sudden longing for a glass of fresh, cold milk. She tried not to think about it.

Emily spoke up, startling Annie from her thoughts. 'Slow down,' she said. 'What's that, up ahead?'

Victor took his foot off the accelerator. Coming out of the night was a small group of people straggling single file along the road. Some of them wore hi-vis jackets. As the lights from the lorry picked them out of the gloom they held up their hands to shield their eyes from the glare.

Victor slowed the lorry to a crawl, inching past the people as they climbed up onto the verges and cowered into the hedge.

A man held up a crying child as they drove past, its eyes scrunched shut, mouth stretched wide to howl.

'Stop, for God's sake,' said Emily.

One of the walkers banged on the side of the cab, and others joined in.

Emily leaned across Annie to roll down the window.

'Don't,' said Victor.

Emily drew back.

The banging got louder. Annie flinched. 'We don't have anything for you.' She mouthed the words exaggeratedly, shaking her head. 'Sorry.' She pictured the scanty meals they'd been invited to share. Farmers and their families with pinched, anxious faces, staying up all night to protect their crops and machinery from local gangs. But… even with their struggles, it was true that some of the farmers had a little more than most – she thought of Caitlin with the eggs from her small flock, and her windfall apples.

'So what do we do?' asked Emily.

'We do our job,' said Victor firmly. 'That's all we can do. Don't get caught up in this. It won't help us if you get worn down by it. And that won't help them either, in the long run.' He turned to her briefly in the light from the dashboard, his face solemn. 'I mean it, Emily. Focus.'

Emily shouted at him then, at his cold heart, at the unfairness of it all. She cried for the screaming child.

Victor set his face impassively and gripped the wheel, and drove on.

Annie saw the tears flashing in his eyes. She turned to watch the people in the road, the howling child, the furious father shouting after them. The rest of the group turned their faces back towards the road and trudged on into the dark.

As the weeks wore on the weather grew warmer – unbearably so. The fields desperately needed rain. Their routine hardly varied: days and nights in the soft-fruit fields, coordinating shifts with the farmers so that there was always someone patrolling the land and keeping an eye on the hives. Sometimes a group of walkers would arrive, hollow-eyed and scrawny, asking for a meal in exchange for some work. The farmers obliged if they could, though they had almost nothing to spare. Where were their ration cards? wondered Annie. Why were they out wandering the lanes when there was food for them in the towns? On those days she and Emily gave their own meals to the walkers. At night, Annie was haunted by their faces.

At each farm, with Emily's help, Annie attempted to count the bees. In addition to the hives they'd lost at Caitlin's farm, numbers were still dropping. It was difficult to estimate the decline but they did their best, regularly checking for bodies in and around the hives. So many new places, such a spread of different habitats and microclimates, not to mention predators – the bees would be encountering numerous organisms they had never come up against before. From living in a tightly controlled environment to this – the open air and the chaos of new things. They could not possibly return to the lab with a healthy number of working hives. It would have been too much to hope for.

Late one day, as Annie wandered back to the farmhouse, she saw Victor sitting outside in the golden early-evening sunshine. He'd taken off his cap; his eyes were closed. He looked peaceful, and for a moment she wondered if she could put off what she had to say. No point, she decided. He had to know. 'I've been counting,' she told him. She paused. But there was no way to sugar-coat it. 'By my estimates we've lost at least fifty-five per cent of the bees.'

Victor winced.

Annie flopped down next to him. 'And that's being generous. I wouldn't be surprised if it was closer to sixty or sixty-five per cent.'

Victor let out a long, controlled breath. 'That sounds about right,' he said. 'I've been trying to work it out too.'

'How much longer?' asked Annie. 'How many more farms?'

'We're still on schedule,' Victor told her. 'With luck on our side I should have you home by the end of August.'

'Luck.' Annie let out a noise – a short, bitter laugh. 'Haven't you noticed, Victor? Luck isn't on our side.'

26

But Victor had judged it right. At the end of August they were packing up to move on to the last farm.

Annie sat in the yard in the early-evening light, surrounded by her near-empty hives, grim-faced, her insides twisting with hunger. Clouds lay heavy in the sky, trapping the day's heat against the fields which lay at the base of the hills. Acres of scrawny bean plants grew from the dusty earth. The farmhouse was a small bungalow surrounded by corrugated iron barns which were collapsing gently towards the ground. There had been no rain for nearly three weeks and the soil in the fields had cracked into deep fissures. In the lane that passed close to the farmyard, the scent of the wild honeysuckle in the hedges was strong, almost sickly. Annie made her notes and took photographs of the interior of each hive, using her smoker to calm the bees before cautiously removing each frame. She documented the number of little bodies, carefully transferring them into plastic storage boxes she'd begged from the farmer – boxes which had once held icecream, or frozen fruit, or leftover dinners, in the long-ago days when people had leftovers. More evidence to add to the boxes stacked underneath Victor's bunk. Once she got back to the Dome she would analyse the causes of death. The poor things – she should have fought harder for them. How long had she been holding her breath? Don't think. Keep going. Do your job.

Emily was inside, packing. From time to time her gaunt face appeared at the open window, checking the driveway, looking this way and that along the lane.

The majority of Victor's hives were half-empty too. He loaded them on to the back of the lorry as carefully as if they were made of glass, and spoke to them as he worked, in a voice that was too low for Annie to hear. She had not spoken to her bees for days now, worried that she may have transmitted her fears to them, that somehow she had been going about it all wrong.

'He's here,' called Emily. The sound of her feet running through the house, then she exploded from the front door and ran up the driveway. Annie could just make out Matt's figure as he walked in from the road.

Annie took a bottle of water and three glasses out to the tree that Matt and Emily sat beneath, their heads together, their voices falling over one another in the still air. Matt had lost weight too. But, unlike Emily, he was pale after his months in the Dome.

'Look at this.' Emily laid her deeply tanned forearm next to his and laughed. She hadn't seemed so animated in a long time.

Annie poured the water and passed it round while Matt

filled her in with news from the Dome – there wasn't much to tell, and Annie didn't want to impose on their reunion, so before long she left them and went indoors, taking her pillow and blanket from the small bedroom she'd shared with Emily and laying it on the sofa in the living room to make it clear that she wasn't expecting to sleep in the bedroom that night. Afterwards, there was really nothing to do. Ordinarily she would have used the time to go over her data, but she couldn't bear to look at it. Emily and Matt were in the garden, Victor was in the yard, the farmers were in their house – Annie desperately wanted to be alone, but where could she escape to? She walked slowly along the edge of the bean fields until she reached the low wall which marked the boundary of the farm, and the lane beyond. She sat down and wiped her face with the edge of her T-shirt. The clouds were a thick, suffocating layer; the setting sun painted them red and orange. There was no chance of the weather breaking any time soon – she'd checked the forecast – day after day of unbroken sun, and warm humid nights.

Annie returned to the farmhouse as the last of the sun was fading from the sky. The farmers had saved her a portion of carrots and reconstituted mashed potato; it sat on the kitchen counter with an upside-down bowl covering the plate. Emily and Matt had gone to the bedroom and Victor was on first watch with the bees. Annie sat in front of the bungalow. Even though the sun had gone, the temperature wasn't falling away. The muggy air barely stirred; there was no relief. She went inside and opened the living-room windows as wide as they would go, then she lay down on the sofa. If she stayed completely still she might cool down. But the sofa was deep and soft, and quickly warmed under her. She lay on her back. Sweat pooled in the dip of her clavicle and she fought the urge to sob. No matter that she was exhausted, she knew she would get no sleep. Mrs Hutchings, the farmer, was listening to loud, discordant music in the kitchen, and Mr Hutchings' voice drifted in from the yard, one half of a fractious phone call.

The heat, the noise, the people, the world – Annie could hardly breathe. She wiped her forehead with the back of her arm. Another sleepless night. Restlessly waiting to leave before the dawn. To be pressed together in the airless cab with an extra passenger, even with the windows open, would be unbearable… She made a decision. Instead of sitting in the overcrowded, claustrophobic cab she would walk to the next farm. If she started out at two am she should arrive at the next farm at about the same time as the lorry. Mr Hutchings and his brother were on the second shift patrolling the fields. All Annie had to do was wait until they had left the yard to walk towards the fields, then she would be able to get up the drive and away without being seen.

When Matt got up for a glass of water at just after two, he passed through the living room on his way to the kitchen. The windows were open wide and the curtains drawn back to let in the night air. There was enough light from the moon to see that the sofa was empty. Annie's blanket was neatly folded on top of the pillow; her bag sat next to it. On top of the bag was a page torn from a notebook, with her careful handwriting.

Can't sleep. Need fresh air – walking on to next farm
– see you there

A

PS please bring my bag?

She was out in the lanes, alone. Matt hurried back to the bedroom. Emily was deeply asleep, one arm flung above her head, her fingers curled loosely, her hair dark against the pillow. He wouldn't wake her. He gathered his clothes and shoes, and padded back to the living room. He dressed quickly, and before leaving the house he added a line of writing to the bottom of the note in his untidy scrawl.

Emily – gone to look for Annie. See you soon Matt x

27

It was a clear night, and the three-quarter moon lit the way so clearly that Annie didn't even need to use her torch. The dry earth gave up its mossy scent, overlaid with the heavy cloying honeysuckle, and Annie breathed it all in gratefully. It did seem a little cooler now. Her shoes on the road were the only sound. She strode out, relishing the freedom. It was bliss. She needed the solitude, the chance to walk at her own pace. In the woods beyond the farm an owl screeched. She hoped it would find food. It would be nice to think someone had eaten well that night.

There was a sound on the road behind her. Feet. Running feet. Thinking of the desperate walkers Annie ducked towards the hedge, crouching down, making herself as small as she could, trying to calm her breathing. A familiar voice called her name. Matt. She stood up again. He came round the corner and stopped when he came to her. He bent over, hands on his knees, breath heaving, soaked with sweat.

Matt stood up straight again. 'What were you thinking?' he gasped. 'Out here by yourself.'

'Don't be ridiculous,' she said. 'Everything's fine.'

'You have to come back with me, Annie. It's not safe.'

'We're the only ones out here, Matt.' Annie stood a little straighter. She wasn't about to be told what to do.

Matt wiped the sweat from his face. 'For just a moment can we pretend you're not my boss?' he said.

Annie folded her arms. 'That's not why I...' she said. 'Listen, Matt. This is the first peace I've had for days. I need this.' What had possessed him to follow her? She wasn't frail or helpless, whatever he might think.

For a moment Matt stood silently, as though weighing up his options.

'You don't have to come with me,' said Annie. 'I don't need looking after.' Take the hint, Matt.

'And I'm not letting you go on alone,' said Matt.

'It's decided then,' said Annie, walking on.

'Looks like it.' Matt fell into step beside her.

'We don't have to talk,' said Annie.

Matt stuck his hands deep in his pockets. 'Got it.'

They continued in silence.

The moon lit up a small creature scurrying across the road, several metres ahead of them, just before the road curved round and out of sight. Out of nowhere a pale shape swept over the hedge: silent, ghostly white. A barn owl. It swooped on wide wings towards the creature and seized it in its talons, then rose, gliding smoothly over the hedge on the other side of the road. Annie grabbed Matt's arm. 'Did you see?' she squeaked. 'Oh, I can't believe it.'

Matt put his free hand on top of Annie's and squeezed. He stopped walking. She understood a warning but... what had he seen? Matt was staring intently at the moonlit place where the little animal had been.

At the point where the road curved, just beyond where the owl had come sweeping down, a tall tree cast its darkness. As Annie watched, the shadows seemed to deepen even further. Something was there on the road, hiding in the gloom. A large and shapeless something – which, even as she stared, appeared to shift and move, growing larger, until it separated and became two somethings, and then four.

'Stay calm,' said Matt, very quietly. 'Let me do the talking.' He took a deep breath. 'If I say run, you run.' He didn't approach them – they were coming out of the shadows now, towards Annie and Matt. Four people, all dressed in dark clothes with dark hoods.

Annie's heart thumped so hard she could feel it in her ears. She noticed that Matt had placed his body slightly in front of hers, putting himself between her and the strangers. She tried to step out from behind him so that they were standing side by side – but Matt held her back with his arm.

'You're out late,' said one of them – a man whose voice was deep and quiet, and even though Annie couldn't see his face she imagined it – the sort of person you wouldn't argue with, because his voice let you know straight away he would win.

'Lost track of the time,' said Matt, easily. 'Just on our way home.'

'He's a bit young for you, love,' said one of the other people – another man, his voice a nasal whine.

One of the others laughed. A woman, perhaps.

'Give us your money and ration cards, and we won't hurt you,' said the first man, his voice so even and apparently lacking in threat that Annie almost couldn't believe she'd heard correctly. But she had, of course she had, and the man with the deep, sure voice was used to getting what he wanted without effort. She looked at Matt.

'Do as they say,' he told her.

'It's all in my bag,' she told him. 'Back at the house. All my belongings. I've got nothing with me at all.'

'Shit,' said Matt, so quietly that only she would have been able to hear it. He raised his voice. 'Neither of us have got anything.'

'Bullshit.' The figures advanced, heavy feet on the tarmac.

'Jewellery,' said Matt. 'What have you got, Annie?'

Annie's hands flew to her ears. 'Silver studs,' she said. 'Probably not worth much, but you can have them.' With shaking fingers she pulled them loose and held them out in her cupped hand.

'Rings,' said the one who sounded like a woman. Annie thought she could see her now; she was a small thing. Slight, like Emily.

'I don't wear rings,' said Annie, keeping the earrings safe in her fist, holding up both hands to show them.

'Fuck's sake,' said the whining man.

The low-voiced man stepped away from the others and swiftly crossed the rest of the space between them, moving so quickly that Annie didn't have time to react. Matt stepped right in front of her then, and held out his arms so that Annie was completely shielded, and couldn't see what happened next – but she heard the sound of Matt exhaling, his surprised grunt, and then the figures silently disappeared back into the void under the trees, vanishing along the road or through the hedge and across the fields, and the next thing she knew Matt was leaning heavily back into her and she sank to the floor, trying not to collapse under him but to support him as they fell.

'What is it?' said Annie, the weight of his torso on her bent knees, her legs tucked under her.

'He… hit me,' said Matt, with an effort. He clutched at his side.

'Show me where,' said Annie, reaching round to the place where he grabbed at his jacket. Her hand came away wet. She couldn't see it – the moon wasn't bright enough. Fear ran through her like a flood. 'Press on it,' she said, and then, fearing that he would not press hard enough, she felt where his hands were and moved them aside, pushing her own hands down on the wound, trying to think of what she might have to staunch the flow, but all she had was what she wore. With one hand she fished around in her pocket for her scarf, then scrunched it into a ball and held it over the area. 'Talk to me, Matt.' She had to try to keep him awake until help came. 'Does it hurt? Tell me.'

'Not so bad,' he said, breathlessly. She felt his chest rise and fall, his quick, shallow breaths.

'Try to stay calm,' she told him, searching the shadows in case his attackers might come back again.

'They've gone,' he told her.

It was all her fault. If she hadn't set off, alone, he would still be sleeping in bed next to Emily. If she hadn't refused to turn around, they would be almost back at the Hutchings farm by now. If she hadn't made such a fuss when the barn owl appeared the killers might not have been seen them. So many points along the way where her actions had led him closer to this moment. 'I'm sorry,' she told him, the tears running down her face. 'I'm sorry, I'm so sorry.'

'It's okay,' he said.

It wasn't okay. How long had they been sitting there in the darkness? She kept up the pressure on his wound. Surely Victor should have been there by now?

A fuzzy pre-dawn light crept into the sky. The scent of the honeysuckle flowers was the sickly smell of decay. How long would it take the lorry to reach them? Annie tried to calculate the timings, to focus on the simple question, but her mind skittered like a wasp trapped in a jar and it wouldn't settle to the task. From somewhere she thought she remembered that it was important to keep talking. 'They'll be here soon, Matt.'

He made a noise which could have been a word, but Annie didn't understand it and she chattered on, trying to fill the silence.

'They... were going to take... our cards,' said Matt, whispering the words between breaths.

'If we'd had something to give them, maybe they would have left you alone,' said Annie, trying to stop crying, trying to stay calm, but God – he was struggling to get enough air, and the scarf was sodden, it was all over her hands. 'They'll be here soon. Hold on, Matt. Hold on. Speak to me.'

'Nothing,' he whispered, 'to say.'

'I don't care,' she said, and shook him gently. 'Keep talking.' Her legs had fallen asleep under his weight, but she was scared to move, didn't want to make it worse. He was getting heavier. She wasn't going to lose him too, on top of everything else. She could clearly see the trees now, and their leaves, and streaks of pink and yellow on the horizon.

'Look at that sunrise,' she said. 'Are you looking? Open your eyes, Matt. Open them.'

He did as he was told. His eyes were glassy and unfocussed. She understood then, that he was going to leave her, and she sobbed, helpless.

The sky bled with colours. Rich and clashing, crazy-bright stripes upon stripes, and gradually the colours came back into the landscape, all the rich greens of late summer leaves. No vehicles came to find them there, sprawled in the middle of the road. Annie talked on, shaking Matt from time to time until he made some kind of response, then she carried on, desperately keeping the pressure on the wound, filling time until somebody came. Where the hell was Victor?

Annie faded in and out. Moments of hyper-vigilance followed by dreamlike absences, when she seemed to be on the very edge of consciousness. Sunlight glinted on the tarmac and the dew-soaked grasses by the side of the road. She felt that she had always been there, that she would always be there. This was her life now – all she had to do was to hold the blood-soaked scarf to Matt's chest and keep talking, though she had lapsed into silence and couldn't remember when.

'Emily?' breathed Matt. Annie could barely hear him but oh, thank God, he was still alive. A wild hope filled her as she imagined the others arriving in the nick of time and getting him to the hospital.

'She's coming,' Annie promised him. 'Stay awake, Matt. You don't want to miss her coming up the road for you.'

He murmured something that she couldn't catch. The waking countryside was near-silent too. 'Stay with me, Matt,' she urged him. 'Not long now.'

She had run out of words. And so she sat silently holding him as the sun rose over them, and the lorry rounded the corner and came to a stop, and Annie could not tell how long she had been sitting there in her blood-soaked clothes, cradling Matt on her lap. Doors opened. Victor and Emily sprinted towards her. Emily reached them first, kneeling in front of them, throwing her arms around Matt, seemingly oblivious to the blood.

Victor knelt next to her and took Matt's wrist, trying to find a pulse. He checked the other wrist and pressed his fingers to the side of Matt's neck, bringing his head down close to Matt's face.

'Do something,' cried Emily.

Victor shook his head. 'He's gone, dear heart.' He lowered his eyes. 'I'm so sorry.' He turned at Annie. 'You can let him go now,' he said, nodding.

Annie's hands were locked around the soaking scarf. Victor lifted them gently from Matt's body and uncurled her fingers one by one while she looked on as though from far away. Emily lay down next to Matt and curled herself into the hollow of his body.

Victor went back to the lorry and returned with a folded tarpaulin. He spread it on the ground next to Matt's body.

'Emily.' Victor knelt again next to her. 'We have to get Matt to the hospital. They'll be able to take care of him there. Will you come with us?'

Emily squeezed her eyes tight shut.

'Emily?'

Victor looked at Annie for help. She nodded, and as Victor lifted Matt's shoulders she slid out from under him. Victor bent to pick up Matt's body and Emily turned towards Annie, crying out with the terrible shriek of an animal in pain.

Victor drove to the hospital. On the flatbed of the lorry Emily and Annie sat with Matt, his body wrapped in the tarpaulin, laid between the hives. The bees were active and came to the entrances of the hives, but the netting stopped them from flying away. 'He's gone,' Annie told them, her hand holding tightly on to Emily. 'He's gone now.' The fields flashed past. Light flickered overhead, then darkness as the road went in under the trees. Coal-black shadows and the killers, hiding there. Why had she just stood and done nothing? She shut her eyes and the darkness closed in. Her fault. Her fault.

The man with the knife lunged towards her again and again.

28

Victor stayed with Emily and Matt's body in the hospital while Annie remained outside with the lorry to guard the bees. People coming through the car park stared at her in horror. She looked down at herself – her clothes, her arms, her hands – all covered with drying blood. The metallic tang of it was in her nose – she swallowed down the bile which rose in her throat and climbed into the cab, pulling the sheet from Victor's bunk and wrapping herself in it, hiding her bloodied hands. The police came and as she told them everything that had happened she relived each moment. She was shuddering now, unable to stop. Somebody gave her a paper cup of water, and her hands shook so much that she spilled half of it before she could get it to her mouth.

She sat on the flatbed of the lorry and sat in the shade of the hives, leaning her head against them, taking comfort from the bees which crawled in and out on the other side of the netting.

There would be an investigation, said Victor, much later. They had given the police the address of the farm and driven there with Emily like a ghost between them. She'd been given something to help her sleep and gone straight to bed. The farmer showed Annie to the bathroom, not meeting her eyes. Annie turned on the shower and stepped into it, watching the water turn red as it sluiced over her. She stood still, letting the water run over her body and through her hair until eventually it ran clear. Then she scrubbed at her fingernails and her face. She found Victor out by the lorry. He opened his arms and came towards her – she shook her head and stepped back. The funeral would take place after the police enquiry, he told her.

'And what happens now?' said Annie.

'We finish work at this farm,' said Victor. 'Then I'll take you and your bees back home.'

Home.

In the end there were hardly any bees to return home with. They drove back to Hattenden with what was left. None of the hives had been untouched by loss. Annie put her hives into the empty nursery rooms at the Dome where she would be able to monitor them for mites and diseases they might be carrying from the outside world. Only when she was sure they were healthy would she reintroduce them back into the simfields. She stacked the empty hives outside the shed and pulled a tarp over them.

For the time being, Victor set up what remained of his hives around the grounds of the college. Annie came out to find him. To tell him how strange it felt to see the bees inside again after so long. To ask him what he would do next. He was going back to Caitlin's, he told her. Back to Iris and his daughters. Emily was going with him (she was already sitting in the passenger seat of the cab, staring fixedly towards the road). Caitlin had offered to take her in for as long as she needed. She couldn't go home, she'd told Victor. Not yet.

'We're all due some compassionate leave,' said Victor. 'Including you, Annie.'

For a long time, Annie didn't speak to anyone except the bees. Soothed by the solitude, the freedom to set her own timetable for each day, she watched as they came and went from their hives and, once she was sure they were free of disease, moved them back into the simfields. She turned to the little bodies in their containers and spent hours in the lab examining them for the cause of their deaths, sleeping in the office when she had to, taking something from her rations when she was hungry, never allowing herself to think about Matt. She didn't know what to do, how to mend the split in the fabric of their lives which had let the darkness flood in.

People brought their news. She asked about Emily, but nobody would tell her anything. Victor came. Because of the riots it wasn't safe to go home. He would be moving to Hattenden with his family. Attica had sorted it all out. He talked about how the remaining bees were faring; he was keeping a close eye on them, guarding them. Maybe next year swarms would move into the empty hives. They were all cleaned and ready. He'd set them all up behind a section of the hedge by the Dome, he told Annie, out of sight from anyone who might be passing on the road or wandering uninvited through the grounds. He couldn't guard them round the clock. It was their best chance. Victor looked at his watch. He looked at the ceiling. He remembered the soup which Iris had sent and took a container out of his bag. 'Potato and onion,' he said. 'It's good.'

Iris brought the girls. They'd drawn pictures for Annie – sunny days and flowers. Annie thanked them but after that she didn't know what to say, and Maria was worried, and sat next to her mother. 'It's okay,' said Iris.

'It is,' said Annie. She made herself smile for Maria. 'It will be.' Annie remembered their time at Caitlin's. While Annie had made notes in her book Maria skipped along the rows chatting to the bees while Sophie lay on her stomach with a sketchpad, drawing. They just liked being a part of things, said Victor. He'd told her to send them back to Iris if they were disturbing her. But – quite the opposite – she had enjoyed their company, and Sophie's quiet concentration had reminded Annie of her own childish fascination with the outdoors.

Sophie came closer and took Annie's hands. Annie stared at their fingers intertwined, Sophie's small slender fingers alongside her own, workworn and dry. She thought of Matt's hands reaching out, his blood covering them both. She withdrew from Sophie and looked away.

'Do you want to come and see our house?' said Sophie. Iris nodded encouragingly. 'It's really near.'

'Maybe next time,' said Annie. She knew they were trying to be kind, but she wished they would go. Before too long, they did.

Attica brought half a dozen eggs and a small loaf of bread. 'Aren't people lovely?' she said, setting the food on the worktop in the tiny kitchen area. 'When I said I was visiting, they asked me to bring you these. Hold on.' She fished around at the bottom of her bag. 'Here. It's butter, fresh made. I'll put it in the fridge.' Attica left soon after, flustered by the effort of keeping up both sides of the conversation. Annie went to lay down on the sofa and watched the sunlight as it worked its way across the ceiling and down the wall.

Days passed. She didn't know how many.

The next time she left the Dome the trees around the village had been painted red and gold by autumn.

29

Victor and his family had set up home in what had been the staffroom at the college – in return for which Victor was working as a sort of live-in security guard and groundsman, tending what was left of his bees, digging over the flowerbeds nearest the building for a vegetable plot, planting it up with potatoes and carrots. There was a small kitchen off the staffroom, toilets and a shower.

One sunny autumn morning Annie invited them up to her house. She had plenty of sheets and towels, and way too many place settings for a single person who never entertained. Someone should get some use from them, she told Victor.

'When was the last time you came here?' asked Iris, as Annie went around drawing the curtains, opening windows. Her little house smelled musty and unloved. There was dust on the countertops and spiders' webs draped across the ceilings and in the corners. It had been months. She hadn't slept there since they'd left with the bees in February – a lifetime ago. Iris seemed much happier. Having Victor at home, Annie supposed. It suited her.

'Everything's so dirty,' said Sophie.

Iris shushed her. 'It just needs dusting,' said Iris. 'Where do you keep your cleaning things, Annie?'

'Oh, no – please don't,' said Annie, but Iris insisted. It was only fair, if they were taking her things. She and Sophie set off with the dusters.

Victor peered through the kitchen window into the overgrown back garden. 'We'll sort that out for you in no time, won't we, Maria?' He let himself out into the garden with Maria hopping after him. Annie trailed behind with the key to the shed – if you can't beat 'em, join 'em, she supposed.

It didn't take long – by the time Annie came in from the garden, Iris and Sophie had made the house fresh and inviting once more. Annie remembered how much she loved it there. It was time to move back home. Together they boxed up her spare plates, bowls and mugs, cutlery and saucepans, then carried them carefully outside to one of the garden trolleys from the college. On top they put sheets, pillows and duvets, then Victor pulled the trolley up the main street of the village with the girls perched on top, giggling. Annie and Iris followed behind.

Some of the villagers came out of their houses to watch the procession. It wasn't often that they heard laughter in the streets anymore. The For Sale signs of the previous year had faded in the sun and many of them had toppled over or been pushed into overgrown gardens.

In their rooms at the college, Victor had set a double mattress near the fireplace in the staffroom, covered with a big quilt Iris had rescued from their house. Sometimes Iris couldn't bear this reminder of her old life and on those days the quilt was banished to one of the cupboards. Maria and Sophie slept top to tail on one of the long sofas, wrapped in blankets Caitlin had given them. During the shortening days, Iris home-schooled her daughters in the mornings. In the afternoons they were free to explore the long echoing corridors of the college and its empty classrooms. They started a new collection of found things. Iris worked her way through the collection of books on the staffroom shelves to distract herself from homesickness. Autumn gave way to winter.

30

Annie sat at her kitchen table with a pencil in her hand, watching the snow blow past the windows, her list forgotten. It was settling now, covering everything. She acknowledged a flicker of fear at the thought that the village might be cut off. Or the electricity might fail, and the simfields would cool.

There was a geranium flowering on the windowsill, its blooms on a long stalk. Like a firework, pink petals bright against the whiteness beyond. She would speak to Victor about the possibility of using the generators if the power went out. They could use the last of the diesel she'd saved. Perhaps he would think she was being extravagant, wasteful, even. But it might be the only way to save her plants and protect the bees.

She got up from the table – instead of sitting here worrying she would go to the simfields and take some temperature readings to check that the systems were managing in the freezing weather. She could search for the generators while she was there.

But there was something else she needed to do first.

Guilt had overwhelmed her since the moment she had caught Matt, mortally wounded, in her arms and sunk with him to the floor. Since she had sat with Emily on the flatbed of the lorry, taking Matt's body to the hospital. Since the last time she had seen Emily's stricken face at Matt's funeral.

Matt's life with Emily, his work at the Dome – she pictured him bent over his laptop in the corner of the tiny office he shared with Emily – his levels of dogged concentration rivalled even Annie's. The undisguised adoration on his face when he'd looked at Emily – Annie had envied their relationship, but she'd been rooting for them too – she'd wished them both well, had hoped for their future.

And then ruined it.

Emily must hate her so much…

There was nothing Annie could do to put things right – she'd been seized by a sort of paralysis and, yes, she'd been avoiding Emily since the funeral. On top of everything else, Annie was a coward.

It was time to try and put things right.

Emily opened her front door just wide enough to peer out. Snowflakes blew in through the crack. On seeing it was Annie, she didn't open the door any further.

Some people were good at knowing what to say. Difficult conversations, awkward moments, on hearing sad news, they seemed to know instinctively the best words of consolation, simply put, genuine and unrehearsed. Annie had never been one of those people. Her mouth was dry. 'How are you?' she said.

Emily's shoulders drooped.

'Could I come in for a minute?' said Annie.

The door opened a little wider – Emily was barefoot in the hallway, barelegged too, it seemed. She wore an oversized jumper and underneath was a long shirt which came down almost to her knees. Her hair was unwashed.

'I'm just off to check the simfields,' said Annie. 'Do you want to come?'

'Maybe next time,' said Emily, turning away. 'I'm a bit busy.' Her voice trailed off as she walked away from Annie, leaving the door ajar.

Annie stepped into the house and quietly closed the door. Emily was climbing under the blankets on the sofa and turning her face so that her hair fell across it. It was cold in the house, and gloomy. The living-room curtains were drawn. Annie could just make out a couple of mugs and a plate on the coffee table. Annie picked them up and walked through to the kitchen, put them into the sink and ran some water to wash them up while she scouted around for other dirty dishes. There were none. She looked in the fridge – only a dry rind of cheese and half an onion which looked as though it had been there for a long time. Annie sniffed at them and made a face. She took them out and tipped them into the kitchen bin, which was full, and smelled terrible. She knotted the bin bag and pulled it out, set it at the front door to take with her when she left.

'Don't help me.' Emily's voice came out of the shadows.

'Just these few things,' said Annie, leaning on the door frame. 'Maybe I could bring you some food later?' She looked at the floor. 'I don't know what to do.'

'I don't want you to *do* anything.' Emily's voice was muffled.

Perhaps it would be better if she left. She would come back, try again another time. Though it didn't seem right, leaving Emily alone in the gloom in her chilly house. Her father's voice came to her gently across the years: *You can't mend everything, Annie.* It was true, she knew that. Her mother's cancer. Climate change. Some things were too big, too broken for a person to fix. But Matt's death? That was on her, and she would never let herself off the hook.

'I'm sorry,' she said, and let herself out of the door into the frozen white world.

31

After the long Indian summer the harsh winter came as a shock. Snowdrifts grew halfway up the windows on the ground floor, blocking out much of the light in the staffroom, filling the place with a dull underwater glow. Ice formed on the inside of the windows and Victor and Iris dragged the sofa and mattress closer to the fire so they would stay warm enough at night. They took turns to get up during the dark hours to put more wood on the fire. Thank God, Victor had thought to stock up the firewood before the snows came. They had all worked hard to carry in the logs they'd salvaged from the woods and stack them along the corridors outside the staffroom. As winter drew on Iris watched the supply getting smaller – by the time the thaw came it would have dwindled to almost nothing.

Iris carried her windup radio to their new home like a prize. It had been a gift from Caitlin. At first, Iris listened to it often, tuning in to the talk stations, trying to find news from their old town. Perhaps, after the riots, things would have settled down. Maybe there would be updates about some of the places she knew. Victor often found her with her arms wrapped around the radio, her face drained of all hope. 'It might be better not to know,' he suggested gently. 'We could try find some music,' he said. 'Songs from before, to cheer us up.' And she shrugged her shoulders and let him find another station. He danced with Maria in front of the fire while Sophie sat and watched. Iris curled herself on the sofa like a cat, feet tucked under a blanket, her eyes half-closed. At other times no matter how carefully she tuned in there was no music, no talking, and Iris speculated that the radio stations had been attacked. More likely to be power cuts, said Victor. It was common enough, these days.

There were weeks of frozen, glassy days and long shivering nights, when the only vehicles which passed through the village were the tractors Attica had organised to drop rations to each house. When the snows finally melted it was strange to see the earth again: the vivid grass, the naked trees and the mud. Annie walked along the road in the direction of the simfields, re-learning her stride. Victor saw her from his window as she passed and waved at her to come in. It was warm in their room. The fire was burning. Maria sat with scissors and a stack of agricultural journals, cutting images which she passed to Sophie, who arranged them on the rug. Iris had taken soup to Emily, he said, and biscuits sweetened with the last of the apples they'd carried with them from Caitlin's orchard. Iris would sit with her and wait until she had eaten. Emily shouldn't be left alone, said Victor. She wasn't looking after herself and had lost more weight. They could only do so much, being here, with the girls. But someone ought to stay with her. He leaned towards Annie. 'Really, the best person to move in with her is you.'

Annie shook her head. 'She doesn't want me in her house.'

'She probably won't even notice that you're there,' said Victor. 'I know you want to help her. This is the way.'

It was a mistake, thought Annie. She was the last person Emily would want to see. But in the absence of a better idea, Annie packed a bag that evening and knocked on Emily's door. Emily held the door open to her without a word, allowing Annie to slip through.

Annie still thought of the house as Matt and Emily's. And since Emily hadn't touched any of his belongings, it was almost as though he had only gone away on a trip and might be back at any moment. Matt's things were still scattered all over the house. In the living room, his personal laptop lay next to pile of journals. Annie leafed idly through them. The future of farming. Industrial food production methods. Artificial intelligence. Why had he been wasting his time on all that when their own research had been so close to paying off? There were other things, too. Articles he'd downloaded and printed off – theories about who was really driving the food shortages. International conglomerates intent on controlling the world's supplies. Dark forces manipulating the financial markets from behind the scenes. Real crackpot stuff. Annie shook her head in despair. What could he possibly have been thinking? She thought about tidying it all away into a cupboard – but it wasn't her place to do that without asking. She drifted through to the kitchen. A mug with Matt's name on it, a Secret Santa gift from the year he'd joined them, was still on the shelf above the kettle.

Since the house was funded by the research money it was just as much hers, Annie supposed. But she would never feel at home here. Her own house was boarded up now, like so many of the others in the village. Windows and doors covered over against thieves, arsonists and looters. Many more people were travelling the roads since winter – looking for work, or money, or the opportunity to force a bit of luck their way. Annie kept the living-room curtains closed – she told Emily it was to keep the heat in. But if anyone came knocking they wouldn't know that two women were there, cowering and silent, waiting for the danger to pass.

Annie passed her old house from time to time, but it no longer felt like hers, despite her boxed-up belongings there, sealed behind the covered windows.

In the simfields a short winter programme had already run its course – enough to kill any harmful bacteria and keep the plants at the correct stages of development. In the nursery rooms the temperature was just low enough to keep the bees in hibernation. Annie didn't need to visit the Dome every day, but it was only a short walk from Emily's house and she told herself it was doing her good to be out in the fresh air, if only for a little while. Victor stopped by, some days, to talk to Annie about what the following year might bring. He'd already contacted the farmers to let them know they couldn't come back in the spring. Hopefully the following year, he'd told them. The coming months would be about trying to raise new broods to replace the lost hives and increasing the numbers as much as they possibly could. At least this was something they could apply themselves to, thought Annie. She liked the idea of getting back to the old routines.

Winter turned slowly to spring and, as the temperatures began to warm outside, Annie adjusted the climate in the simfields to keep them more or less in sync. When Maria and Sophie had done their lessons with Iris in the morning, she set them free to explore. Often they would appear at the Dome in the afternoons, their faces against the front doors, waiting for Annie or Victor to let them in. They loved to watch the bees as they returned from the simfields to the nursery rooms – where glass panels allowed them to see the inner workings of the colonies.

'Let's go in,' suggested Victor, and Maria hopped nervously from foot to foot. 'They won't hurt you,' Victor reminded her. 'If you are calm, they will be too.' Sophie knew where the protective gear was kept and went to fetch it. Though Victor never wore it Iris made sure Maria and Sophie (but especially Sophie) were always safely covered whenever they were around the bees. Once the girls had pulled on the overalls, gloves, hats and veils, Victor led them through into one of the nursery rooms to meet the bees.

Some afternoons they helped with hive repair in the shed, sanding the new sections Victor cut from reclaimed timber, painting them and leaning them up against the fence outside to dry. Iris joined them too, sometimes. In the old days she would have worried about the girls getting paint on their clothes. It didn't seem so important any more. Sometimes one or two of the children from the village would venture through the college gates to see if Maria and Sophie could play. 'Don't go too far,' said Iris, fighting the urge to keep them in her sight, always.

32

The villagers who'd stayed in Hattenden turned over their gardens to food production. Chickens and geese scrabbled and rooted up lawns which had once been checked obsessively for dandelions and moss. Pigs grubbed around in newly fenced paddocks; sheep and goats were tethered to posts during the day to graze and locked in sheds overnight. Flowerbeds were dug over for potatoes and carrots and beans and squash. Included in their weekly rations were packets of seed: Government Issue in paper packaging. The villagers set up walking patrols around the village to protect their livestock and crops, circulating rotas for day and night shifts. Attica embarked on a crusade of leaflets through letterboxes, urging villagers to get planting. Their efforts now would be rewarded in due course. There were instructions on how to sow, thin out seedlings, plant out and harvest. Recipes and information on how to store and preserve their harvests would follow.

Annie looked doubtfully at her leaflet and wondered out

loud how they would succeed at growing any crops without pollinators.

'There are ways,' said Victor, enigmatically. They sat together the simfields, watching his daughters play in the long grass. 'When's Attica getting here?'

'Soon, I think,' said Annie. She surveyed the quiet fields, leaning back on her arms, stretching her legs out in front of her.

Victor's gaze shifted from his children to something beyond, out at the edge of the fields. 'There she is now.'

Annie turned to look. In the distance, Attica stood behind the two sets of glass doors which allowed Annie to control the environment in the fields. Annie rose and walked to the doors, motioning to Attica that she should remove her shoes and slip on one of the pairs of boots lined up along the wall, then stand in the airlock. The fans ran for two minutes, allowing the vacuums to sweep any stray pollens or particles from her clothes and hair.

Attica was somewhat breathless as she emerged through the doors. 'Thank you for meeting me,' she said. 'And for allowing me to visit your fields. How interesting this all is.' She scrutinised her surroundings as though making calculations, measuring up with her eyes. 'Victor.' She extended a hand and walked towards him; he got up off the grass, wiping his hands on his jeans.

Attica's involvement with anything came with requests and demands. Victor and Annie stood, waiting.

'I'll get right down to it,' said Attica, rubbing her hands together. 'I'd like to use these fields as part of the effort to feed the village.'

'No,' said Annie, hollowed out in an instant. 'Absolutely

not.' How could this be happening again? 'Against my better judgement I let you take my bees. Now you want my land as well?'

'Your land?' Attica looked at her enquiringly. 'Your bees?'

'Yes,' said Annie. She would not be intimidated on her own turf. 'My project.' She looked at Victor. Why didn't he say something? The simfields were completely silent. Even the girls had stopped their game and stood watching. 'Most of my bees died during your little plan last year,' said Annie. 'It was a terrible, unconscionable waste. All those years of research ruined in a few short months out on the road. For what?' (The man with the knife lunged again, and Matt fell back into her arms in a warm gush of blood.)

'Your bees provided us with a harvest,' said Attica. 'Not in the quantities we needed, but so much better than nothing.'

'The project is more important,' said Annie. 'We have to get back to the research. It's the best way to ensure we have better harvests in the future.'

'More important than human lives?' asked Attica, her voice gentle. 'Do you know how many people starved to death in the District over the winter, Dr Abrams?'

Victor looked down at his feet.

Annie nodded. 'I take your point, Attica, but…' Anything she said now made her a monster.

'But? You still have objections?' Attica's face softened. She knew she was winning, thought Annie.

'Turning the simfields over to unapproved plants and seeds? If we squander the few insects we have left, we're in real danger of losing the lot,' said Annie. 'Victor, help me out here.' Why was he still standing there like a wet blanket when he should be helping her to make their case? Maria and Sophie had crept closer to him during the exchange, and now they stood either side of him, their arms lightly around his waist.

'I'm sorry,' said Victor, glancing at Annie. 'I agree with Attica. It seems like a fine use of the space,' he said, putting his arms around his daughters' skinny shoulders. 'The soil must be good, and we can create ideal growing conditions...' He tailed off.

Just for the promise of a few short-term gains – but they would all lose in the long term. Annie tried to keep her voice steady. 'I have nothing to add,' she said. 'Attica, I assume you have a plan of action?'

'Of course,' said Attica. She had the grace not to look triumphant.

Every Monday morning Annie walked the length of the village, from the old bakery near the base of the hill, along the high street and past the ancient church, passing the small grocery shop with its fading government-issue notices: *Please Don't Ask for More Than Your Share. Think Food, Think Fun! Don't Waste: Be Wise with Leftovers.*

Leftovers – such an old-fashioned word. They were a thing of the past, along with second helpings and snacks between meals. Along the High Street the terraced houses had tiny front gardens; in the houses that were still lived in the little squares of lawn were now given over to tomato plants where they would catch the best of the sun, and strawberries grown in tubs on windowsills, upstairs and down. Smaller roads led off the High Street here and there;

most of these houses were now empty. Annie pulled the big gardening trolley. She knocked at the doors, although by the time she'd visited the old bakery there was really no need. Her arrival was expected, and often people were waiting at their doors with plants in pots and empty food containers, worn-out Wellington boots, rolled-up paper, scraps of material or whatever they could find. Some of the seedlings were carefully labelled on pieces of card tucked into the soil alongside the tender green stems; others were handed over with a shrug. 'We'll work it out,' said Annie, who was becoming an expert at identifying the seedlings. She had learned the names of all the villagers, too. She tucked each pot carefully in amongst the others so that they wouldn't tip as the trolley rolled along. At the very end of the road, when her trolley was almost full, the houses gave way to the first of the college residences, student halls long-empty, and then the campus itself with its old gateway twined with flowering vines carved into the stone, peppered with stone birds and insects long-ago frozen in flight.

She carried the plants from the trolley to the double doors of the simfields and passed them into Sophie's eager hands, who then ran with them to Maria. Annie thought again of all the new bacteria they were introducing to the restricted atmosphere, all the foreign soil microbes. She no longer had the luxury of playing God in her own little world, and every day she had to let go of it again – the urge to constrain and control. She watched Maria walking away with the pots held level like cups she was trying not to spill, towards the makeshift allotments they'd created in the centre of the fields where the soil was richest. She and Emily and Victor had dug them – even Iris had been persuaded to help out – cutting away squares of meadow grasses to expose the earth. It was deep loamy brown and easy to dig, unlike much of the heavy clay soil in the village. The plants would thrive here. Victor and Emily received each plant from Maria, then planted them one by one. They knelt in the earth, using trowels and fingers to make a hole, tipping the young plants carefully from their pots and tucking them into their new beds. Annie had turned the weather programme to occasional light showers during the nights so the plants would get enough water without making it too muddy to work during the day. Iris carried watering cans from the standpipes at the edge of the simfields, giving each new seedling a good drink once it was planted. 'This isn't how I wanted it either,' said Victor, seeing Annie's anguish at the vandalised meadow. 'But we still have to eat, don't we?' It was for the best, what they were doing. Maybe if Annie told herself often enough, she might start to believe it.

'We'll have bees to pollinate the simfields,' said Emily. 'How will it work outside?'

'Ask Victor,' said Annie. She filled her glass from the water jug and took a long drink, exhausted by the day's work.

Victor's voice floated up from the long grass – all they could see of him were the tops of his bent knees. 'Mechanical pollination,' he said. 'Pollination by hand. It'll work in a small garden. All you need is a small paintbrush and a lot of spare time.'

'I expect Attica has a leaflet for that,' said Emily.

'Count on it,' said Victor.

'But… what about the fruit trees?' asked Iris, from where she lay next to Victor.

Annie thought of Caitlin's orchards, and the trees came flooding in. Apples and pears, row upon row upon row upon row. The farms they'd visited: the strawberry fields, the cherry trees, the plums and raspberries and currants. With wild pollinators now so few and far between, would there be any fruit at all come harvest time? She took a deep breath. She tried so hard not to think about the farms or the trees since Matt – she forced herself to turn away from the images waiting in the wings. Iris was looking at her, waiting for an answer. 'I don't know,' said Annie. 'I just don't know.'

33

Late August and although it was only seven o'clock in the morning the day was already stiflingly warm. Annie stood in Emily's kitchen. Their neighbour had given them each an egg. She cracked them into the hot frying pan.

Emily came down the stairs holding a sweatshirt of Matt's. Faded blue and soft after years of wear. 'How long am I supposed to keep his things?' asked Emily. 'I don't want to get rid of it, but…' Her voice caught. Her eyes were red-rimmed. 'But every morning when I wake up and see his clothes I almost can't get out of bed.'

Annie turned off the heat under the eggs and went to stand as close to Emily as she thought she could. 'I don't think there's a rule,' she said. 'You'll just know when it's time.' When her father had died, there had been very few possessions to speak of, very little to show for a life. Perhaps he had spent the years after she left home whittling his belongings away so that when Annie was required to take care of the estate only the essentials were left – a few important papers, passwords and a box of old photographs.

In the kitchen one saucepan, one frying pan and one of everything else: plate, bowl, cup, knife, fork, spoon. In his wardrobe, a couple of changes of clothes and one spare pair of shoes. He had filled his e-reader with enough books to last another lifetime and given all his paper copies away. He had even cast off as much of the furniture as he could, making his footprint small. Drawing in the edges of his life until he existed in a circle just big enough to stand in.

'Maybe I could help you,' said Annie.

Emily looked at her with empty eyes. 'No, thanks.'

But, a few days later, when Annie was about to leave the house to check on the simfields, Emily appeared at the top of the stairs. 'I'm going through his things,' she said. 'I wondered,' she paused and swallowed, 'I wondered if you might stay.' The shadow of an almost-smile. 'Just stay in the house, until I'm done.'

Annie settled herself on the sofa in their little front room. She could check her emails and catch up with the news. The morning sun slanted in through tiny front window and shone onto Annie's legs as she turned on her tablet and idly scrolled through her news feed. She had long ago tailored her selection to items relating to her own interests, filtering out the rest of the world's noise. It did no good to read it. Anyway, internet access was patchy and becoming more unpredictable, along with the electricity supply. She waited patiently while the icon turned and turned in the centre of the screen, above her the sound of Emily dragging boxes from under her bed.

She had no idea how long she had been asleep, but when Annie woke the patch of sun had moved across the wall and Emily was standing in front of her with a piece of paper. 'Read this,' she said.

Annie took the paper. It looked like a printout from another one of the conspiracy theory websites Matt had been so fond of. She read: "'How's this for making the most of a bad situation – anyone for black-market deliveries via drone? Robotics engineers are making the most of shortages by offering food deliveries to anyone who can afford it.'" Underneath there was an out-of-focus photograph of a drone – the sort which they saw daily flying overhead. Some of the farmers who could afford them had drones fitted with cameras so that they could patrol their fields from the comfort of their farmhouse. "'Our reporter met with Connor at his London workshop to find out more. Connor designs drones of all shapes and sizes, from large delivery drones to something small enough to carry out surveillance tasks and minor repairs in pipes and ducts.'" So?' Annie waved the piece of paper. "'Names have been changed to protect our sources.'" She turned over the paper. There was some writing on the back – Matt had scrawled an address in Bermondsey. 'I don't get it.'

'Think about it.' Emily shifted from foot to foot. 'Matt was on to something.'

A pause, while Annie re-read the piece, then looked from the paper to Emily's encouraging expression.

'Sorry,' said Annie. 'You'll have to explain.'

'What is it that we need, while the bee numbers are low?' asked Emily before pressing on, not giving Annie the chance to reply. 'Alternative methods of pollination. We can't just hit the pause button on food production while we wait for insect numbers to recover, and hand pollination will only work on a very small scale. We need to broaden our horizons, Dr Abrams. Tiny drones. Just think about it.'

'Tiny drones,' repeated Annie. 'For mechanical pollination?' She looked at Emily, her eyes wide, and Emily nodded, smiling. 'I don't know,' said Annie cautiously. She felt a shiver of unease. How could a tiny machine possibly replace the complexity of a bee? 'In theory, perhaps,' she said. She skimmed the report again. 'But in practice? You mean outside, on the farms? In the orchards? The scope is just too vast. I don't see how it could ever work.'

'Let's talk to him, at least,' said Emily. 'This Connor. He'll be the best person to tell us, won't he? Whether it'll work or not?'

Annie hesitated.

'I want to try, at least,' said Emily. 'For Matt. He was always falling in love with ideas like this.' She looked imploringly at Annie. 'Let me go talk to him.'

Annie owed it to Emily, after all. She owed it to Matt too, for all the times he'd tried to speak to her and she'd shut him down without listening. And, doubtful as she was, goodness only knew they needed a short-term solution. 'Okay,' said Annie. Emily showered her with thank-yous and began to cry, and Annie insisted that she'd be going too. Not only because it wasn't safe for Emily to go alone. Annie wanted to meet Connor for herself, to see what he had to say – and to make sure Emily didn't agree to anything in her absence. 'See if you can find a contact number, would you, Emily? I'll go and tell Victor.'

34

Despite their best efforts, nobody was able to find a contact number for Connor. 'Nothing wrong with keeping a low profile,' said Emily.

'A self-employed drone designer who doesn't want to advertise?' said Annie. 'This guy doesn't want anyone to find him.'

They would go and knock on his door then, said Emily. She'd been so happy since finding the interview with Connor. She was transformed.

They didn't know how long they'd be away, but they were adept now at living out of rucksacks. A couple of changes of clothes, their laptops and notebooks, and they were ready to go.

Victor came over to ask Annie a few last-minute questions about the simfield systems before they left. 'I think that's everything,' he said, checking back through his notes. He looked at Annie. 'For God's sake, be careful,' he added.

'Don't,' said Annie quietly, forcing the thoughts away.

A horn sounded from outside.

'That'll be Attica,' said Annie.

Victor looked out of the window. 'That's her,' he said. 'Better hurry. You wouldn't want to keep her waiting.'

Attica was giving them a lift as far as Sevenoaks. She was collecting a defibrillator for the village Emergency Readiness Provisions. After that, they would walk, or hitch lifts. If they were still travelling when the night came Annie would make sure they were off the roads. She wasn't above breaking in to an abandoned house if it meant they had a place to stay. She put her hand over her jacket to check one last time – inside the zip-up pocket was the Swiss army knife her father had given her on her tenth birthday. 'Let's go.'

As they approached the ornate front gate of the college they spotted Iris and the girls, waving. 'Good luck,' they shouted, as the car went past.

Attica dropped them on the outskirts of Sevenoaks, only a short walk from the motorway on-ramp. They set down their bags and stood together in the long grass. The road was almost deserted, just the occasional van heading out towards the coast, one or two private cars, windows closed, sealed against the world. The lanes were pot-holed by the hard winter. Plants grew wild over the road signs and along the central reservation. Annie knelt in the grass in order to search around the base of the stems. Maybe she would find some beetles, or a woodlouse hiding in the cool of the leaf litter. 'Dr Abrams.' Emily's voice reminded her of why they were there. A van had pulled over for them: a heating repair man on his way to a call-out. 'I can take you as far as Woolwich,' he told them. He looked legitimate – clean-shaven, dark blue overalls with a company logo on the breast pocket. Annie sat in between the driver and Emily and made small talk. She was unable to block out memories of the damage a stranger could do. Beside her Emily sat quietly. She was thinking about it too, Annie knew. He didn't seem to mind having them in the cab, said he enjoyed the company, but it didn't stop Annie from counting down the miles on the signs along the road, each minute on the clock taking them closer to their destination. When the driver dropped them off Emily checked the map on her phone. They could easily walk the rest of the way there, she said.

The closer they got, the more excited Emily became. She talked and talked about all the wonderful possibilities for the scheme – once they had a working prototype, what would stop them from building enough to pollinate the whole of Kent, or the whole country – and why stop there? Her face was pale, her eyes glittering. She was pinning all her hopes on an idea so flimsy it amounted to nothing, and Annie would have to pick up the pieces when it didn't work – although – nervous as Annie was, she was almost as eager as Emily to find out what Connor thought. They walked quickly along the route, through near-empty streets, then past a snaking queue at a community kitchen, its doors open wide, the smell of overcooked vegetables drifting out into the air. People stood patiently with their mugs and bowls. There were couples and families, young children sitting on the kerb, kicking their feet in the gutter. An elderly woman perched on a folding stool while she waited. Two policemen watched over the line.

They traced their way through the streets, reaching

Bermondsey just as lights were coming on behind some of the windows. They arrived at the address: an old warehouse on a side street which had been redeveloped into houses and workshops. There was no sign on the door to say what sort of work Connor carried out, nothing to confirm it was his place at all.

Annie hesitated, trying to compose herself, not sure of what she was going to say to the stranger who would open the door. The light was fading rapidly from the sky.

'Do you want me to do it?' asked Emily.

'No, no.' Annie took a deep breath, stepped forward and knocked boldly on the door. There was a small patterned glass panel in the door through which Annie could see a shiver of movement, then a shape grew larger and larger as someone came towards them on the other side.

Annie took a deep breath. 'Here goes,' she said.

35

Scott Edwards wasn't your typical nerd. At least, he'd been trying really hard to shake off that image – from the day he got to the top of the class at school for maths and computing until graduating with an honours degree in Artificial Intelligence Design. Yes, he liked comic books. Yes, he was prepared to fight anyone who said they didn't like *Star Wars*. And yes, he found it difficult to talk to anyone if the subjects didn't include any of the above. He'd moved to London to study for his postgrad in Applied Drone Technology, then taught for a couple of years when the AI boom was taking off in earnest. Sensing the opportunity to launch his own design studio he found a workshop where he could develop his machines. He bought a vintage-design Harley Davidson, one of the first electric models off the line. He grew a beard, got a tattoo and prepared himself for wild success. It was around that time when the first World Crash happened, and, just like that, success was no longer an option.

Scott moved out of his flat into the small rooms above his workshop, then set about trying to find enough clients to keep his head above water. He was managing – just. He did a lot of freelance repair jobs – drones which had fallen out of the sky for no apparent reason, control panels which refused to communicate with their units, dents and scrapes and spare parts – and he'd built up a steady stream of clients who appreciated his fast turnaround on their jobs. When he had the time, he worked on his designs. Custom-designed bots and drones for repairing hard-to-reach electrical and plumbing jobs. In his grand scheme, every household would have them, with different programmes for different tasks. Not so very long ago he would have been fighting off investors and homeowners would have queued up to buy them. But since the chaos of the Crashes people had other concerns.

Scott's favourite designs were for nanodrones; he had a collection of them in the workshop, each with a slightly different specification. Most were fitted with tiny cameras. Basic drone technology was old news, but Scott had developed the tech to the point where it was possible to use small tools he'd fitted to them, fine-tuning them until they were able to solder fine wires and use tiny screwdrivers to mend a pair of glasses. He'd come to terms with the fact that, for the time being, it could be no more than a hobby.

The sun had almost gone from the sky, and it was expensive to keep using the daylight bulb he'd set up over his workbench – he would stop soon. Scott picked up the drone he'd been working on the previous day for the guy who ran the old cinema, using it to scan the auditorium for black-market food sellers. Someone in the audience had brought it down with a well-aimed shoe and two of its propellers had snapped off. It was a pretty basic repair but Scott had quoted him a price which was well over the odds. He could afford it, thought Scott. He took a sip from the cup of miso soup which sat cooling next to him while he worked. The draggle-tailed cat who'd recently adopted him mewed from its bed on the old blanket which Scott had folded and laid under the workbench. The cat kept him company while he worked. So long as nobody found out about it, he'd be fine. The cat yowled at him. 'Yeah, yeah. We're all hungry.' Scott looked down at him and poured out some of the soup into the cat's bowl.

There was a rap on his front door which sounded loud and official – not like the tentative knocks of most of his clients. He tried to pick up the cat to put it out through the back door but it darted away into the shadows at the back of the workshop. Scott kicked the blanket further under the desk and went to answer the door.

36

When the door opened, Annie opened her mouth to introduce herself. But the person who stood there was so unexpected that she was unable to say anything at all. Beer-hazed memories of the student union crowded suddenly in. Messy shared houses, the damp smell of her attic bedroom. Late nights in the tiny pub round the corner. A bedroom with a low ceiling and a Luke Skywalker duvet cover on the narrow bed. He stood straighter now, had grown into his broad shoulders, stopped shaving. But it was still, unmistakeably, him.

They stared at each other.

'No way,' said Annie.

Scott gave a half-hearted sort of laugh. 'Why, Ms Abrams,' he said.

'Dr,' corrected Annie.

'What's going on?' asked Emily.

'He's, he's…' Annie stopped, paused, tried again. 'We… uh…'

Emily turned to Annie, widening her eyes, then looked

back at the man in the doorway. 'Connor, isn't it?' she asked.

'I wish I'd never spoken to that sodding reporter,' said Scott, opening the door a little wider so that Emily and Annie could come inside.

While Scott cleared papers, pieces of equipment, half-made drones and protein bar wrappers off the collapsing leather sofa in his workshop, Annie stood near the doorway with her arms folded tightly across her body, taking in the glare of the artificial lights in the roofspace, the scuffed grey industrial flooring, the bare brick walls, the mismatched furniture. And everywhere the chaos of Scott's work, wires and drone parts on every available surface. Emily kept up a stream of chatter. She worked backwards from finding Scott's address on the back of the printout, to why she had been clearing out Matt's things, at which point Scott stopped what he was doing and turned to her with his arms full of clutter. Emily ploughed on; everything brimmed over and spilled out, unstoppable.

'So, let me get this straight.' Scott looked around the room for somewhere to place the stuff he was carrying. There was nowhere, so he set it all on the floor next to his workbench and pushed it into the space beneath with the side of his foot. 'You want me to build you a colony of drone bees capable of pollinating crops?'

'That's right,' said Emily.

'More than one colony,' added Annie. 'For this to work we'll need lots.'

'What sort of numbers are we talking about here?' asked Scott.

Annie and Emily looked at each other.

'We've done some estimates,' said Annie. We think at the very least we'll need fifty colonies.' She took a deep breath before continuing, 'With a bare minimum of one thousand drones per colony.'

Scott gave a bark of laughter. 'O-kay. And, how long exactly have I got to construct these drone swarms?'

'Pollination starts mid-February,' Emily told him.

'Six months? Six fucking months? You've got to be kidding,' said Scott. 'I'm sorry, but that's impossible.'

'No need for profanities,' said Annie, automatically.

'Oh, this one always hated swearing,' said Scott, jerking his head in Annie's direction. 'One of the reasons it never worked out.'

'Not the main one,' said Annie, under her breath.

'Getting back to the point of our visit,' said Emily. 'You won't be working alone, Dr Edwards. You'll have us.'

Scott didn't even bother trying to hide his laughter.

Emily balled her hands into fists and stood up a little straighter. 'We're the best,' she told him. 'Dr Abrams has dedicated her whole career to studying the behaviour and culture of bees. She's taught me everything, and taught me well.'

'Think of how this will enhance your portfolio,' said Annie. 'Responding to something like this – filling a gap, finding a solution to an urgent problem—'

'You've seen the news, right?' interrupted Emily. 'Without bees, we're fucked.'

Scott raised his eyebrows approvingly.

'And, using this project as a test case,' Annie continued smoothly, 'you could patent your design, roll it out countrywide, make a fortune.'

149

It was well past midnight by the time they finished talking through the idea – Emily sitting on the edge of the sofa, leaning forward eagerly to explain, with Scott opposite her on a plastic chair, echoing her posture. He hadn't agreed to anything yet; he'd have to sleep on it, he said, adding that they were welcome to stay overnight, if they wanted. Annie and Emily gratefully agreed. 'Wait here,' said Scott. 'I should tidy up a bit.' He disappeared up the metal stairs against the far wall and his heavy footsteps moved back and forth overhead. Annie and Emily sat side by side on the sofa with the cat purring round their ankles. Annie longed for sleep. Emily dug through her rucksack and pulled out a couple of protein bars. She passed one to Annie, who peeled back the wrapper and ate slowly, making each small bite last as long as she could. The artificial flavours didn't bother her as much as they once had. There was no pleasure in eating it, though.

'You can come up now,' called Scott.

They carried their bags up the narrow flight of stairs to a small living area. A kitchenette, small table and two chairs, a grey fabric-covered sofa and, on the grey-carpeted floor, an inflatable mattress. A broken blind half-covered the window. It was a bare, serviceable space, like a neglected office staffroom.

'One of you can sleep on the sofa,' said Scott, coming back through from another room carrying pillows and blankets. 'It's basic, but…'

Annie, numb with exhaustion, said nothing.

'Thank you,' said Emily. 'Just, thank you.'

'You take the sofa,' said Annie. Emily was far shorter; she'd be able to sleep there more comfortably. Emily slipped off her shoes and lay down, pulling a blanket over her.

Scott and Annie looked at each other. 'I… I'm grateful,' said Annie.

'No problem,' said Scott. 'Bathroom is through that door. I'm back here.' He indicated the room behind him. 'Night.'

Annie settled herself down on the mattress, covering herself with a blanket which smelled disconcertingly like Scott.

'What's the matter?' murmured Emily, on the brink of sleep.

'I don't want to talk about it.' Why did it have to be him? She turned restlessly on the mattress, trying to get comfortable, trying not to think about how awkward it was to see Scott again, and how much she wished she'd asked Victor to go with Emily instead until, despite everything, tiredness overtook her and she fell asleep.

37

The day Annie had arrived at King's College as an undergraduate – almost from the very first moment she stepped out of her father's car – she'd had a terrible feeling that it wasn't going to work. Her father drove off with a cheery wave and Annie stood in the road in front of the student house with a cavernous feeling. She had been tipped out of the nest. Was she supposed to instinctively know how to fly? She wasn't ready. Annie watched as his car slowed and stopped at the junction at the end of the road, the left indicator light flashing, then it turned out into the traffic and was gone. She stood, blinking hard, the late September sun warm on her back. Then she turned and went into the house, running up the stairs to the attic bedroom where they'd carried all of her things. At least she was the first one there. She began to unpack, to make the room incontrovertibly hers, before anybody else arrived. She laid her suitcase down on the floor and unzipped it, releasing the smell of home. Only the day before she'd been packing, ready to leave. 'You think you don't need other people,' said her father, sitting on the side of Annie's bed, folding Annie's favourite black jumper, laying it neatly into her suitcase. 'But you do. You do need them. Try to take an interest, Annie, even if sometimes you're just pretending.' Her father didn't understand, of course. Annie was fine all by herself.

She sat on the floor next to the open case for a moment, aware that she could let herself be overwhelmed by the feeling but choosing to pull back from the edge. She took out her clothes one by one and hung them in the rickety wardrobe. She dropped her underwear into the chest of drawers, then lifted out her sweaters, still thinking of home. There was a bang downstairs, the sound of the door being thrown open, and voices in the hallway.

Her housemates were all going down to the Backs Bar to meet some of the other freshers in what had been advertised as a First Night Icebreaker. The thought of it had filled Annie with a cold dread, but she'd allowed herself to be swept along by the rest of them and she sat obediently while Rachel, whose room was just below Annie's, had perched in front of the mirror on Annie's desk and put on her makeup, then offered to do Annie's eyes – adding perfect dark sweeps of eyeliner to her lids, finishing each one with an expert flick. Annie looked at her own reflection. She looked less like herself. She liked it.

The bar was close to the river. They crowded inside, joining the crush of people all shuffling about, some trying to get to the bar for more drinks, others trying to get back to their tables without spilling anything. Too hot, too close, too many people pressing in around her. Once they'd managed to get their drinks they created a smallish space for themselves by a narrow shelf along the wall where they could set their glasses, and stood watching the rest of the room, talking and moving to the music which pounded through Annie's head. Someone behind her knocked her elbow so that her glass tipped. They didn't even notice. Annie felt herself to be flotsam in this sea of bodies and a flicker of panic lit in her chest. She picked up her glass and motioned to Rachel that she was going outside, then inched her way to the door and edged through into the fresh air.

She leaned against the wall of the bar, closing her eyes, taking deep breaths, waiting for the pattering of her heartbeat to subside.

'Hi.'

Annie opened her eyes. How long had this tall young man been standing next to her, watching? *Try to take an interest, Annie, even if sometimes you're just pretending.* She smiled a self-conscious smile.

'You okay?' he asked.

'I will be.'

'Scott.' He held up his hand in greeting.

'Annie.'

'Too much for you?' He tipped his head in the direction of the door.

'Not really my thing,' she admitted.

He nodded and raised the bottle of wine he held in his other hand. 'We could sit by the river? It'll be quieter down there.'

It was a warm evening, and in the gathering dusk a few people still steered their punts about on the golden water. Annie and Scott shared the wine, and their stories. He was gawky and awkward, but not difficult to talk to, and she had been surprised at how uncomplicated it was to arrive at that point – alone on the riverbank with him, the soft splash of oars in the river and the liquid song of a blackbird in one of the trees along the bank, and before too long the tentative pressure of his lips on hers, and her kiss in answer.

And just as simply as that she had fallen into her relationship with Scott Edwards, slipping into step beside him as though they'd always been walking along next to each other, her hand fitting perfectly into his.

38

When Annie and Emily went out to collect their week's food rations three days later, autumn had already started to turn the leaves in the little squares they passed. Even though it was early in the morning and the shop was not yet open, a queue had already formed, and they joined the back of the line.

The queues for shops were always so quiet. Annie fingered the plastic ration card in pocket. The thought that the food might run out before it was your turn to go in – it made people suspicious and silent. Gone were the exchanges of pleasantries, the little comments about the weather. Annie sneaked a look at Emily, who stood next to her – she seemed like her old self again, even down to her old short bob. Perhaps sensing Annie staring, Emily tucked her hair behind her ear and turned to meet Annie's gaze. There was a flash of pain, but just as soon as Annie had seen it, it was gone.

'I still can't believe he said yes,' said Emily. 'I really thought he was going to tell us to get lost.'

'You and me both,' said Annie, thinking of his expression when he'd opened the door to them.

'Is it going to make things too complicated?' said Emily. 'With all of your history?' She quickly bit her lip as if worried that she'd overstepped the mark. 'Sorry.'

'No, no,' said Annie – *all of your history* – like they were both dinosaurs. Emily was right about the complications, but that was all in the past. Annie had to – somehow – separate her long-ago feelings from the work which lay before them. 'It was just a shock at first, that's all.'

'I'm glad,' said Emily. 'Because, he's so nice, isn't he? Easy to talk to.'

There was a ripple of anticipation as, way down at the front of the queue, the doors opened, and the line began to move forward. Distribution was swift and efficient – no problems with the network today. The people around them in the queue murmured their approval.

When they returned to the workshop, four brand-new 3D printers had been squeezed into the already crowded space. Scott was cramming papers and files onto bookshelves, and stuffing drone parts and wiring into the overflowing drawers under his worktop.

Annie set down her bag of shopping and went to inspect one of the printers.

Emily whistled. 'These are top of the range,' she said. 'Where did you get them?'

'I called in a favour with a client,' said Scott. The truth was, for a small percentage in any future profits, one of his clients had sourced them, and Scott knew better than to ask where they'd come from. The people whose drones he repaired didn't like to talk about their work, and Scott's policy was never to ask. If they could pay him for his work on the repairs that was all he needed to know. 'Are you okay, Emily?'

She reassured him, yes, she was fine. 'It's just...' Her voice trembled. '...Matt would have loved all this so much.'

'I wish I could have met him,' said Scott, and meant it. Poor kid – what a thing to have to deal with. He admired her initiative, deciding to come and find him. And convincing Annie? That couldn't have been easy. 'First lot of materials have already been delivered,' he said. 'Shall I finish setting up the printers? Then we can get started.'

Emily nodded eagerly. Annie hardly even turned round from the printer – her nose was clearly out of joint about something but he wasn't going to ask.

'Let's begin with a basic drone body.' Scott walked back through to his desk and began scrolling through his files.

The 3D printers were capable of extruding the shape of each tiny nanodrone and its propellers, the interior – the brain, as Scott described it – and a small yet powerful solar battery on the top of each drone. Minuscule pollination parts would then be attached. Scott showed them his plans for filament-like pollen collectors on the front and back of each drone and more underneath of a different, flatter design, so that they could approach any flower, whatever its shape or size.

Annie watched Scott as he explained his designs, her thoughts scattered. Her memories of him had been safely locked away for a long time. Truthfully, she hadn't really thought about him for years – but now, face to face with him again, the lid had been lifted. Her insides churned.

Scott held one of the drones up behind a large magnifying plate on one of the work benches.

'How will you get them to pollinate the plants?' asked Emily. 'I mean, my brother used to have one of these drones – you had to control it remotely. Don't tell me each one of these things will have its own controller.'

'You're right,' said Scott. He peered at Emily over the top of his reading glasses. 'Things have come on a long way since then. And I've developed some really good stuff.' Annie remembered that infectious self-confident smile. The AI technology, he explained, would allow the nanodrones to learn to identify the flower or blossom of each plant, and learn its various parts so that it could target the pollen. Then, it would select the best pollination tool for the plant, depending on the shape of the flower, and would go from flower to flower, doing just exactly what a bee did.

'How will it know if a flower has already been pollinated?' asked Annie.

'It'll be able to read whether pollen has already been taken from a blossom,' said Scott. 'And it will also be able to read how much pollen has been added from different blossoms.'

'What about bad weather?' asked Annie. Despite her assurances to Emily, she found herself wanting to take the wind out of his sails, determined to find a flaw.

'They can cope with a rainy day,' said Scott. 'But very heavy rain, powerful winds – I'll admit that's a problem.'

'How will you control the drones once they've learned their tasks?' asked Annie. 'What's to stop them flying off and never coming back?'

'Whoever is in control sets the parameters for each colony,' said Scott. 'Range, flight time, we can programme all the details before they're released, and then monitor their remaining battery capacity. They will self-monitor, staying within control range, returning to base if they fall below five percent battery power. We have the override option to call them all back in again at any point.'

'This is incredible,' said Emily. 'How many tests have you run?'

'Plenty of lab tests for these basic models,' said Scott. 'Flight handling, balance, control.'

'But how do we know if these will work in the open air, with real weather, and real plants?' pressed Annie.

'That's where you come in,' said Scott. He was beginning to sound irritated. 'You know all there is to know about the flight behaviour of bees, their methods, their design. I want to know how they operate. I want to incorporate the very best of their skills into my drones. There's no reason why we can't design them to be just as good as the real thing.'

39

(Presenter walks to the edge of a field where wildflowers have been planted. He is dressed in a hat, veil, long-sleeved shirt and trousers, gloves.)

Welcome to a new series of *Biology for Today*. In this series of programmes, we'll be learning how to identify the various species we might meet every day. This week we're looking at insects – specifically those useful species which we want to encourage because they pollinate our fruits, vegetables and flowering plants.

(Presenter squats down to level of grasses and flowers.)

At the edge of this field, the farmer has planted a mix of wildflower and plant species which have been shown to attract pollinating insects.

(Presenter touches a small plant with small slipper-like egg-yolk yellow petals.)

This plant, bird's-foot-trefoil, is a member of the pea family. It got its name because its seed pods look a little like bird's claws. It is particularly attractive to the caterpillars which will eventually become common blue butterflies.

Look! There's one now. Can you believe it! Just goes to show, doesn't it? No CGI here.

This is garden sorrel or narrow-leaved dock. (Presenter moves to a plant with long, arrow-shaped dark green leaves. They are shiny and growing close to the ground.) Attractive to the caterpillars of small copper butterflies, the leaves are also edible to humans. The flower is a red to yellow spike.

Amongst the mixture of flowers which you'll see here are cowslips, field scabious, meadow buttercups, clover and ox-eye daisies. (Camera zooms in to show individual flowers.) The wealth of pollinators they draw in is phenomenal: not only bumblebees and honeybees, but many other bee varieties, plus butterflies, moths, beetles, hoverflies, flies and wasps.

You might not be able to hear them now because I'm talking, but I'm going to stop and ask my cameraman to keep filming, and I'm hoping that the sound engineer will be able to pick up the sound which I can hear – the sound of thousands and thousands of busy pollinators going about their work.

(Presenter puts his gloved finger to his lips and mimes being quiet. Camera pans round field. Sound of amplified insect noise – an industrious hum.)

Biology for Today
Presenter J.C. Ravensworth BBC Programmes for Schools
(first shown March 1998)

40

The first test was to check that the printers would produce viable drones. Scott chose five newly printed drones at random. Once their batteries were charged he cleared the paperwork and mugs from the coffee table and set them down. Emily laughed with delight when Scott demonstrated the take-off and landing.

'It's pretty clunky,' said Scott. 'But we'll soon iron out the kinks.' He grinned at Emily.

From the other side of the workshop, Annie watched them chatting happily, their heads close together, examining the drones, making sure they were evenly spaced prior to take-off. Under the bright, chilly lights, the tiny drones rose and hovered then landed perfectly, one after the other. Annie had a sudden queasy sense of foreboding. In Scott's expert hands this was going to work – and there would be terrible consequences.

Emily turned to Annie, her eyes shining. 'Did you see that?'

Annie stood completely still, her jaw set. She had

163

been wrong to support Emily's determination to come – she should have said something, put her off the idea of contacting him. It had all been a mistake.

'Thoughts, Dr Abrams?' said Scott in the same lazy way which always used to infuriate Annie. It had exactly the same effect on her now.

'These… things… you're making.'

'We're making,' he said, oblivious.

'If they work—'

'They'll work.'

'*If* they work,' she repeated, 'then we'll have no further use for pollinators, will we?' Emily looked at her, open-mouthed. 'Who will fight to protect the bees then,' said Annie, her voice rising, 'when we have machines to do it all for us? Don't you see?' How could she make him understand? He was so pleased with what he'd done. 'We're just going to carry blindly on towards our own oblivion, aren't we? More animals driven to extinction, but it needn't affect us.'

Scott threw his hands up in exasperation. 'The only reason I'm doing this is because you fucking asked me to.'

Emily stepped between them with her hands held out placatingly. 'It was me who asked,' she said, facing Scott. Then she turned to Annie. 'Dr Abrams, with the utmost respect, we have to try to make this work.'

Annie reached for the chair behind her and sat down. 'You too, Emily?' she said.

Behind Emily, Scott ran his fingers through his hair, then stood with his hands on his hips staring furiously at the ground.

'Or people will starve, Dr Abrams.' Emily held Annie's gaze, pleading. 'But… it doesn't mean we have to stop fighting for the bees.'

41

The first time Annie had slept with Scott was at a party at his student house. She'd slipped away with him before midnight, up to his room, Scott evicting the couple who were already on his bed. Next morning, while he slept, she got dressed and made her way down the stairs from his room. The sitting-room floor was strewn with bodies – some in the sleeping embrace of another, some alone, curled on the rugs, still holding beer cans. She couldn't see any of her housemates as she picked her way across the floor, so she left by herself, letting herself out of the front door, trying to remember which classes she had that day. It was cold, and her head thumped with the previous night's music and wine. Annie had crossed the wide lawns of the campus, grinning at the few other souls who were also out and about. Probably they were also returning from beds not their own. Back in her room she'd checked her timetable – no classes until two pm. She could go back to bed for a while – but she wasn't tired at all, despite her lack of sleep and everything she'd had to drink. She was blissfully distracted, her mind filled with Scott. She'd tucked her notebook and pens into her bag, grabbed her laptop, and headed back out to see if she could find some breakfast while she waited for the library to open.

Those were the days, thought Annie now, remembering breakfast at the little off-campus cafe. Fried eggs, bacon and sausages, a stack of thickly sliced toast, butter in little foil packets, hard and cold from the fridge, spread so thickly she could see her teeth marks when she bit into it. And the coffee. Real coffee, dark and deep, and a free refill if you asked nicely.

Annie tried not to think too much about food. She tried even harder not to think about coffee. The only things awaiting her today were protein bars, protein shakes, simulated flavours. Eating and drinking were no longer pleasures; they had become a simple act of refuelling. Think about something else, she told herself, and her brain lighted on the unhelpful memory of Scott reaching for her in bed. No. She shook her head to clear it. Drones. Pollinators. Balance gear. The problem of how to programme the simulated insects to recognise certain blooms. Forget all that, she told herself for the millionth time since he'd opened the workshop door, forget all that and get on with your work. Though she couldn't help but smile. That's what she'd had to tell herself back at college too, for different reasons. When he found her in the library or trying to study in the corner of the cafeteria, she could see exactly what he wanted. She'd wanted it too – but after she'd finished her essay, she told him, or once she'd finished reading the paper she'd unearthed on one of the quieter shelves of the library. It had taken every ounce of her self-control to turn him away, but she always did, promising to make it up to him later. Another image: Scott in her attic room, standing at the end of her bed, racing to rid himself of his clothes.

42

He had a child now, Scott told her. And an ex-wife. They lived in California. She – Rebekah – was American. She'd moved back to be closer to her parents. They were helping with childcare. She could do her research there. It had been easier for her to find funding.

'You have a son,' said Annie. Reminding her of just how much time had passed. Annie could imagine him. A little version of Scott: large dark eyes, charming grin. 'How often do you get to see him?'

Scott looked away. 'We have a video chat from time to time.'

Of course. Aeroplane travel had become something that was only for the seriously wealthy. 'The skies are so empty,' she said. Gone was the time when the air above them was sketched with contrails. Annie thought of the security drones which flew over the farms. She shook her head. 'I'm sorry about yesterday – it was clumsy, what I said. I was angry. I shouldn't have…'

'What is it?' Scott was at his workbench, the nanodrone

prototypes spread out before him. He peered at a spindly drone held delicately between his thumb and forefinger and picked up the tiniest screwdriver she'd ever seen. How did he manage such intricate work with those big hands?

'I can't be part of this project,' she told him.

Scott set everything carefully back on the bench before looking at her. 'But, I thought, after Emily said—'

'It feels like I'm turning my back on the one thing I care about,' interrupted Annie. 'I believe the natural world can recover – we just have to give it a chance. And I want to be part of that. But this, this…' She gestured at the computers and 3D printers. 'It's all part of the problem, isn't it?' Her face was getting hot. She pressed the backs of her hands to her cheeks.

Scott sighed. 'I know you're not that naive,' he said. 'It's not one thing or the other. Nature and technology aren't mutually exclusive. Why can't they work together?'

Annie looked around the windowless room: flashing lights on the machines, stark overhead LEDs. No view, no fresh air, no way of knowing whether it was night or day, sunny or cloudy – she felt her throat constrict.

Scott put out his hand to touch her arm, reassure her, but she took a step back. 'First of all,' he said, 'this is our only hope of getting any crops from insect-pollinated plants at all next year. Second,' he paused, trying to catch her eye, 'it doesn't seem as though no is an option. And third…' Annie finally looked at him – was she starting to come round to his way of thinking? He wasn't counting on it. 'What do you take me for? Some kind of robot? Of course we need bees. Listen, Annie.' He reached out to her again and this time she let his hand rest on her forearm. 'It's just a stopgap,' he said. 'It's temporary. Once insect numbers are viable we can park the drones and crop pollination can go on just as it always has before.'

Annie narrowed her eyes. 'You don't really believe that,' she said. 'Who'll be interested in investing in species conservation when a drone can do the same job with fewer complications?'

Scott rolled his eyes. 'I don't think you want this to work.'

'Of course I don't!' Annie clapped her hand to the side of her head. 'If the drone technology is effective, what's to stop people from continuing to use pesticides and fertilisers? They won't affect the technology, right? Producers could have their cake and eat it too. Higher yields, fewer pests and diseases, and all with no knock-on effect on pollinators, because drones don't get sick.' She paced around the room. 'It won't matter if farmers do away with trees, hedges, wild areas... Think of all that unexploited land, which up until now has only been protected for the sake of the wildlife. It's perfect for the big food producers and chemical companies. Meanwhile, not only the insects will disappear, but other dependent species will decline and fail. It's a short-term fix with potentially irreversible long-term effects. Think about it, Scott. Try to imagine it, five years, ten years down the line.' She appeared to be on the brink of tears but fought to control herself.

Scott remembered Annie on the stage at the climate rallies, striding about, trying to whip up a reaction from their fellow undergrads. It was impossible to get them to care about anything beyond getting a job and trying to scrape together enough money for somewhere to live after graduation. The environment was an important issue, of course it was, it had been for as long as any of them had been alive – but it hadn't been at the top of their list of priorities back then. Annie couldn't understand why other people didn't seem to see things the way she did. Frustrated, her voice would rise and her face would burn. Scott would stand at the back of the crowd where he could get a sense of the general response, fiercely proud of her.

'Try to imagine the future without the drone colonies,' Scott said now. 'Insect numbers are already so low as to make a viable harvest impossible next year. You've told me yourself there's no way the country could breed enough bees to make a difference, no matter how hard we try. So, tell me your solution, Annie. Do we sit here and do nothing? Feel sorry for ourselves and go hungry? Doesn't sound like a plan to me.' His brow furrowed. 'Annie, you know more about this than most people – you have to be one of the leading experts in the field. So, tell me. What should we do?'

Annie said nothing. She would not look at him but sat facing the opposite wall and its bank of computer screens. Her mind seethed with the things she could say to him – resentments she'd dredged up from all those years ago – but there was nothing constructive she could think of as a solution to the current problem, nothing that was a better idea than the drone colonies.

43

How to share a life with someone? It wasn't something Annie had had much practice at. No brothers or sisters, no pressure from her parents, allowing her to be alone if she wanted to be. And she often wanted to be. But with Scott it hadn't been so very difficult after all, during those first dreamlike months. She'd been comfortable with him. He made no demands on her, was more than happy to see her if she came by but was equally happy if she didn't. The terms drew on and Annie, though unfamiliar with the workings of a romantic relationships, was skilled at finding patterns.

'You always wait for me to find you.'

Scott leaned towards her and stroked her hair. 'I came and knocked on your door the other night, if you remember.'

'For sex,' said Annie. 'Sex doesn't count.'

He pulled a face. 'I beg to disagree.'

'When was the last time you thought about going out for the night, or what we'd get to eat? When was the last time you surprised me with anything that didn't involve us getting naked?'

He'd smiled his lazy smile. 'You're making me quite distracted.'

'I mean it, Scott. I love you.' They'd been saying it to each other for weeks. 'But... here's the thing.' She stopped. He had a distant expression on his face, which almost certainly meant he was thinking about coding. She sat looking at him – he didn't seem to have noticed that she hadn't finished the sentence. 'Don't worry about it,' she said, leaning across to kiss him, getting up, grabbing her bag from the floor. 'I've got to finish this essay. Call me later?'

44

'Don't tell me what to do, Annie,' said Scott. He set the nanodrone down carefully and put his hands against the edge of the workbench. 'I know what to do.'

'Then stop trying to immobilise the pollination tools,' said Annie. 'If you attach it like that, the drone won't be able to adjust to the anomalies within the blossoms, and the pollination will fail.'

'Who's running this operation?' said Scott.

'I'm not trying to step on your ego, Scott, I'm trying to make this thing work.' After a long sleepless night she'd grudgingly accepted that she should contribute to the nanodrone project after all. Could he not, just this once, admit that he was wrong about something?

Emily looked at the ceiling.

'Trust me,' said Scott. 'If I don't immobilise the pollinators, it throws the balance out of whack and the drones won't fly with any precision.'

'And if you do immobilise them,' said Annie, 'I'm telling you that nine times out of ten you're not going to be able to perform the operation these things are designed to do.'

They stood facing each other, hands on their hips, glaring.

'Jesus, Annie. Just let me get on with my job, would you, then we can run the tests.'

'Let the record show that I tried,' said Annie, gesturing to Emily as her witness before stalking away to laptop on the other side of the room. She put her headphones on and busied herself with her data.

Three hours later, Scott announced that he was ready to test the prototype again. They pushed back the coffee table and set several large pots of fresh-smelling echinacea plants in the centre of the floor, their candyfloss-pink blooms supported by tall narrow stems. Anne perched on the edge of the sofa with her notebook, scowling – Scott was not forgiven. He switched on the prototype and placed it carefully on the ground. He set his laptop and controller on the table. 'Emily, are you filming this?'

Emily nodded, checking the camera on its tripod, turning it on and giving him a thumbs-up. 'Recording now,' she told him.

'Mark two drone, running pollination test,' said Scott, looking into the lens, his brow furrowed with concentration. He took his seat at the desk and used the controller to control take-off. The tiny drone rose and stabilised about a foot off the ground. 'Approaching flowers now,' he said, biting his lower lip with a seriousness that Annie remembered. They'd successfully managed this part of the operation several times. 'For the echinacea flowers we have selected the pollinators on the underside of the drone,' said

Scott, bringing the drone level with the upturned flower. In the centre of the petals sat a perfect, deep-copper disc of pollen-bearing spines. It was in perfect position, the petals fully open, the flower almost completely flat. He moved the drone alongside the flower and then manoeuvred it over the flower, lowering it little by little until the pollinator was touching the florets in the centre. 'Bingo,' said Scott, keeping the drone in contact with the surface of the flower and allowing it to hover there. 'Are you getting this, Emily?'

'Yes,' she said, 'I've zoomed in as close as I can.'

'Right, I'll go to a different flower now,' said Scott. He adjusted the controller up a fraction, raising the drone from the flower and taking it across to the next. This one was growing at an angle, tilted to about forty-five degrees, its petals not yet fully open. Scott struggled to bring the drone alongside and then he tried to introduce the pollinator underneath the drone to the central florets of the bloom. At his first attempt he overshot completely. Bringing it back, he tried to tilt the drone so that the underside was parallel to the flower, but the angle was steep and the propellers struggled to maintain the position of the drone. Scott's face grew red with frustration. Annie pretended not to notice. In Scott's attempt to touch the drone down on the flower's surface, the flower head was pushed this way and that on its thin stalk and it was impossible to maintain contact with the centre of the flower.

'Don't say it,' said Scott. 'Just don't say it. You were right, okay?'

Annie bent her head and concentrated on her notes, as though he hadn't spoken at all, as though it was nothing to do with her.

'Continuing test,' said Scott, his voice back under control. He gave up on the tilted flower and moved on to the next, achieving contact with the correct parts. Once the test was over and the drone had landed back on the floor, they watched the video back, confirming that out of eight flower heads, the drone had successfully made contact with five of them.

'Not bad,' said Emily.

Neither of them looked at Annie. She said nothing. Scott picked up his prototype and took it back to the workbench, where he immediately began work on disabling the mechanism which had immobilised the pollinators.

A long time passed with Scott bent over his workbench, saying nothing. At about eight thirty, Emily asked if Scott still needed them. 'Sure,' said Scott, not looking up from his work. 'I suppose everyone is deserting me?'

'We can start again early tomorrow,' said Annie. 'As always.'

'Can I get you anything?' asked Emily. 'Protein bar? Shake?'

Scott didn't even look up. 'I need to finish this,' he said.

Once Emily and Annie had gone up the stairs, Scott put on his music and borrowed the lamp from Annie's desk, angling it so that it cancelled out the shadows thrown by his own desk lamp. It would be easier to see with a bit more light. He bent back over the prototype, adjusting his magnifying spectacles and trying to focus on the task of allowing the pollinators to move flexibly once they made contact with a surface, yet stay stable when in flight. He made hundreds of tiny alterations to the drone until he was satisfied then took the drone back to the test area and set up the camera on its tripod so that he could film it.

'Mark two drone, running pollination test two,' said Scott, concentrating on take-off. Manoeuvring the prototype to touch down on each flower, he could see that the modifications he'd made were a step in the right direction, but the pollinators were not sensitive enough to react on contact with delicate flowers on very flexible stems. The camera recorded him swearing loudly and repeatedly as he landed the drone and walked over to turn the camera off.

45

Annie woke early. She couldn't get back to sleep and lay on her back on the deflating air mattress turning over the conversation of the night before. What was the matter with her? Falling back so easily into behaving like her defensive nineteen-year-old self, just like when she'd been going out with Scott. She'd been won over then by his easy-going manner and self-assurance. Funny how those same qualities were now irritating her more than was reasonable.

No more time for teenaged sulking. There was too much at stake.

Annie got up and dressed quickly, pulling on her jeans which lay draped over the side of Scott's sofa, finding an almost-clean T-shirt, picking up her socks from the day before and tucking them into her trainers; she'd put them on downstairs. Emily was fast asleep, one arm flung out from her sleeping bag, her face almost covered by her hair. Annie checked her phone – it was far too early to wake her. She perched her glasses on top of her head before quietly closing the door and tiptoeing down the stairs to the workshop. While she was the only one up, she would see if she could familiarise herself with Scott's designs, see if there were any amendments she could suggest, surprise him with them when he came down. As an afterthought she ran her fingers through her hair as she made her way down the stairs. She sat on the sofa and switched on her laptop to see if there were any messages from Victor or Attica.

A memory came up on her social media feed. A photograph of the room she'd lived in during her second year at university – her desk under the window, her files lined up neatly along the shelf above her bed. The year things had started to go right with her studies.

'I think I need to spend more time working,' she'd told Scott, as gently as she could. She sat on the uncomfortable chair she'd dragged upstairs from the kitchen. 'I think I've been spending too much time with you.'

'Isn't that what's supposed to happen, when you go out with someone?' said Scott. 'Spending time with each other?' He'd been lying in her bed. He poked one foot out from under the duvet and traced it along her leg.

Annie pressed her fingers to her temples, where a headache was beginning. 'Of course. Of course it is. Except… I can't manage it like you can.' She drew a breath, thought carefully about how to say it best. 'I'm not as clever as you are, Scott. I have to work twice as hard as you to get anywhere. And a lot of the time, when I should be working, I'm thinking about you, and when I can see you next, and whether you'll like the new dress I bought, and whether or not I can afford to go see a film with you. I'm not good at this, Scott. All this.' She waved her hands about. 'It's really difficult. And I don't think it's supposed to be.'

'But… this is easy,' said Scott.

For you, perhaps, she wanted to say. You wait to be found, and I can't help myself – I always come looking. You're totally absorbed in your own work – but you expect me to be there whenever you look up. 'I worked really hard to get here,' she told him. 'I'm not a natural genius like you are.' (He looked very pleased when she said that.) 'I need to put in as many hours as it takes to get things done, and I'm just not managing it.'

Enough, Annie told herself now. She closed the tab, shut her laptop and went in search of one of the drones.

But she wasn't alone.

Against the far wall, two lamps shone pools of light down on to the figure of Scott, slumped over his workbench. She felt the adrenaline rush in her blood, and her breath caught somewhere in her chest. She hurried over to check that he was okay. But she needn't have worried. His breathing was regular, his eyes lightly closed, a faint blush on the cheek which was turned upwards towards the light. The camera Emily had used to film the test runs was on the desk, near his head.

Annie took the camera to the sofa to watch the footage back. There were obvious drawbacks to one person running test flights alone – when Emily recorded them she could follow the drone around. He'd set the camera at slightly the wrong angle and so the drone was often out of shot, but she got the idea of what wasn't working properly each time because of the soundtrack of disappointed remarks and muffled curses. The balance was completely off. The adjustments were throwing all of his other measurements out of whack. With each new test, he'd tried to fix the error, but in doing so he had affected something else. But – he'd used her idea, she realised, as the test films went on. He'd made changes to his design to allow for the pollinators to move. She could hardly believe what she was seeing. She watched as the drone gradually became more responsive to the different angles of the flowers, and the greater ease in which it positioned itself at each bloom.

'This doesn't mean you get to pick holes in the rest of my design,' said a voice from the other side of the workshop. Scott stood there, his face slack with tiredness, his hair sticking up in all directions.

Annie resisted the urge to say something – she'd been right, he'd been wrong, they both knew it. 'That was a good night's work you put in,' she said. 'What's next?'

'We start work on the AI component,' said Scott. 'The brains. I'll need to input information about flower shapes and sizes. Which is your area, if I recall correctly.' He sat on the stool he used for the workbench and hooked his heels over the rung. 'So. What've you got for me?' His eyes crinkled at the corners.

Had the words of the previous night been forgiven? Perhaps even forgotten?

She sat on the sofa and took up her laptop. She'd been hard at work inputting details about the varieties of flowers and blossoms they'd be encountering, along with information about how insect pollinators negotiated them to get to the nectar. Her database of flower types was extensive, detailing the shapes and locations of the sexual parts, highlighting the ways in which the drones could best approach them. She'd let herself be distracted by the test flights and the design errors, letting herself be drawn in to Scott's struggles – but not any more. It was her turn to step up. 'There's lots to be getting on with,' she told him. 'I'll email it to you now.'

46

Now that the prototype was operational, the pressure was on to produce the vast numbers of drones. They began to eat at their computers – breaks up in Scott's flat took up too much time. Late evenings turned into all-nighters, the printers clicking and whirring, churning out nanodrones. Scott checked and rechecked the specifications, honing and smoothing and streamlining and making hundreds of minor modifications to improve their performance. Annie added to her research where she could; the more details she was able to provide Scott with, the better the final versions would be.

They only left the workshop to collect their rations. Not enough sunlight or fresh air. Having spent so many weeks out in the orchards in the spring sunshine, Annie noticed it now, more than she ever would have before, when her life had revolved around lab work and the simfields. The urge to be out of doors in the wild had left her, she'd reasoned, trained out of her by years and years of research – but that brief spell, those few short months in the sun, had awoken it in her again and now she craved it. In the windowless workshop she didn't know whether it was day or night unless she checked the time on her screen.

Every so often, one of them would take a turn to bring the others half a protein bar or a mug of miso soup or a watered-down protein shake. When it was time to sleep, Annie climbed the stairs to Scott's living room and laid her air mattress on the floor. Sometimes, if it was still light outside, she would stand at the window and look out over the street. There were generally very few passers-by. It was cold, and the clouds blanketed the sky with grey. Leaves whipped past in the wind. Sometimes she caught sight of the person who lived in the house opposite as he stared out of his window. An elderly man who always wore a knitted hat pulled down low, heavy-rimmed glasses whose lenses reflected the light from the window. She couldn't tell whether he was living alone or what his state of mind might be. In the early days they had waved at each other, and Annie had smiled, in an attempt to connect. But now that they knew each other by sight, it felt strange to keep waving. Infantile, pointless. And so they stood and looked at each other, and Annie hoped that he was not living by himself. Sometimes people walked past underneath her window in the direction of the nearest supermarket. It was about ten minutes' walk east of Scott's flat, and people rarely went there alone, preferring to go in groups of four or more, arranging with friends and neighbours when they might go together; safety in numbers and all that. On their return journeys people walked quickly, furtively, hurrying along the street with their rations in bags slung over their shoulders, or pulling wheeled trolleys or suitcases. Very few people used their cars. This was perhaps the strangest thing of all: the demise in city traffic. Some days Annie saw no cars at all, only bicycles and, occasionally, a double-decker bus, near-empty, the top deck almost level with her window. One afternoon as she watched, the bus slowed then stopped right outside. A small boy, his face pressed to the window, stared at her with hungry eyes as she sipped her mug of watery soup. The person he was sitting next to – his mother, she presumed – sat looking straight ahead. Annie made a face to distract the boy, but his expression didn't change, and after a couple more attempts to make him smile she gave up and they simply watched each other from only a few metres away until the bus began to move again and drew away, taking the boy out of sight.

The days ticked on to December. Soon it would be Christmas. Annie felt nostalgic for shops full of mince pies and puddings, advent calendars and tubs of chocolates. Adverts showing large family get-togethers and programmes dedicated to cooking the perfect turkey dinner. Last year there had been no tinny Christmas songs on a loop in the shops, and very few festive treats. This year the only things on the shelves were artificial sweeteners, clothes pegs and bleach. Everything else was rationed, kept carefully locked away until people arrived to collect their share for the week. People often used to say that Christmas wasn't about the presents, or the food. This year they would all find out if that was true.

'Shall we call it a day?' Scott looked up from his screen, his eyes bleary with tiredness.

'Thank Christ,' said Emily. While she waited for the printers to finish, she did a brief tour of the workshop, picking up the empty mugs and setting them on the stairs to take up with her.

'You don't have to do that,' said Scott.

'I know,' she said, lightly.

Annie drew a deep breath and pushed down the lid of her laptop. She stretched out her arms, lacing her fingers together and pushing her palms upwards and away, easing the muscles in her back and shoulders.

Later, upstairs in Scott's living room, Annie lay on her mattress and tried to rest. She knew sleep would not come quickly, but she willed her mind to become calm. She listened to Emily's breathing until it deepened and became even. Then Annie closed her eyes and conjured images of the trees in Caitlin's orchards, their branches spreading overhead. Blossoms, whispering in the breeze, papery and pale, the promise of fruit. The sleepy hum of the bees as they bumbled from flower to flower.

If she'd known what was coming she would have paid more attention to it all. She would have gone out at sunrise every day and stayed out under the trees until last light. She would have slept outside in the summer under the canopy of leaves. She would have savoured each bite of apple, every bursting segment of orange. She would have been more grateful for it all.

She turned her thoughts away from what was no longer possible – back to the trees, and the warmth of the imaginary sun.

Eventually, she slept.

The alarm sounded. Without thinking, Annie rose from her mattress to start all over again.

47

As a way to escape the confines of the workshop, Annie reinstated the news ticker across the bottom of her screen while she worked. When she noticed a breaking news headline she switched into a screen-in-screen live news feed, turning up the volume so that Emily could listen as she passed.

'The long-awaited International Food Summit begins tomorrow at Versailles, near Paris,' said the newsreader, her hair a perfect helmet, her face a smooth mask. Sydney Clark, the familiar NewsOrg anchor: dependable, unbiased, the friendly face of British news. 'As anticipated, security is at an all-time high, with the leaders of twenty nations in attendance. Protesters have been prevented from approaching the venue.' The camera cut to footage of thousands of people crowding the streets approaching Versailles. A barrage of concrete barriers, several metres thick, lay across the road. In front of that, water cannons and row upon row of riot police with shields. Mounted police waited nearby, the horses stepping nervously, unable to keep still. The protesters looked desperate, thought Annie. The placards were few, as were the children. Nearest to the barricades stood a jostling phalanx of people, their faces covered by scarves, their fists punching the air. There was raw fury in their shouts.

'Several arrests were made today when a small number of protesters jumped the barriers and attempted to approach the venue on foot,' said Ms Clark. 'They were quickly apprehended and removed from the scene. A number of international leaders arrived today; they were greeted by the French President Yves Falcon.' Footage of helicopters landing on the lawns and various well-dressed delegates walking carefully down the aircraft steps, holding on to their hair. The British Prime Minister, Henry Ellison, was first, waving to the cameras, his expression impassive. He seemed like a good person, thought Annie. Principled, with an appetite for fair play. But the last few years had taught her well – the Prime Minister's intentions meant nothing. The narrow margin held by his party meant that he was, essentially, powerless.

None of the leaders smiled at the world's press, there to capture their arrival. And there was no footage from inside the building of any of the usual niceties – delegates taking afternoon tea or talk of what would be served at the first night's banquet. But there was no doubt in Annie's mind that these things would be happening behind closed doors, while the protesters went home to their meagre rations.

'Tomorrow, talks will begin in earnest, with world leaders discussing the current situation and ways our nations might work together to solve the crisis.' Sydney's voice was expressionless. Under her heavy makeup her face was pale.

48

The server was down again. It happened almost daily. Unable to access their data from the cloud, they used the time to build up drone numbers with the 3D printers. 'I want you to check the network every five minutes,' Scott called to Emily. 'As soon as we're back up I need to get my hands on the AI programming.'

'Absolutely,' said Emily, her head bent over one of the printers.

Scott positioned himself behind Annie's chair. 'We need all hands on deck,' he said.

'I'm listening,' said Annie. She was in the middle of writing an email to Victor – as soon as the server was back up she'd send it. 'I need to check on how things are going in Hattenden,' she said, not lifting her eyes from the screen. 'And before you say I can leave it all in Victor's capable hands, it's essential I let him know the protocols for checking the systems in the simfields. One day we'll get more bees. In the meantime we need to maintain their environments.' She frowned in concentration and finished typing a sentence.

'The priority isn't your simfields,' said Scott. His voice was controlled – but barely. 'The priority isn't your precious bees.'

Annie stopped typing. It was one thing for Scott to have completely taken the lead on the drone project – she and Emily were doing everything he asked – but to question her own work at the Dome? Annie closed the lid on her laptop and turned in her chair to face him.

'I need you to focus, Annie. If we don't get fifty thousand drones online we're all going hungry.'

'Shut up, Scott,' said Annie. 'Just, please, shut up.'

A beat. Emily looked from one to the other, her eyes wide.

'We're all doing the best we can, aren't we?' said Emily, her voice pleading. 'Listen, the printers are all set up and ready to go. I'm going to check the network.' She turned to leave the room, adding quietly, 'Please try not to kill each other while I'm gone.'

Scott and Annie sat in the off-campus snack bar which had always been their favourite place for coffee. They had finished their drinks and cake. Soon he would be thinking about going back to his project; most of their conversation had swung back to how well it was going, and how he couldn't wait to show it to his tutor.

Annie took a deep breath and launched into the speech she'd been mulling over for days. She'd thought so much about what she wanted to say that she accidentally started somewhere in the middle. 'I got the mark back on my last assignment,' she said, no longer able to look him in the eye, concentrating on the grains of spilled sugar on the table top instead, stirring at them with her finger. 'I can't keep compromising. My work has to come first.' Her voiced cracked a little. She kept going. 'It means less time with you.' Tears threatened. 'I don't want less time with you.'

'Me neither,' he said. 'Course not.' He sounded cross. 'Though I still don't see why we can't have both.'

But I don't know how, Annie wanted to say. And she'd made her decision. She would not let him stand in the way of her chance of a good degree. So she stopped turning up late to lectures and using her study time to pop round to his room. When he knocked on her door late at night she would let him in, but then she'd leave early for the library the next morning. It took all of her strength to step back from him, but as the weeks went on she began to feel as though she was finally getting on top of her essays and lab work, and at the end of term when she'd handed in her last essay she texted Scott to tell him, and to ask if he was free to grab a drink later. His reply was brief. He was busy. Maybe some other time. He didn't phone her over the holidays or reply to any of her texts. He was in a pout, she knew. She would leave him to stew for a bit. She was proud of herself for sticking to her guns – and cross with him that he hadn't even tried to distract her.

At the beginning of the next term she saw him sitting on a bench on the other side of the quad deep in conversation with a girl she didn't recognise. As Annie watched, she saw Scott pass one of his ear buds to the girl, who laughed and popped the ear bud in, and they sat with their heads tipped together, almost touching.

49

They worked on, despite the furious silence between Scott and Annie. Scott uploaded data and worked on the coding. Emily and Annie printed and packed hundreds of nanodrones.

On the way back from taking another box of drones to the storage area, Annie stopped to check the news ticker on her laptop. She broke the silence. 'You two,' she said, quietly, taking a seat on the sofa. 'Come and have a look at this.' She opened the breaking news page so that they could watch the bulletin.

'At the International Food Summit today, there was an unprecedented attack on a number of prominent delegates.' The Breaking News ticker scrolled across the bottom of the screen. Beneath her foundation Sydney Clark's face was ashen. Her hair was not as carefully styled as usual, suggesting a rush to get to air. 'It has been confirmed that the French President and the Prime Minister of Great Britain have sustained critical injuries resulting from knife and gunshot wounds. A number of other individuals are confirmed injured. We do not currently have any further details of these persons.' Cut to footage from a news drone circling over Versailles showing a large number of ambulances and police cars in the immense courtyard. From the air it was possible to see the activity: paramedics running from their vehicles into the building, police and security personnel circling the perimeter.

'It is not known how the attackers managed to gain entrance to the grounds and building despite the overwhelming security presence,' continued Sydney. 'We understand that all of the attackers have been killed at the scene and the location has been made secure.'

Annie turned from the screen. 'How can this have happened?'

'I expect somebody took a bribe, let them in.' Scott turned back to the drone he was working on. 'Lots of desperate people out there.'

Emily moved a little closer to Annie, her hand hovering over her mouth as she watched the story. 'I can't believe it,' she said, her voice breaking. 'This was probably our last chance of…' She shook her head.

'This will strengthen the opposition parties,' said Annie. She closed the lid of her laptop.

'Break's over,' shouted Scott from his desk.

'Any chance we could call it a night?' asked Annie. Emily's face was pinched and fearful. She looked as though she might cry.

'We've got just over a hundred to finish before we reach our target for today. It's only seven o'clock,' said Scott. 'Sooner we get back to it the sooner we can stop.'

Emily rose to her feet and went back to the printers.

Annie got up to follow. As she passed Scott, Annie paused. 'Don't push Emily too hard,' she said.

'We haven't got time for politics,' he said, but his expression had softened.

'Are we calling a truce?' said Annie.

Scott gave her the smallest of nods. 'Just… we can't afford to get distracted.'

50

Annie checked back in on the ten o'clock bulletin. Sydney Clark's face was more impassive than usual as the studio lights came up.

'Something's happened,' said Annie, motioning for the others to be quiet.

'The death has been announced of Isabella Belasco, the Spanish Prime Minister, due to injuries sustained in today's attack,' said Sydney. 'Her husband was at her side in hospital when she passed away. Our own Prime Minister is still in a critical condition, according to a statement from the hospital. Five more deaths have been announced: two members of the United States' delegation and three members of catering staff at the venue. Their names will be released once their families have been notified. This brings the death count to nineteen.' They cut to a photograph of the Spanish Prime Minister and her husband at an unnamed event. She looked like a jolly, warm-hearted sort of person. Her husband stood rather awkwardly at her side, very formally dressed; his smile didn't quite reach his eyes. Not comfortable in the limelight, thought Annie, feeling sorry for him, at the road life had led him down.

'Police are investigating a number of lines of enquiry regarding the identity of the attackers.' Sydney lowered her eyes for a long moment before turning back to the camera and announcing, 'And in other news…'

51

In a windowless room illuminated by light from beyond a plexiglass ceiling, a white-haired man sat watching film of the attack on the international food summit. This footage was not the distant view shown on the online news by cameras in circling drones, but had been filmed at ground level by cameras hand-held or attached to somebody's clothing, recording jerky movements and muffled sounds as the camera moved rapidly towards a group of men and women seated at a long table. There were antique mirrors, gilt-framed portraits, flashes of luxurious wallpaper and tapestries. The table was covered with plates of food, the sort of meal which should not have been possible. Roast meats on carving dishes, platters of potatoes glistening with butter, dishes of peas and carrots, asparagus and green beans, and baskets of fresh bread rolls. Silverware, elaborate china and glasses of wine. Crystal decanters were dotted up and down the long table. The camera jumped and jerked but the scene was clear enough to those watching.

'Parasites,' said the white-haired man, wiping the back

of his hand across his mouth. The self-composed young woman who stood next to his chair, hands clasped in front of her, said nothing.

At first, only one or two people in the gilt-edged room noticed the disturbance; they raised their hands (some of them still holding forkfuls of food) to point in the direction of the camera. Some of the others turned in the same direction to watch, their mouths falling open. Somebody screamed. From either side of the camera, out of the peripheral view and into the foreground, came a number of figures dressed all in black. They fanned out wide, raising their guns, taking aim. 'Security!' shouted the man at the head of the table – somebody immediately opened fire and the man crumpled to the floor, his head hitting the edge of the table as he went down.

Pandemonium. People running, pushing back chairs, knocking them over in their haste. People clutching at each other as they ran, pulling each other out of harm's way. People cowering under the table, crouching low against the ornate carved legs, covering their eyes against the attackers. They'd followed their instinct to hide but now they were trapped, and the camera, swinging wildly from left to right, recorded their deaths. Blood on the antique carpets, blood on the priceless mirrors. Blood on the buttered potatoes and the small, juicy peas. People crying for help as the gunmen picked off the final few who remained in the room. Nobody left standing. Muffled orders from one of the gunmen and the cameraman turned to retreat, showing glimpses of gilded corridors and flashes of faces appearing at doorways and just as suddenly withdrawing as they saw who was running towards them. Then: the noise of shouting coming from a distance, armed bodyguards rushing towards the camera, more gunshots. A carved chair thrown through the window to the right-hand side of the shot and the cameraman tumbled after it. Blurred footage of grass and sky then up again, dashing across a garden, the gunmen in black flanking the cameraman. The footage ended abruptly.

'How did you get hold of this?' asked the man.

'Found it on Tor. Someone had posted it.'

'Who's behind this?'

'Nobody knows, Mr – John – I mean, sir.' The young woman blushed.

The man twitched with irritation. 'Keep an eye on it, would you, Rae?'

'Yes, sir.'

52

Five days later and the attack was still headline news. 'The doctors have put the Prime Minister in a medically induced coma,' said Annie, scrolling through the news feed. 'The summit has been abandoned—'

'Of course,' interrupted Scott. 'They couldn't very well continue with talks.'

'…any delegates who are able to travel home are on their way back,' said Annie. 'The pound is tanking, so's the dollar.'

'Again,' said Scott. 'We've been here before. Let's not panic just yet.' He kept on tapping away at his keyboard, adding data to his latest spreadsheet.

Emily was quality checking the latest batch of drones before carefully placing them in sectional boxes.

'I've uploaded the latest data,' said Scott. 'Keep it coming, Annie. I'm on a roll.' He fell silent again. For a long while there was just the tapping of keyboards.

Scott's single-mindedness was something Annie remembered from university. Sometimes to the point of forgetting to eat, drink and sleep. Not because he was aware of deadlines or dates, simply because of his fascination with the tech.

Six hours on, Scott was still hunched over his computer. Annie and Emily sat scrolling through news websites, trying to find any updates on the attacks. The only footage available was what they had already seen dozens of times on the news.

'There's nothing new,' said Annie. She clicked through to a different site. 'See, exactly the same clips.' She sighed and closed the window. 'Hey, Scott. How much longer until you're ready for this test?'

'Just a few more tweaks,' he said.

'You said that two hours ago.' Annie pushed her glasses up so that she could rub her stinging eyes. 'Can we stop for the night?'

'Uh… no,' said Scott, his fingers not slowing on the keys. 'We're already way behind schedule.'

'I'm going to make a hot drink,' said Emily. 'Think there's some of that packet soup left.'

Annie couldn't remember the last time they'd stopped for food. 'Good idea,' she said.

53

'This is your Christmas Eve NewsOrg news bulletin.'
The lights in the studio came up, revealing Sydney Clark
in a black suit jacket, a small sprig of holly pinned to the
lapel. She showed signs of terrible strain, wearing her worry
around the corners of her eyes, her mouth – her lower lip –
quivering. She was struggling to maintain her composure.
Annie's heart clutched with fear as the newsreader began to
speak. 'Today, after eight days of round-the-clock treatment
in a Paris hospital, our Prime Minister, Henry Ellison,
finally succumbed to his injuries. He will be flown home
tomorrow. A state funeral will take place in one week's
time on New Year's Eve. The Deputy Prime Minister has
declared three days of national mourning and urges the
people of Great Britain to respond appropriately and with
consideration. A hospital spokesman confirmed that the
Prime Minister's wife and two children were present when
he died.' There was no cutaway to footage of the attack.
There was no conjecture from experts, no outside broadcast.
Only the newsreader in the studio, dressed in funeral black,

trying not to cry. 'On behalf of everyone here at NewsOrg, our hearts go out to the Prime Minister's family and friends at this tragic time.' The camera remained on the newsreader and the dark shadows under her eyes which makeup had not managed to conceal. She took a deep breath. 'And from all of us, to all of you watching,' she gave a small, trembling smile, 'we wish you a Merry Christmas and a Happy New Year.'

'My God.' Annie closed her laptop. With Ellison gone, there would be another power struggle. He'd somehow managed to hold together a fragile peace between the fractured parties in Westminster. Annie feared what might happen now that his voice had been silenced.

'What's that noise?' Emily put her hand on Annie's arm.

The sound of running feet from the street outside. One person, then another. A pause. Front doors slamming, shouts, more people running.

'Stay there,' said Scott. He hurried to the front door and locked it, then ran upstairs. 'Crowds of people,' he called down. 'God knows where they're going.'

The sound of breaking glass, a whoop, a scream.

Annie got up from the sofa, pulling Emily after her. 'Upstairs,' she told her.

There were no ground-floor windows in the workshop; the only glass was the panel in the front door. Scott beckoned to Annie to follow him back down the stairs, and together they cleared everything from the desk in the workshop and heaved it along the hallway, tipping it on its end and pushing it up against the front door. 'Now the back,' said Scott, racing down the hall. There were boxes of drones packed and ready to go out the back via the service alley. He checked that the back door was locked and dragged a filing cabinet in front of it, then the drone boxes. Annie began to shake; the surge of adrenaline had swept away the months, taking her back to the night walk with Matt, his stabbing – the silent knife flashing out of the dark – a blurred reality since she had no recollection of seeing the knife, Matt's body the solid wall between it and her. The blood – oh, the blood. She would never be free of it. She sat on the sofa in the darkness and pressed her hands between her knees.

'It's okay,' said Scott, appearing at her side. 'Everything's secure. Come upstairs.' His voice was soft, understanding. She was safe. He held out his hand. It would be so easy, now, to relax, to allow herself to be absorbed back into his orbit. She took his hand, and he pulled her up, towards him. 'It's okay,' he said again, and bent to kiss her, his arms a shelter, his lips just as soft as she remembered. She felt herself soften, her edges dissolving.

A shriek from outside, very close. Something hit the front wall, shaking Annie from her dream. From upstairs, a scream. She pulled away. 'Emily,' she said, racing back up the stairs.

Upstairs, together in the dark, the three of them watched the flow of people up the street towards the river. For hours they came, holding up their phones, filming, the screens bobbing brightly above their heads. Shouting, chanting, running, windows breaking. Fires burned. While they swarmed below her, Annie couldn't bring herself to leave the window. When at last the crowds began to thin out, she turned and saw Emily asleep on the sofa, her knees drawn up to her chin, the blanket half-covering her face. 'What time is it?'

Scott sat on one of the dining chairs, his face in shadow. 'You should get some rest,' he said.

'I won't be able to sleep.' Nothing felt safe any more.

He knelt in front of her. 'Annie.'

Whatever he thought he'd felt in their kiss, whatever he thought he saw in her eyes, he was mistaken. Too much water under the bridge.

'Annie?'

She shook her head.

He stood up and put out his hand to her.

Such a small space between them.

The thought of being by herself that night…

Annie reached out to him, and in a moment they were back in each other's arms. She nestled into his familiar warmth. Oh, she remembered that feeling of security – nothing could touch her while they were together. Don't think, she told herself, as they found their way to his bedroom and quietly closed the door. It was one night. They could have one more night.

When Annie woke it was still dark. Scott's breathing was deep and rhythmic, his warmth radiating from the other side of the bed. She rose swiftly, gathering her clothes from the floor. She didn't want Emily to wake up alone. More than that, she wanted to keep it a secret – something between her and Scott alone. She slipped from his room, pulling the door gently closed behind her, padding back to the living room. She peered out through the window. The streets were empty now, and the fires had burned themselves out. Annie wriggled back into her underwear and T-shirt and laid her mattress on the floor. As she lay down she noticed flakes of snow beginning to drift past the window. She pulled the blankets around herself and thought of Scott, of how their bodies had remembered each other. And the snow fell more thickly, faster and faster, settling on the windowsill, already a couple of centimetres thick by the time she finally fell asleep.

54

Christmas Day – and a white Christmas, too. The streets were blanketed with snow and all of the previous night's chaos had been erased. Snow over the remains of the fires lit in the street, the broken glass from shop fronts and windows, the mangled remains of bikes and cars. Their shapes were gentle, their edges softened. Lumps and bumps that could be anything or nothing. The darkness was gone now, the noise and the panic. It was no longer scary – it was blank and quiet and cold. A fresh start.

Annie came away from the window. She pulled the blanket from her mattress and draped it around her shoulders. The room was freezing. The heating must have cut out during the night. Annie went down the stairs to the control panel and set about rebooting the system to get it running again.

Scott came down soon after, dressed, with two mugs and a couple of protein bars. He set them down and turned to Annie. They drifted back together without a word and fell into a kiss. They sank onto the sofa, curled into each other, Scott's hands warm on her body.

Then, from upstairs, the sound of the toilet flushing. Feet at the top of the stairs. Annie leapt up, pulling the blanket after herself. Scott crossed the room to his computer and logged in so that by the time Emily appeared Scott was scrolling through drone specifications and Annie was checking the news headlines on her tablet.

'Happy Christmas,' said Emily. She held her hands over the nearest heating duct.

'Same to you,' said Scott. 'Okay, folks.' He rubbed his hands together. 'AI test in ten minutes. Emily, if you could bring me five of the latest drones, I'll upload the coding. Let's get started.'

Emily went through to the back of the workshop to search the packing boxes, and while she was out of their line of sight Scott slunk up behind Annie and wrapped his arms around her. She turned to him. 'I'd better get dressed.' She stepped gracefully out of his embrace and hurried up the stairs. Focus, Annie. Focus.

When she returned, Emily was setting up the camera on its tripod while Scott arranged the drones on the floor amongst the variety of flowerpots. Under the artificial light the plants looked sickly and seemed to be paling.

'Poor things,' said Annie. 'They need some natural light.'

'Let's move upstairs,' suggested Emily.

In the living room they pushed back the sofa and set up the pots and tripod again. Annie settled on the sofa with her notebook and pen, sitting cross-legged, leaning slightly forward, excited.

'Here goes,' said Scott. He grabbed the controller and guided the drones through take-off. It was eerie to watch them all moving as one, following the same trajectory.

They hovered over the flowers. 'Now,' said Scott. 'See the drone with the red spot? It's the lead drone, the one I'm controlling – the others are programmed to follow. The idea is, I guide the lead towards a flower and the others will follow the movements but will sense if they don't have a flower beneath them. That's when the AI should kick in. They are programmed to find a flower to land on. Here goes.' He manoeuvred the lead drone towards an echinacea flower, its petals splayed open and back to welcome insects. He carefully guided it down so that the pollinators on the base of the drone came into contact with the bloom. 'I'll hold it there,' said Scott. 'Are you getting this, Emily?'

Emily nodded.

They all turned their focus to the four other drones, the followers, hovering at the same height as the lead drone, none of them over a flower.

Scott bit his lip.

'How long until they get the signal?' asked Annie.

'Shh,' said Scott. 'Any second now.'

Annie, Scott and Emily held their breath. The only sound in the room was the whirring of the propellers. The moment stretched – waiting for a response, waiting for movement, waiting for… anything.

And then with no help from the controller, with no instruction from Scott, with no outside interference at all, the four drones changed direction and moved out in their own – slowly, slowly, as though searching for something.

'Yes,' said Scott, taking a breath.

The four drones explored their immediate surroundings. Where they had all moved off together, simultaneously, in the same direction, they now moved out on their own trajectories, a little jerkily, rising a fraction, falling a fraction.

'There,' whispered Emily as the second drone connected with a flower, its pollinator grazing the mound of dark golden florets. 'Oh,' she said, as the third drone landed on another.

Within five minutes all of the drones had made contact with a bloom. And then, as the lead drone rose once more into the air, the others followed. Scott guided them all back in to land on the floor, carefully bringing them down to rest while the others whooped and cheered.

'You did it! You totally did it!' Emily punched the air with her free hand.

Annie pressed her hands to her mouth in relief. It worked. It worked.

Scott grinned crazily. 'Things to work on,' he said, pacing again. 'Make a note, would you please, Annie? We need to speed up reaction time. We need to work on flower identification – if the lead drone lands on one type of flower, they all need to seek out the same species. It's no good if they land on anything with pollen.' Scott walked as he talked, striding around the floor, between the plant pots, stopping to pick up the lead drone, moving on, running his fingers through his already messy hair. 'Oh – and we need to improve pollination time. Once the lead has pollinated the first flower we can't have it waiting around for the other four, or twenty, or five hundred drones to land. Once the lead drone has landed and pollinated it must be free to go find another flower. The same with all of them. We need to make sure that after the initial instruction to find a flower to pollinate each drone is capable of operating independently

– until I call the lead back in. Got all that?' Annie nodded. 'Okay, let's get to work,' said Scott. 'Bring them all back through, would you, Emily?'

There was no time to think about Christmas, or to worry about what might happen now that the Prime Minister was dead, or for Annie to go over what had happened the previous night. She glanced over at Scott. He seemed completely absorbed by his work – but then he looked up and caught her eye, and winked. She looked away, her cheeks flaring with heat, pretending to take an interest in her screen. Emily was once again completely involved with the 3D printers. She flitted from one to the next, gathering up the completed drones and bringing them to Annie for a final quality check. Their delicate structure, all joints and angles, did feel almost insect-like. She turned them over, checking all the pollinators, feeling Scott's eyes on her. She didn't need to look up to check – she knew, and felt a flush once again rising over her chest, her neck, her face. She shouldn't have done it. Things were suddenly more complicated than they had to be.

Test followed test, with Scott making tiny adjustments between each one. They stopped for a protein shake at noon, and another one at six. The streets were still empty; the snow lay untouched. While Scott worked to develop the AI, Emily and Annie printed more drones and fitted them with solar batteries and pollinators.

They ran a test at eleven pm. Scott had managed to cut reaction times to a few seconds after the lead drone had made contact with the first flower head. But their biggest breakthrough was independent movement after the first instruction. The first drone was free to take off again once it had pollinated the flower, at which point all drones worked separately.

'Congratulations,' said Annie, as Scott guided the drones all back in to land. He looked dazed, exhausted.

'You're amazing,' said Emily, looking at him with admiration.

'We've done it,' said Scott. He pushed his fists into the small of his back.

'I'd kill for a drink right now,' said Emily. 'Beer. Ice cold.' She stretched out on the sofa with a sigh.

'Whiskey for me,' said Scott.

Annie remembered. The smoky burn of whiskey, no ice. He'd kept a bottle and two glasses on the bookcase under his window and sometimes, at the end of an evening when they were both drowsy but not yet ready for sleep, he'd slip from under the duvet and pad across the carpet to fetch them, clinking, back to bed.

55

Much later, Scott went back down to the workshop to put away the drones. Emily had fallen asleep, so Annie pulled a blanket over her, then she arranged her mattress and bedding on the floor and went back down the stairs. Scott sat on the floor, the nanodrones around him. He turned the lead drone over in his hands, squinting at the pollinating parts, making notes on his tablet. He looked up at her as she came into the room, his eyes softening. She'd better say something now, before she lost her nerve. 'Last night,' she said, sitting down next to him.

Scott smiled at her goofily, all at once looking exactly as he used to. 'Some things we were really good at, weren't we?'

'We were,' said Annie, with a sudden rush of affection for those long-ago days and nights. 'We *are*.' She paused. She didn't want to hurt him. 'But, can we just... could we—?'

'I was selfish, back then,' he said. 'I've changed.'

She bit her lip. I haven't, she thought.

'Annie.' Scott took her hands in his. 'We don't need to stick a label on it.'

I do, she thought, pulling away from him. I need that. 'Sorry,' she said. She ran her fingers over one of the drones; the pollinators were soft under her touch. 'I'm no good at this.'

Scott gave a dejected laugh. 'Can I be the judge of that?'

'Of course,' she said. 'I only meant—'

His voice was gentle. 'Don't worry, Annie.'

It was dark in the workshop now. The only light came from the glow of the computer screens. 'I've been on my own too long,' said Annie.

'It's okay, I get it,' he told her. 'Last night we were scared. We were lonely.'

Relief.

'It was one night, Annie. It doesn't mean things have to go back to how they used to be.' He sighed. 'But… let me say this. We don't know, any of us, how this is going to end. Wouldn't you rather be with someone? Do you really want to face all this alone?'

She leaned forward, taking his face in her hands. One last sweet kiss. 'I'm not alone,' she told him.

56

Broadband was patchy, but they managed to get a video call with Victor. It was good to see his face again. He sat in their living room at the college, the image pixelated and halting, but there he was. In the background the girls' voices came quietly.

'Have you got snow?'

'Absolutely. They're only here now to get a hot drink and to dry their socks by the fire.' Victor grinned, and the image snagged between a smile and a half-turn back to look at them. There was a piercing metallic sound and the image jumped back to life. Victor brought his face closer until it filled the screen. 'Iris found some jigsaw puzzles in one of the old classrooms and wrapped them up,' he said quietly. 'And we were so sure that Father Christmas wouldn't make it this year.'

'How have things been,' said Annie, 'since the news?'

'It's all anyone can talk about,' said Victor. 'I think they're going to open the church on New Year's Day so people can be together to watch the funeral.'

'Is it quiet there? Are you all okay?' The streets outside the workshop were deserted now but once the sun set Annie expected there would be more unrest.

'Sure.' Victor's voice was reassuring. 'Everything's fine. Listen.' He took a sip from whatever was in his mug. 'I've been looking at the long-term weather forecasts and running cross-checks against the last ten years. Seems that we can say with some certainty that this year we'll still be following the trend for an earlier spring.' He turned away from the camera, looking out of the window where the blank glare of the snow had erased the gardens. 'If you can believe it.' He turned back to the screen. 'Best estimate is, the first signs of spring will be even earlier this year, with the pollination window beginning on February first.'

Scott, who had been sitting at his own desk, scooted across towards Annie on his wheeled office chair. 'What does that mean for us?' he asked.

'It means,' said Victor, rubbing at the stubble on his chin, 'that we'll need to be ready to go two weeks earlier than we'd planned, based on last year's pollination dates. It means that you've got a bit less time than we thought.' The picture froze with Victor's furrowed brow gathered over his eyes. It seemed to hold a question: can we do this?

The connection was lost. Annie closed the lid of her laptop.

'Less than five weeks to get the glitches smoothed out, pack up and get down there,' said Scott. 'Jesus Christ, we haven't even run a full colony test yet.' He paced about. 'Emily, where are we with numbers?'

'We've got almost twenty-five full colonies now,' said Emily.

'It's not enough,' said Annie. 'We need fifty. Let's say forty at minimum.'

'We don't have time to print out that many drones,' said Emily. 'Not even if we run the machines twenty-four hours a day.'

Scott got up, stretched, ran his fingers through his hair. 'We could split the colonies,' he said, rubbing his eyes. 'But that would mean spending longer at each farm. We don't have time for that.'

'Wait. Wait a minute.' Emily got to her feet. 'The nanodrones can start and finish whenever we want them to. We're not restricted to daylight hours, right? When it gets dark we can fly them until they run out of charge. What do you say?'

'It could work,' said Annie doubtfully.

'You might be on to something,' said Scott. 'But we still need as many drones as possible. Emily, work out a shift pattern on the printers for you and Annie.' His face looked almost grey. 'You'll be working back to back. We haven't got a second to waste.'

57

Globally, it's believed that there are over twenty thousand species of bees. They have effectively colonised every place in the world where flowering plants exist, evolving to manage in a wide variety of different habitats and climates. Here in the forests of Madagascar, and indeed in many tropical and subtropical regions of the world, live bees without stings. These stingless bees, or *Meliponines*, are closely related to our own honey and bumblebees. They produce honey which is highly prized for its medicinal properties.

After walking for several miles through the forest our guide found a nest in the hollow branch of a tree. With my years of conditioning, growing up to understand that such an insect can cause a painful, if not life-threatening, sting, it was, I must admit, difficult for me to stand quite so close to the hive.

Inside their hive the bees store pollen and honey in beeswax pods, roughly egg-shaped. Unlike honeybees, the eggs of *Meliponines* are placed into a cell containing pollen and nectar on which the larvae can feed. The adult bees then emerge after pupation.

In the case of honeybees, we are of course used to seeing swarms or bees in search of a new hive. In the case of stingless bees, new nests are established by workers who build up a hive in a new location. Once the nest is complete, a mated queen moves in to establish her hive.

J.C. Ravensworth, *Insect Life*
(Associated University Press, 1995)

58

They were all feeling the pressure of the deadline now. Scott cursed and crashed around the workshop. His mood affected everybody's work; Emily's fingers, sweaty and nervous, snapped off several of the delicate pollination brushes and she had to start printing them all over again. 'Don't tell Scott,' she whispered to Annie. 'It'll only make things worse.'

A hurried test flight went disastrously wrong. The group of twenty drones did not respond to the instruction to learn the new flower shapes and attempted to pollinate all of the different plants in the test area in the same way. Their pollinators missed the majority of the pollen on the blossoms.

'Fucking things,' shouted Scott, flinging the controller on the floor and stalking out of the workshop. Emily guided them in as best she could. Scott had allowed them both to practise take-offs and landings but she wasn't very adept.

Annie held out her hand for the controller. 'He just needs some time to vent,' she said. 'Let's power these down and get them put away.'

While Emily was busy with the drones, Annie found Scott upstairs on the sofa with his head in his hands. 'Lighten up, would you?' she said. 'We're all stressed out here.'

Scott gave her an icy look. 'I was quite happy before you came knocking,' he said. 'Just getting on with my life. I could do without all this.' He gestured around the living area strewn with Annie and Emily's clothes, pot plants and drone parts. 'So spare me the lecture, would you?'

59

On the twentieth of January Annie packed her few things back into her bag. In the early morning she moved around Scott's living room, checking that she had everything.

'I should come with you,' said Emily. 'It's not safe to travel alone.' She sat up on the sofa and hugged her knees.

'It won't take two of us to help Victor get the lorry ready,' said Annie. 'And Scott needs one of us here. You know the printers better than I do – it makes more sense for you to stay.' Hopefully Scott would lighten up a bit once she was gone.

'Be careful, for God's sake,' said Emily. 'Call me as soon as you get back?'

'I promise.'

Annie walked through Bermondsey as the sun was coming up, past the soup kitchen on the corner of East Road with its usual snaking queue, out towards the motorway. There wasn't much traffic on the road but it wasn't long before a car stopped: an older man driving on his own to visit his son and family. He could take her as far as Aylestone, he said. She looked him over. He was slight and hunched a little over the steering wheel. The car was clean inside, and on the back seat was a small suitcase which seemed to tie in with his story. The skies were grey and heavy with rain; she didn't fancy waiting for another offer. 'Thanks,' she said, opening the passenger door, climbing in, setting her bag on her lap.

'It's nice to have some company,' said the driver, who said his name was Gideon. He was politely chatty, happy to talk about the weather and his grandchildren. It was a relief to Annie, who had had enough of discussing flower parts, pollinators and drone specifications. She leaned back and let Gideon talk, speaking only when he paused for a response. 'What's your business in Hattenden?' he asked.

'Visiting friends,' she told him. 'It'll be good to get out of the city for a few days.'

Gideon nodded his head in agreement.

At the off-ramp for Aylestone, Gideon pulled the car over and Annie put her hand out to open the door. 'Wait,' said Gideon. He got out of the car and opened the back door, unzipping his case and digging around inside. He returned with a packet of shortbread biscuits, which he passed to Annie.

'I couldn't,' she told him. She hadn't seen shop biscuits for years. The packaging was bright red with a photo of the shortbreads laid out on a plate next to a cup of tea. The words printed on the outside were in a language she didn't recognise. Where on Earth could he have found them? 'It's too much,' she told him. 'I should be giving you something, for your kindness.'

'You look hungry,' he told her. 'I want you to have them.' His smile was gentle. 'You don't owe me a thing.'

Showering him with thank-yous Annie climbed out of the car and waved to Gideon as he drove away. She walked across to the other side of the roundabout to the top of the on ramp and perched on the crash barrier while she waited for another lift. The rain was falling steadily now. She put up her hood and tucked the packet of shortbread into one of her jacket pockets, intending to take them home to share with Victor, Iris and the girls. But as she sat waiting her stomach growled and she ran her fingers over the crinkly packaging. She would have just one. She opened the plastic packet with her teeth. The biscuits were round, golden, perfect. A sprinkle of sugar on the top. She crunched the grains between her teeth and the rush of sweetness was almost too much to bear. She took a bite. The shortbread was just as she had imagined: buttery, crumbly, almost sandy. She nibbled at the edges of the biscuit to make it last a little longer. Despite her efforts to take her time it had soon disappeared. She reached again into her pocket for the packet but made herself count to one hundred as slowly as she could before she allowed herself to take another one, savouring the taste of the first one in her mouth, determined to slow down. One, two, three biscuits. Enough. She twisted the top of the packet, unzipped her rucksack, tucked the biscuits in amongst her belongings. She could feel the sugar coursing around her body, darting in her blood.

Annie waited for a long time. Only a few vehicles passed, many of them already full; the drivers indicated apologetically as they passed – no room. The water soaked through her coat; she could feel it seeping along her shoulders and down her back. She sat with her body stooped against the falling rain. She would give the rest of the biscuits to the next person who stopped. She let the thought drift away from her. Less than a minute later a rusty red hatchback drew up. The steamed-up window opened a couple of inches. 'Where you going, hun?'

Annie squinted in. 'Hattenden,' she said.

The driver, a skinny young woman, leaned forward to look at Annie. 'Take you as far as Ashbridge,' she said.

'Thank you so much.' Ashbridge was the closest large town to Hattenden, only about six miles from the college. Annie opened the door and climbed in. The interior of the car was very different from Gideon's. Empty protein bar wrappers littered the passenger seat and footwell. In the back was a toddler in a car seat. The child slept, his hair plastered damply to his head. Around the car seat and in the rear foot wells were bags of belongings, pillows, blankets, packets of powdered protein shakes. Annie unzipped her rucksack and pulled out the biscuits. She held them out to the driver. 'For your trouble,' she said.

'There's no need,' said the young woman, her hand shooting out for the packet, tucking it into the cupholder next to her. 'Where'd you get them?'

'They were a gift,' said Annie. 'They're good.'

'I'm Angel,' said the young woman. 'In the back, that's Wren.' She wiped the condensation from her window and checked the road before pulling back out. She kept to the near-deserted motorway for most of the journey, then joined the B-roads for the last section to Ashbridge.

Things had changed since August. More of the little grocery shops were vacant, their windows broken or boarded up. The few people who were out walking looked unkempt and aimless. Outside those few shops which were still in business, queues stretched along the road, watched by armed security guards, hands hovering over their weapons. The supermarket in Ashbridge was gone. The illuminated sign had been pulled down; a hand-painted cardboard sign outside read Merciful Heart Homeless Shelter. People spilled out of the doors, standing about in groups, sitting on the pavement. They stared at the car as it went past.

'What's happened here?' said Annie.

'Same as everywhere,' said Angel. 'No food, no money. Things 'ent safe. At night, when I charge the battery…' She stopped talking, switched on her indicator and turned right. They were on the outskirts of Ashbridge; the road curved north towards Stelling Common. 'Okay if I drop you here, hun?' she said.

The few miles to Hattenden were easiest along the river on the old footpath. Annie hitched up her rucksack, pulled her sodden hood up over her head, and set off walking through the wet grass. Scott had insisted she should take one of the tasers he'd sourced. She kept it in her pocket, her hand closed around it, vigilant.

60

The college was part boarded up now. Annie saw the panels over the windows as she rounded the last bend in the river, like eyes closed against the fading light. Despite the tiredness which dragged at her she forced herself the last few hundred metres to the gate on the footpath which led through the college grounds. It was overgrown now with brambles and tall nettles, knitted together with bindweed. She took her rucksack off and held it in front of her like a shield, pulling her jacket sleeves over her hands to protect them. The gate was in there somewhere – she walked forward, forcing herself through the thicket.

Maria had her hands over her eyes in the centre of the overgrown lawn, counting out loud. 'Ninety-nine, one hundred. Coming, ready or not,' she shouted, removing her hands, seeing Annie coming towards her over the grass. Maria whooped and ran towards her. She'd grown taller since Annie had left. Thank God, with all the shortages, there was still enough food to keep the girls in good health. But then Sophie emerged from the bushes next to the main building, skinny and frail. She picked her way cautiously over the grass, tripping, falling, getting back to her feet, her limbs as spindly as a new calf. What had happened? Annie hid her worries as the girls threw themselves at her, squeezing her tight. Their clothes were soaking wet, their hair straggled in tendrils down their backs.

'Come on,' said Maria. She took hold of Annie's rucksack, put it over her shoulder and held Annie's hand. Sophie took the other, and they led her towards the house.

Iris threw open the kitchen door, her face gaunt with anxiety. 'Come inside,' she said. 'You look exhausted. Come, sit by the fire.' Iris spoke, all the while drawing Annie towards the warmth of the living room. 'Maria, go get some towels and find something dry for Annie to wear. Sophie, my God. Get out of those wet clothes, would you?' She plucked at Sophie's wet jacket, fumbling for the zip, pulling off her wet shoes.

Maria came back and laid a pile of folded clothes next to her. She handed Annie a towel.

'The girls and I will find you something to eat and drink,' said Iris. 'We'll let you get changed.' They left the room.

Annie could hear Sophie's wheezing cough, and Iris berating Maria for letting her sister get so wet. She didn't want to move – but she knew she must, to get out of the wet things before she began to shiver.

Before too long there was a quiet knock at the door. Annie had changed and was gathering her wet clothes into a ball.

'I'll take those,' said Iris, sweeping into the living room with a tray. There was a mug of hot miso soup, and some tinned tuna on a plate. 'Don't ask me where Victor finds these things,' said Iris. 'All I know is, he's keeping us fed.' She set the tray down on the coffee table and stood back, holding out her hands for the wet clothes. 'We've got some dried apple rings for after,' said Iris. 'Caitlin came – she brought us some of her fruit.'

'How was her harvest?' Annie put her hands around the mug, sighing with relief at the warmth.

Iris shook her head. 'Not good. She spent days and days trying to pollinate by hand, but…'

A chill ran through Annie. 'Were there no insects at all?'

'Very few, she said. I don't know what kind.' Iris forced a smile. 'I'm glad to see you, Annie. Victor is over at the simfields. He should be home soon.'

'I should go.' Annie set down the mug, began to struggle to her feet.

'Stay put,' said Iris. 'Wait until you're warm and dry at least. If he's still not back by then, well.' She shrugged.

'Tell me how things have been,' said Annie. 'Tell me everything.'

Iris lifted her armful of wet clothes. 'In a while,' she said.

Annie moved her chair a little closer to the hearth. She picked up one of the cut logs from the basket and laid it carefully into the fire, sending up sparks. Sophie crept in wearing a baggy sleeveless dress and tucked herself at the end of the sofa. Her eyes were fever-bright. Her arms were painfully thin. She tucked them quickly under a blanket. Iris came back and Annie caught her fleeting glance of anguish as she looked at her youngest daughter, before it was swiftly masked and gone. Iris sat next to Sophie and stroked her hair while she told Annie about the harvest in the village – how most of the gardeners had managed to grow enough to supplement their rations, enough to see them through the winter, though even the preserved fruits and vegetables were beginning to run out now. The simfields had done very well; the few bees in the confined space had managed to pollinate their collection of crops. Attica had directed Victor and Iris in the distribution of produce so that everyone had a fair amount. It had been very moving, said Iris, to see everyone working and sharing together. No squabbles, no arguments. There had been some deaths during the cold weather. Mrs Featherstone from the old Post Office, Mr and Mrs Sladden from number fifty-eight. Miss Tanner who had lived with her sister, she had passed, too. It wasn't just the cold. She'd been giving her sister some of her own rations – hadn't they all been doing it, said Iris. Victor was running workshops in a couple of the classrooms. Simple things to help out. Repairing broken appliances, repurposing furniture. He'd always been good at mending things. Her face glowed.

The sound of shuffling footsteps in the corridor. 'Victor,' said Iris, her face breaking into a smile. He came into the living room, filling the doorway despite his obvious weight loss. They were all thinner, Annie supposed. She rose from the chair to greet him, standing back awkwardly while Iris hugged and kissed him. Once his wife had released him Victor stepped forward and gave Annie a bear hug. 'Hello, stranger.'

That evening Annie sat with Victor and his family in their kitchen, over reconstituted potato and something Iris called leftover soup. 'I shouldn't be eating your food,' said Annie. 'Tomorrow I'll go for my rations. I can pay you back.'

'None of that,' said Victor, waving her offer away. 'So tell me. How was life in the big city?'

Annie looked out at the wet garden, the dripping trees. It felt like she'd been holding her breath for months and now, at last, she could exhale. 'It's good to be home,' she said.

They had less than a week to make all the necessary adjustments to the lorry: fitting a watertight section to the flatbed with bolts and catches where they could store the nanodrones securely. Victor spent any spare time chopping fallen branches from the woods and dragging them back to their living quarters. Maria had grown several centimetres while Annie had been gone. She was wearing her mother's clothes and her body, though lean, was strong. She helped her father to stack the firewood along the corridors until he was satisfied that they would have enough fuel until his return. Next to Maria, Sophie's failure to thrive was even more apparent. 'I think all her energy is spent on fighting to breathe,' confided Iris. 'Medicine is hard to find. Thank God Attica knows someone who…' Maria came into the room with an armful of firewood for the basket, and Iris said no more.

On the last day of January Iris stood in the driveway with her arms around Maria and Sophie. Victor gave each of his girls a hug and a kiss, leaving Iris till last. Annie stood at a distance, her hand over her eyes against the bright mid-morning sun. They had enough time to drive to the workshop, load up and recharge the battery, then come back before dark.

It was a clear run to Bermondsey, where Scott and Emily were ready and waiting.

Annie followed Emily up the stairs to Scott's flat where Emily was checking round to make sure she had everything. 'How's it been?' asked Annie.

Emily slid her laptop into her bag and pulled the zip closed. 'It's been fine.' She bent her head so that her hair fell forward, hiding her face.

Was Annie imagining things, or was Emily blushing?

61

On February first they drove out to the first farm. Annie, sitting nearest the passenger-side door, wound down the window and tipped her face up towards the sun, breathing in the fresh air and the very particular scent of spring: the warming earth, new growth.

Scott was sitting next to her. 'Perfect day for it,' he said. He turned to Emily, who was perched on Victor's bunk. 'You okay?'

Emily murmured something in reply. Annie didn't quite hear – she was still blindsided by Emily's confidences at Scott's flat, where she'd confessed that she thought there was something between her and Scott, and she hoped Annie wouldn't mind, she didn't want things to be strange. Things *were* strange, whichever way you looked at them, thought Annie, and she'd hid her surprise as best she could, though why should she be shocked when Emily so clearly carried a torch for him and Scott had as good as told Annie he didn't want to be alone? Of course she didn't mind, Annie had said. It was a good thing and she wished them both well.

She was glad for Emily, that she'd found someone. (There was a moment's awkward silence when Annie pictured Matt's face – she wondered whether Emily was thinking about him too.) Privately, Annie let it sting; it was an ache that was both bitter and sweet – it would pass soon enough. She turned her face once more towards the passing fields.

They were close to the first farm now. Victor turned onto the long driveway lined with birch trees, their paper-peeling trunks almost glowing in the sunlight. The farm was exactly as Annie remembered it: the red-brick farmhouse surrounded by barns and outbuildings, all softened by the rapid growth of the early spring. Jed Shull, the farmer, was waiting for them in the yard, and his weathered face creased into a smile when he saw the lorry.

Scott had decided they would arrive and set up in daylight until they became familiar with their routine. He unzipped his rucksack, taking out the box containing the first lead drone and its controller. 'All powered up and ready to go,' he said. He set up his laptop on a nearby wall and began to search for mobile data connections.

Victor climbed up on the back of the lorry and passed the boxes carefully down to Annie and Emily. Once they were all unloaded he jumped down and helped to open the crates, unstacking the pallets so that each drone stood open to the air and ready for take-off. Scott and Emily worked methodically, setting the pallets out in rows, walking up and down to check them.

'Very excited that you chose my orchard to be the first one for your little experiment,' said Jed, pacing around the pallets, unable to keep still.

'Wouldn't have had it any other way,' said Victor.

'By the end of this operation your crop should be pollinated,' said Annie.

'We've been praying for a miracle,' said Jed. 'But I hardly dared to hope.'

'Okay,' said Scott. 'This is the moment we've been waiting for. Please confirm that all of the pallets have been checked.'

'All checked,' said Emily.

'Please confirm that all of the drones are standing clear,' said Scott.

'Confirmed,' said Emily.

'Let's do this,' said Scott. 'Launching Colony One.' He placed the lead drone on the ground and stepped back.

This was the moment. Jed and Victor stopped talking and came closer. Emily put her hands to her mouth. Annie crossed her fingers behind her back.

Silence.

Nobody moved.

The lead drone twitched and rose into the air with a barely audible hum. A second later, out of the crates, the rest of the swarm began to climb. The white noise of the propellers drowned out every other sound as they ascended into the air, each one maintaining a perfectly safe distance from the rest, like a murmuration of starlings on the wing. And then, following the lead drone, they moved together across the short distance to the orchards.

Scott's mouth worked in concentration as he sought to keep an eye on the lead. One of his final tweaks had been to change the colour of the lead drone completely, abandoning the red dot on its upper surface, making the whole thing scarlet so that it stood out from its dark grey counterparts.

He walked beneath the swarm, over the tarmac, onto the grass, and guided the lead down towards one of the lower blossoms so that he could more easily monitor its connection with the bloom. He held his breath as the drone made contact. A second later, he watched the other drones fan out over the trees in a perfectly coordinated swathe, all of them coming in to land on their own flowers.

'They're doing it,' squeaked Emily.

'Not yet, not yet,' said Annie. She held out her hand. 'Wait for the next bit.' This was the crucial moment. Would the lead drone take off before all the others had finished pollinating their flowers? Would the whole swarm be able to move independently from that moment on?

The answer to both questions was yes. The lead drone rose from its flower and took off in search of another one while all around it drones were still landing. Soon after that, Annie watched as other drones took off in their own time.

Scott lifted his hand from the controller. 'It works,' he shouted. 'It works!'

Now was the moment to celebrate. Emily and Scott rushed to embrace one another.

Annie looked at Scott over the top of Emily's head. 'Can you believe it?' said Annie, suddenly awkward.

'We did it,' said Scott. 'Now let's get Colony Two prepped and ready.'

62

At eleven am on the twenty-seventh of February Rae hurried in to John's office with her tablet. 'Something's happened,' she said.

John leaned back in his chair. 'Yes, what is it?' He indicated that she should sit.

'We've had a report of activity around the orchards, sir.'

'It's too early.'

'That's correct. But with the mild winter, it's possible—'

'Yes, yes.'

'One of the bee farmers is on the move.'

'Impossible,' said John. 'The bees are gone. Find out as much as you can and report back to me.'

'I have information, sir,' said Rae. 'I've been sent some video footage.'

John smiled. Occasionally his contacts surprised him with their initiative. 'Go ahead.'

Rae pressed play on the screen, then passed it across the desk to John. The video showed a large lorry turning in to the access road at a farm. The cab and trailer were both unmarked, though the brief shot of the licence plate would perhaps prove useful later. The camera zoomed in on the lorry as it drove further away along the drive. The lorry came to a standstill in the yard, parked as close to the blossom-covered trees as it was able to. Four people got out of the cab. Three of them went round to the rear of the lorry and opened the large doors. One of them jumped up into the back and began to hand out crates to those waiting on the tarmac.

'Where have they managed to find more bees?' said John, bringing his fist down hard onto the table.

'Just wait, sir,' said Rae.

The footage continued. Once all of the boxes were out of the lorry the people went round to all of them, opening the lids, squatting down on their haunches to peer inside.

John peered more closely at the screen. 'What the hell are they doing?'

It was impossible to see. After some time, when all of the boxes had been opened, the people stood back from them, around the outskirts of the crates. One of the people – a man – had a holdall. He took out two small objects, placing one down on the ground and holding the other. He took a step back. There was a moment's pause. And then – the tiny thing on the ground rose into the air. The camera zoomed in once more; the close-up shot was almost too unsteady to see.

John gasped as a cloud of… things… simultaneously rose into the air out of the crates.

'I know, sir.'

The things moved in a coordinated cloud across the short distance between the yard and the first line of trees, then dispersed and disappeared. The video stopped abruptly.

'Apparently it was impossible to get any closer,' said Rae. 'Our contact stayed put for several hours, sir, and managed to film what happened at the end of the day.'

'Play it, for God's sake,' said John.

After a short moment to find the next bit of video, Rae pressed play and passed the tablet back to John. A view across the tops of the apple trees. Nothing seemed to be happening. And then, a dark scattered cloud seemed to build over the nearest trees and became denser and more compact as it moved over the yard. The cloud lowered over the tarmac, settling itself down. Somebody bent over to pick one of the things up. The other people jumped around, screaming and hugging each other and clapping.

John paused the video and zoomed in on the image. 'What the hell is going on?'

63

Maria came into the kitchen and held out her hands for inspection.

'Where's Sophie?' asked Iris.

'Just coming,' said Maria. She pulled one of the heavy wooden chairs back from the table and sat down, tucking her hair behind her ears, stretching her arms out on the table.

'Here you go.' Her mother set a tall glass of protein shake, pale pink, on the table in front of her, scanning her daughter for any signs of weight loss. It was difficult; both of her girls had always tended towards slightness, and now that they were growing it seemed that there was even less spare flesh on their bones than before. She hoped Maria wouldn't notice she'd adjusted the proportions again. A little more powder, taken from her own rations. Iris had been doing it for months, making the changes gradually so that the girls wouldn't spot the difference. They had never liked the taste, and it was a struggle sometimes to get them to finish the whole glass.

Maria took a sip of the drink and made a face. 'Thank you, Mummy,' she said. Iris smoothed the hair on the top of Maria's head. It was as fine and soft as down.

Sophie skipped into the kitchen.

'Hands,' said Iris. Sophie stretched them out and showed her mother – front, then back. 'Here you go.' Iris pulled out the chair for her younger daughter then set her glass in front of her. Sophie's arms were definitely thinner since the last time she'd checked. They had a translucent quality, and last year's T-shirt hung baggily off her shoulders. Iris turned away to the sink so that she could fight back her tears without the girls noticing. They were both observant, her daughters, Sophie in particular, and there was a lot Iris wanted to hide from those deep blue eyes of hers.

Slowly, almost imperceptibly, people were beginning to starve. Hunger was no longer reserved for those people who used to be considered vulnerable. It was affecting everyone in the village, even those she'd thought of as blessed – the well-off, the highly respected. It touched them all now, eating into everybody's lives.

'Mummy?' said Sophie, setting her empty glass down on the draining board. 'Is everything all right?'

Iris nodded, blinking. 'Of course, chicken.' She cast about for a reason to be sniffing over the sink. 'I was just missing your daddy.'

'Me too,' said Sophie.

'Let's check the map, see where he is,' said Iris, swiping beneath her eyes and turning from the sink. She fetched the map from the living room and came back, spreading it on the table. 'They started here.' She laid her index finger on the Shull farm. 'Then on to the Slatter farm, the Abbotts', the

Hutchings". She traced her finger along the country roads of east Kent, through the Weald, towards the Downs. 'They came through the farms around Canterbridge. And then, last week, they were at Caitlin's farm.' The girls whooped and leaned over the map to see where Iris was pointing. 'Then the Ruck farm, and all the neighbouring orchards. Last of all, they'll end up right here.' She pointed to the Milsteds' farm, in the fields outside Hasting Green.

64

Caitlin walked through her orchards, her daily walk, moving from row to row. She scrutinised the fading blossoms, the bases of the flower where the petals would drop and, if pollination had been successful, the ovary would begin to swell into fruit. It was too early to tell. Nothing was showing yet – after all, Victor and the drones had only been gone for about a week. This wouldn't stop her from checking, every day, when she walked the orchards. She whispered health to each tree, and fertility, and muttered unformed prayers to – who knew? Maybe somebody was out there listening. On a bright spring morning like this one, the plants bursting with life, it was still possible to conjure up the idea of benevolent gods.

On her way back through the last field she saw that a vehicle had parked in the yard – an ancient four-wheel drive, one of the first generation of cars which had been converted to electric engines. Two men in jeans and T-shirts were walking about in the sunshine, peering in through the gap in the machine shed doors, taking photos of her tractor, checking their phones. One of them carried a clipboard. Some new instruction from the Warden, she supposed.

'Mrs Walker,' oozed one of the men. 'I'm Mr Bradley, this is Mr Roberts. We hope we're not disturbing you? We're here about the pollination trials. Just following up after last week's operation. We wondered if you might have a few moments to speak to us.' They flattered her, telling her how well-kept her farm was, how beautiful her house.

'Okay,' said Caitlin. She walked round to the back door and eased off her boots, leaving them side by side on the back step, holding the door wide open to let them in. 'Can I get either of you a glass of water?' They thanked her for her kindness. No, that would not be necessary. Would she mind if they filmed the interview while they took some notes? She touched her hair self-consciously; it was wind-blown after her walk. Would it be shared with anyone? Just for their records? She supposed that would probably be okay.

They sat in her tidy living room; the threadbare rug between the sofas was spotless, as were the windows. The ancient sofas had throws across them, not quite disguising the tears in the covers. When Iris and the girls had lived with her it had been impossible to keep everything as clean and tidy as she was used to, and for a while she had resented it. Now, the tidiness underlined her solitude. The house was too empty. She thought again about emailing Iris, inviting them all to stay, even if it was just for a few days. She sat with her hands in her lap and waited for the men to begin.

'How did you find the experience?' asked Mr Bradley. He appeared to be senior to his rather younger colleague.

'It was fine,' said Caitlin. 'They arrived when they said they would, set up quickly. It all went very smoothly.'

'How much did they tell you about the operation?' asked Mr Bradley.

'They told me it was an experiment,' said Caitlin. 'They said only a handful of people knew about it.' Why hadn't Annie mentioned a follow-up visit?

'Of course.' Mr Bradley chuckled. 'We have to check.'

'It's all top secret,' said Mr Roberts.

Mr Bradley winced. 'I'm sure Mrs Walker understands,' he said quickly. 'Now, at any point during the operation, Mrs Walker, were you at liberty to see what was going on in the orchards?'

'Of course I was. They said I could come and watch. They're funny little things, aren't they, those robot bees? I couldn't hardly believe it when they all started flying about.'

'Did you get a good, close look at one of them?' asked Mr Roberts, leaning forward in his chair.

'As a matter of fact I did. Sorry, who was it who sent you?' She glanced from one to the other. 'Could I please see some ID?'

The two men exchanged looks.

And Caitlin watched in disbelief as Mr Roberts put his hand to his jacket and, from the inside pocket, drew out a gun.

65

Did you know that not all bees are yellow and black? *Augochloropsis metallica* has an astonishingly vivid green body. *Agapostemon angelicus* wears a metallic blue-green jacket. While *Megachile lanata* is a warm and furry marmalade, the diminutive *Perdita luteola* is a pale lemon all over its body with diaphanous wings – a ghost bee. Bees come in all different shapes and sizes, having adapted to all different shapes and sizes of flowers. It's believed that bees use a variety of senses to locate flowers. Their sight is keenly developed to spot colour and the availability of pollen. Their sense of smell is acutely sensitive; a bee's antennae can detect molecules in concentrations of parts-per-trillion.

So, I urge you, look about you as you walk, through your garden, through the fields which encircle your town. Look carefully and you will see things you never dreamed of. The bright unexpected colours of nature, the tiny unseen jewels which surround us. The bees, the hoverflies, the moths and beetles and butterflies. Take the time to notice them. Their lives are but fleeting. And we, in our greed, disregard them at our peril. They are not only beautiful. They are not only fascinating. They are one of the very cogs which keep us in our fragile existence.

J.C. Ravensworth, 'Of Bees and Men'
(article, *Nature Monthly*, pub. 2014)

66

'They did what?' John stood abruptly, knocking over his chair. It clattered against the floor.

Rae took a step back, pressing herself against the office door. 'Just passing on a message, sir.'

'Idiots. *Idiots*. How could they have let it get that far?' He ran his fingers agitatedly through his hair. 'She was an elderly woman, for God's sake. How much of a threat could she have posed?' He bent to set his chair upright. 'It was not part of the plan.'

Rae shook her head slightly. 'I'm sorry, sir?'

'Take a seat, Rae.' He sat back down. 'The breeding programmes are doing well. Insect numbers are soaring. It's time we moved on to Phase Two.'

She waited for him to continue.

'In order to keep the numbers of pollinators in the greenhouses at optimum levels we should allow the mature colonies to move on so that we can breed new ones. And who are the people who need pollinators?'

'Farmers,' said Rae, obediently. She was used to him

speaking to her like a child.

'The bees are worth their weight in gold,' said John, lacing his fingers together, his eyes gleaming. 'They won't come cheap. Of course, I understand that not everyone will be able to pay up front for new hives, but I have worked out a very reasonable payment plan so that everyone can afford to have their own bees, no matter what their circumstances.'

Rae thought of the text message she'd been sent. The photograph of the woman in patched work clothes lying on a tatty old rug on the floor. She did not look like someone who had money to spare. What would a payment plan involve? She glanced at John. His face was still flushed from the news of the woman's death. She would not ask him now.

'Arrange for Bradley and Roberts to meet with me, would you, Rae? It seems I must explain it to them again – I simply can't afford to lose any more potential customers.'

67

Fruit tree pollination was nearly complete, and Scott started to turn his mind to the soft fruit fields. In the evenings he worked on adding the new AI specifications so that the drones would recognise the different blooms. They had just one more apple orchard to go: the Milsteds' at Hasting Green.

The lorry pulled up into the yard and Emily and Scott jumped out. Annie watched as, without speaking, they began to unload. Scott, on the flatbed, unharnessed the crates. Emily took the tapes from him and rolled them neatly for storage. They worked with the quiet assurance of people who had known each other for years, or as couples do, their movements synchronised. They volunteered to walk the orchards in the evenings to check for fallen drones, slipped away after dinner to check on the progress of charging, went over specification updates. It's okay, Annie, don't worry, we've got this. She noticed other things – the way Scott touched Emily's hand when he passed her a crate, her secret smile in return. Annie turned and went in search of the farmer, stamping on her jealousy. It was what she'd wanted, wasn't it?

The farmer came out to join them for the moment of take-off. Annie loved to see their faces as the drones rose as one into the morning air and across the orchards. She spent the day in the fields with her notebook. Now that Scott and Emily were together she tried to give them space. She was self-conscious about it – newly awkward. Victor came to find her in the late afternoon and they sat under one of the trees, listening to the hum of the drones, marvelling at them.

Victor checked his watch. If things were running to schedule, the drones should be nearly finished by now. He got up and went to find Scott. Annie got to her feet, woozy in the warmth of the afternoon. She tucked her notebook into her back pocket and followed him.

Scott stood at the edge of one of the fields, watching the sky. He checked his tablet – the drones had been out for seven hours. Pollination was at eighty-nine percent. He would give them another half hour then intercept the signal and call them back in. He loved this part. He felt like the shepherd of a huge flock. He knew, of course, that the nanodrones weren't sentient but it was hard not to feel as though they were responding to him in some animal way – something more than the instructions from one computer to another. 'Hey, Annie.'

She waved to him and pulled out her notebook again. She was writing observations about their work so far, not just data this time but personal reflections – her journey towards understanding. It would form the beginnings of a book she would write, one day, about the use of technology and drone insects and how they could complement the pollination process as the number of insects gradually recovered. Man and nature working in harmony. Imagine, the potential for increasing food production, to feed a hungry nation, a hungry world. If the land could sustain it there was no reason why crop amounts couldn't be built back up to the old levels and perhaps beyond. Even in places where insect numbers had long ago ceased to flourish, here was a chance to change all that. She hugged the thought to herself.

'Earth to Annie.'

She looked up, blinking into the sun. It was Scott.

'Have you seen Emily?' he asked.

She shook her head. Here was an opportunity to ask him about Emily. But she wasn't ready – not yet.

'You look happy,' he said.

'I am.'

'Me too,' said Scott. 'We're still on schedule and everything's running smoothly – sometimes I have to pinch myself. I really think we're making an impact, Annie. Things are going to get better.' He pushed his hair out of his eyes and grinned at her – she saw again the nineteen-year-old behind the man he'd grown into. 'Nearly time to call them in,' he said. 'Do you want to come?' He held out his hands.

'Sure.' She reached out to take them and he pulled her to her feet.

'There you are,' said Emily, coming towards them out of the fields. 'Scott, I was looking for you.'

'Perfect timing,' said Scott, letting his arms drop. 'We were just heading over.'

Together they walked back to the place where they'd left the crates, at the very edge of the orchards where the grass met the cement yard. Scott retrieved the controller which had been charging off one of the vehicles and Emily checked the connection. She stared at the screen for so long that Annie asked her what the problem was. 'Oh – nothing,' said Emily, with a little shake of her head. She gave Scott a thumbs-up.

'Okay, my beauties.' Scott pressed the button on the controller which switched the drones back into manual mode, and hit the button which signalled to the lead drone and from there to the rest of the swarm, instructing them to return. 'Come to Daddy,' he said.

They waited. Sometimes it could take a while – depending on the size of the orchards and the wind speed and direction.

Scott checked his watch. 'That's three minutes,' he said. He paced up and down along the edge of the grass, craning his neck, checking the trees, looking at the sky. There was a high haze, and not even the trace of a breeze.

'Four minutes,' he said. 'The longest they've ever been is five minutes twenty. We give them until five minutes twenty.' He carried on pacing. Sweat prickled the back of Annie's neck. She passed the back of her hand over her forehead and looked at Emily for some sort of clue as to what might be happening.

'Okay,' said Scott. 'That's five twenty. Let's go in there and find them.' He set off into the trees, slipping through the rows so quickly that Annie soon lost him. She walked a row of her own, checking the blossoms, the upper branches, the grass, in case they had for some reason fallen to the ground. She could hear Emily behind her calling to Victor, urging him into the orchards, telling him to hurry.

There was nothing. Annie could see no trace of the drones. They had perhaps run out of power and all ended up stranded on the other side of the orchards or encountered some kind of fault which Scott had never envisaged. She estimated it might take several more minutes to cross to the other of the fields. She started to run, trying to check for drones at the same time, the unaccustomed exercise taking its toll almost immediately; her leg muscles were weak, she had no stamina. She slowed down a little, heaving the air in and out of her lungs. 'Scott,' she shouted. 'Where are you?'

She heard him in the distance. Was he somehow far ahead of her? She pushed on along the row, until she could see the trees beginning to thin. There was an access road. Scott was standing on the tarmac holding the controller, his face ashen.

'What's the matter?' she shouted, getting closer. 'What's happened?' She still couldn't see a single drone. They had vanished. But… that wasn't possible. As she closed the last of the gap between them she saw him raise his hand, pointing out over the fields beyond the access road.

'They're over there,' he said. The cloud of drones, as familiar to her now as her own bee colonies, was a field away at least, the dark shape of them clear against the blue sky. They were densely packed yet somehow still not touching, flying in the close formation she'd witnessed many times.

For a moment she stood, staring. She squinted into the distance, sure that she must have made some kind of mistake. It was a trick of the light, or the way that a certain landscape could make things look closer – or further – than they really were. 'Are they… flying away from us?'

68

Late that night in the farmhouse kitchen, Victor, Scott, Annie and Emily sat round the table. The farmer set a pot of artificial coffee in the middle of the table. His wife filled the kettle and set it on the range to heat for more. She pulled her dressing gown around her and retied it, rinsed a cloth under the tap and wiped down the already spotless countertops.

'What the hell happened?' said Victor, looking around at the team. They had spent hours wandering the fields and driving around the area to try to locate the nanodrones but with no luck. They sat, shoulders slumped, exhausted.

'I've been checking the flight report. Something interfered with the secure connection,' said Scott. He looked at the screen in front of him. 'We were unable to re-establish a link in order to call the swarms back in.'

'How did this happen?' said the farmer. 'Didn't you know something was wrong?'

Scott closed his eyes. 'Not at first,' he said.

The farmer turned to fetch some mugs from the

cupboard, filled each one from the pot, passed them along the table.

Emily cleared her throat. 'At the moment to manually override the AI systems, I checked the connection and I did notice a slight anomaly in the signal strength,' she said. 'I put it down to atmospherics, or perhaps the demand on the local server. It all happened so fast.' She hung her head.

'All gone,' Annie said to herself. She was having trouble believing it. 'What could have happened?'

'There could have been a massive glitch in the system,' said Scott. 'They might simply have gone in search of more orchards. When the sun comes up we can go out again to look.'

'They're all fitted with tracking devices,' said Annie, 'so that we can monitor them in the fields. Can't we just—'

'The systems are currently offline,' interrupted Scott. 'I'm trying to get them back up.'

Victor took a sip from his mug, grimaced, pushed it away. 'What else could it be?' he asked.

'If it's not an error with the AI technology or the internet connection, there's only one more possible cause I can think of,' said Scott.

Annie looked at him expectantly. 'Yes?'

'We have to consider the possibility that the signal was hacked.' Scott squared his shoulders. 'They might have been stolen.'

Annie was numb, as though her mind had detached from her body. Their hard work, their days and nights of toil, all shut away in that workshop with no natural light, obliged to spend all that time in such close proximity when it was at times so painful, but they did it anyway, didn't they? Because they'd had to. For the greater good. And now, everything they'd worked for was gone.

'What are we going to do now?' asked Victor. He looked defeated.

Annie willed herself to carry on. She would not allow herself to stop until they were back home. 'We mustn't impose on Mr and Mrs Milsted's hospitality a moment longer,' said Annie, nodding at the farmers in thanks. 'We'll head back to Hattenden tomorrow morning.'

69

Rae knocked on John's door. 'We've got them, sir,' she said, unable to keep a note of triumph out of her voice.

'All of them?' asked John. He sat at his desk, peeling an apple. The knife blade was long and slender; it slipped easily through the skin. The peel came away in a single elegant curl.

'They're as sure as they can be,' said Rae. 'They hacked into the server and changed the destination command.'

'Where are they now?'

'They've been packed away, sir. Tomorrow our contacts will bring them here.'

John finished peeling his apple.

Rae stood waiting, motionless.

He took a large cotton handkerchief from his pocket and wiped his fingers carefully, one at a time.

With extreme care he cut the apple in half, then into quarters, eighths, sixteenths. He set the knife on the table, next to the plate.

He ate each piece of apple one by one, pips and all.

Then he ate the length of peel as though it was a liquorice shoelace.

Only the stalk was left on the plate.

He wiped his fingers again, the length of each one, making sure that not a trace of juice remained.

He folded the handkerchief and placed it to one side of the plate.

'We should prepare for visitors,' said John. 'It's only a matter of time before they come looking.'

70

Annie woke in the night, as she often did. It felt good to be back in Hattenden, even if she was still in Emily's spare room. She lifted the heavy covers and slipped out of bed. It was a chilly house, even in the summer. She felt around at the end of her bed until she found her socks and fleece, pulling them on, opening the door to the small landing; the two bedrooms and the door to the bathroom led off a small square of floor at the top of the stairs. But... the space was filled by a shape, a looming, shuffling darkness. She screamed and darted back into her room, then leaned against the door with all of her weight.

'It's me,' said a familiar voice.

She opened the door. 'Scott?'

'Sorry, Annie,' he whispered. He put his hand on the door handle to Emily's room. 'Didn't mean to scare you.' He slipped through and closed the door quietly behind him. Annie padded down the stairs to the kitchen, her heart pounding.

A noise from overhead: the old bed frame protesting.

Annie imagined Scott getting back into the warm bed beside Emily, his broad back and shoulders, his sheltering arms. Would he curve himself along Emily's body as he used to do with her? She tried not to think about the way he would settle into her bed after a late night, warming his cold feet against her legs, pinning her with his arms so that she couldn't escape. She'd hated it when he did that. She'd loved it too, having someone else in her bed. Listening to him breathe. The wonder at finding him – at being found. The belonging.

She reminded herself that she didn't feel lonely. She did not want someone only to stop her bed from being empty. Except at that moment, at two in the morning in the living room of the little cottage, with Scott and Emily sleeping above her – she longed for someone.

When Annie came down to the kitchen early the following day, Scott was already there, sitting at the table, a mug in front of him, tapping at his laptop.

'How long have you been up?' she asked him.

'A while. I've been awake for hours.' He looked up sheepishly. 'Sorry about last night. I didn't mean to scare you.' He looked away. 'Or make you feel awkward.'

Annie poured a glass of water and sat opposite him. 'I'm very happy for you both,' she said, proud of herself for her business-like tone. 'Do you want to talk about it some more?'

He made a face. 'Not really,' he admitted.

Relief. 'Right then,' she said. Keep it professional. 'Have you made any progress with the drones?'

'The trackers are still offline, so there's no way to locate them.' Scott sighed. His eyes were fixed on the screen. 'But I'm working on the assumption that they've been stolen.'

At the college, there was no answer when Annie knocked, but the door was open a crack, so she cautiously went in. She found Iris in the living room with Sophie, both of them lying on the mattress, the curtains drawn. Iris lay on her side, one arm draped across her daughter. At the sound of Annie's footsteps in the hallway Sophie turned lethargically to look at her and Iris opened her eyes.

'I'm sorry,' whispered Annie, backing out of the fusty room.

Iris found her in the kitchen. 'She can't shake off the sickness,' Iris told her. She leaned on the counter. 'We've all had it – just a cold, really, but Sophie was already so frail.'

Annie put out her hand to Iris's arm. 'Have you been able to find a doctor?'

Iris nodded. 'Attica knows somebody, thank God. He brought medicine for her fever and some high-calorie formula.' She made a face. 'Sophie won't eat it unless I spoon-feed her.'

'Let me help,' said Annie. 'What can I do?'

Iris stared out of the kitchen window at the patchy dry lawn.

'I can sit with her,' said Annie. 'While you get some sleep. You can go back to Emily's house, get away from here, take my bed.'

'That's kind of you,' said Iris, in the polite tone she had perhaps used with the rest of the village.

'I mean it, Iris,' said Annie. 'Please?'

Iris gripped the edge of the counter and gave a

shuddering sigh. 'Thank you,' she said. 'Later, maybe? Give me a chance to tidy up?'

'There's really no need—' started Annie.

'This afternoon?' said Iris.

'I'll be here,' said Annie. She walked across the campus to the simfields, worried for Iris, desperate for Sophie. Her little body, weak and tired. She had seemed so listless. From nowhere Annie was struck by the beginnings of an idea. She walked a little faster. She had something to ask the bees.

That afternoon Annie returned to the kitchen door at the college. When Iris came to answer it Annie help up a jar of cloudy, viscous gold. 'For Sophie,' she said. 'From the bees. May I?'

Iris smiled and nodded. She headed towards Emily's cottage to sleep, while Annie took a spoon from the kitchen drawer. She found Sophie in the living room. The sofa had been moved over to the window and Sophie sat at one end, looking out into the sunny garden. She rested her forearms along the back of the sofa and rested her head on them.

'I brought you some honey,' said Annie.

Sophie nodded eagerly. 'I tried some once, a long time ago,' she said. 'Dad said it would be okay.'

Annie unscrewed the lid and dipped in the spoon. Sophie took it and popped it into her mouth, her eyes widening at the sweetness. Annie's mouth watered, remembering the taste of flowers, and sunshine, and summer.

Scott was in Emily's kitchen for days. Morning until night, sometimes all night, staring at his laptop. Annie never saw him take a break. He was there when she came down in the morning, there when she left for the simfields, still there when she came back in the late afternoon. Hunched over his keyboard, looking at incomprehensible websites, conjuring long complex codes. He didn't talk to anyone if he could help it. He seemed transfixed by the glow from the screen.

The simfields were in a poor state. There were so few bees that not many of the fruiting plants would be fertilised. The frequent power cuts had overridden the weather settings and the meadows were dry and brown. Annie set up a hose with a sprinkler attachment and moved it from place to place, trying to make up for the lack of rain. She searched the internet daily for bee suppliers with stocks of nucs and queens – there were none.

The following afternoon once she'd finished work in the simfields Annie went round to the back door of the staffroom. She found Iris in the kitchen in front of her laptop. 'I'm looking for advice,' she said. 'Sophie's taking the honey,' she said, 'but she's refusing to eat any more of that high-calorie powder – she says it's disgusting.' Her face crumpled. 'She's so weak. I don't know what to do.'

'You can go and rest,' said Annie, twisting the edge of her shirt between her fingers. 'I'm here for as long as you need. She might eat something for me.'

'When I was Sophie's age, I had a lot of pets,' said Iris, wiping her fingers under her eyes. 'A whole menagerie. A rabbit, three guinea pigs, a hamster. We had a couple of dogs, too.' She shook her head. 'I don't know why I keep thinking about that.'

Annie came round to the other side of the table and took a seat.

'I keep going round and round in my head,' said Iris. 'Wondering what sort of world we're leaving our children. A world where they can't have pets. They've got no family home, no security. The girls have gone to bed hungry every night for as long as I can remember.' She wrapped her arms over her stomach and leaned forwards as though she was in pain. 'They haven't gone to school for over a year. But… what's the point? What's the point in them learning anything at all? Sometimes…' She dropped her voice so that Annie could hardly hear what she was saying. 'Sometimes I don't think Sophie will see another Christmas.' She began to cry again. 'What have we done, Annie?'

When Annie got back to Emily's house early in the evening she heard Scott and Emily snapping at each other in the kitchen.

'What's the point in looking for them any longer?' she heard Emily say. Annie slipped in through the front door and left her shoes on the mat. 'When can we start to rebuild?' Emily asked. Annie went through to the living room and lay down.

'We can't rebuild,' said Scott, his voice carrying clearly. 'There are no more resources. There's no money.'

'We'll have to find the money,' said Emily.

'How exactly?' Annie recognised the sarcastic edge to Scott's voice.

'More drone repairs, maybe?' Emily suggested.

'My clients are all in London. I'd have to build my business back up. Besides, I don't have a spare second,' he snapped. 'Jesus.'

Emily came through to the living room. 'Sorry,' she said

to Annie, her face red. She let herself out of the front door. Annie pressed her fingers to her temples as Scott mumbled and swore in the kitchen, pounding on his laptop keys. She was so tired. The feeling descended on her so rapidly, so insistently, that she was powerless to resist it. She tucked a cushion under her head and closed her eyes. She was asleep within seconds.

Raised voices. Annie opened her eyes. The living room was dark; a sliver of wavering candlelight showed from the slightly open kitchen door.

'Well, I'm sorry.' Emily didn't sound particularly sorry. 'But I'm going to bed.' The sound of the door opening and Emily's feet on the stairs. Scott muttered to himself; Annie couldn't make out the words but she understood their meaning. It was cold in the living room. Annie felt around for the blanket which lay along the back of the sofa. She would get up soon, she thought, and climb the stairs to her soft bed. In a minute. She closed her eyes and drifted back into sleep.

'Annie? Hey, Annie.' Scott's voice broke through Annie's dreams. What time was it? Where was she? Her body was stiff and sore. 'Quick,' he said. 'I think I'm on to something here.' Annie sat up on the sofa, blinking, and tried to stretch out the kinks in her neck and back. It was a new day – she could see the light through the curtains. 'Come and look at this,' said Scott. 'I think I've found them.'

The trackers had briefly been switched back on – the tracker for one of the lead drones, in any case. Perhaps somebody was fiddling about with the mechanism, said Scott, trying to work out how they functioned. He'd managed to bring up the location: a field right on the Kent coast. 'There,' said Scott, stabbing at the screen with his finger. 'Thanet. They aren't so far away.'

'Well, let's go,' said Annie, checking the time, slipping on her shoes.

Scott laughed. 'Hang on. We don't know who's got them, or where they're being held – we have no idea what we're getting ourselves into.'

'We haven't got time for all that,' said Annie. 'We've got to get them back as soon as possible. There's the soft fruit harvest to think of, not to mention the vegetable crops. Those farmers are relying on us – we can't let them down.'

Scott bit his lower lip. 'You're right,' he said. 'But, Annie.' He put his hand on her arm. 'It could be dangerous.'

'So?' Annie was already thinking about what she'd need to take. Bottle of water, phone… 'We have to get going, Scott. Right now.'

71

Annie hurried round to the back of the main building and knocked on the kitchen door.

'It's open,' called Iris. She was picking over a collection of tired-looking vegetables on the counter top: a couple of parsnips, some carrots, several wrinkled potatoes. She looked up. 'Come and see Sophie.'

In the living room the jar of honey sat on the mantelpiece next to Sophie's nebuliser, inhalers and medicine bottles. Sophie sat on the sofa, reading one of the books from the college library.

'She hasn't had the energy to read for weeks,' said Iris.

As she spoke, Sophie looked up from the page. Was it Annie's imagination or was she much more alert, smiling like her old self? 'Annie,' she said, and pulled back the blanket which covered her legs.

'I'll come to you,' said Annie, crossing to the sofa, and giving Sophie a gentle hug. She looked back at Iris, whose expression was a complicated combination of worry and joy. 'You're looking brighter, Soph,' said Annie. 'Keep up the good work.' She turned to Iris. 'Is Victor about?'

Iris pointed towards the far side of the grounds. 'Down by the hives,' she said.

Annie found him talking to the bees, so quietly that she couldn't hear what he was saying, bending his tall body close to the hives. As soon as he heard her approaching he stopped and straightened up, waving her over.

'I've come to say goodbye,' she told him, and explained as briefly as she could.

Victor would have none of it – the idea of Annie and Scott going alone. 'I'm coming with you,' he said, and started immediately back towards the house with Annie protesting in his wake. 'No,' said Annie. 'That's not why I came. You need to stay here,' she said. 'Iris needs you. And Sophie, and the simfields. We'll be fine, the two of us.'

Victor stopped and turned to her. 'You don't know what you're walking into,' he said. 'Wait for me at the main gate.' He opened the back door of the house and closed it firmly behind him.

Back at Emily's house Annie could hear raised voices from the street: the panic in Emily's voice as she pleaded with Scott not to go, and Scott's low rumble, trying to reassure her. Annie went round to the back door to fetch her rucksack. Emily was sitting at the kitchen table, crying silently, her face streaming with tears. 'Promise me you won't let anything happen to him,' she said to Annie, not trying to hide her blotchy face, scrubbing at her nose with the edge of her shirt. 'You have to promise me. I'll go mad.'

Annie stood behind Emily, put her arms around her shoulders. 'I promise I'll try.' She rested her cheek for a moment against the top of Emily's head. 'Will you keep an eye on Iris while we're gone? I think she's struggling.'

'We're all struggling,' said Emily.

Annie felt the shudder which passed through Emily's body. 'I know,' she murmured.

Forty minutes later, Annie walked out of Hattenden with Scott and Victor. Emily stood next to Iris under the main arch at the college entrance, hand in hand with the girls. Annie turned back to look at them one last time before they rounded the corner. Emily was standing straight, her eyes dry. Annie knew she was staying strong for Iris.

72

A van driver set Annie, Scott and Victor down at the last motorway exit before the port. He was hoping to find some bargains on the incoming tide, buying and selling goods to the small boat owners who made a living along the coast. 'Wish me luck,' he said, as Annie opened the passenger door to get out.

Scott climbed out beside her and walked round to the back of the van to let Victor out from where he sat surrounded by boxes.

The sun was high in the sky now and the heat bore down on them as they walked the road towards the coast. There was no shelter – no trees, no hedges, just wide flat fields bordered by shallow ditches. The dry earth blew across them in a fine dust as they walked.

'Why isn't anything planted here?' asked Scott.

'The soil's been over-farmed,' said Annie. 'It's dead.'

'This was all cabbages before,' said Victor. 'When I first started travelling with my bees.' He squinted out across the land. The fields began a gentle climb out in the direction of the sea, where the cliffs rose above the English Channel, and they all fell silent. Annie's breathing came faster and deeper; the sweat stood out on her skin. It was nothing, almost nothing at all, but her body reacted as though she was running, hard.

She pressed on, leaning into the incline, her hands pushing against her thighs, head bent, until she could go no further, and stopped to rest, looking towards the brow of the hill, trying to gauge how much further until they would reach the top.

There was a gleam at the brow of the hill, a sliver of light, as though the topmost edge of the field was made of polished metal, or glass, or perhaps was even on fire – but there was no smoke. The silvery line stretched the length of the ridge, almost from one side to the other. 'What is it?' Scott stopped to catch his breath, narrowing his eyes against the light.

'I know this place,' said Victor. 'They're greenhouses. You wouldn't believe the size of them.'

'What are they for?' asked Scott.

'Tomatoes,' said Victor. 'Peppers, cucumbers. Growing all year round, more or less.'

They carried on walking. No cars came. It was as though they were the only people left on Earth. As they got closer the greenhouses rose up to meet them, filling the whole of Annie's vision: a great wall of greenhouses, or rather one great greenhouse, its roofline a series of peaks and valleys and the glass, the acres of glass, reflecting back the rays of the sun so that they could not look directly at it but had to focus their eyes only on the little bit of road in front of them. The only sounds came from their laboured breathing and the wind, which whipped the dry soil across the fields and into the road, and settled in the creases in Annie's jeans and socks, and made her eyes gritty and the skin on her face feel tight.

A sign on the road read Private Property and warned them to contact reception immediately on arrival to state their business, but the sign looked old, and was cracked down the middle and daubed with graffiti so that it was difficult to read the words. A little further on another sign had been pulled half off its post and the post pushed down nearly to the ground. They looked at each other and asked, looters? Protesters? And, why had the signs not been replaced?

'It looks deserted,' said Annie, now that they were close enough to see.

Scott checked his phone. 'This is the place,' he said. 'According to the trackers.'

They walked more cautiously now, up to the side of the greenhouse, along the path which followed the wall. The glass walls were translucent, revealing blurred colours on the other side. Some of the panels had been replaced with fibreboard pieces, or corrugated iron, or planks of wood fixed into place. All holes and gaps had been filled. There was some damage to a section of the frame, too, as though a large vehicle had made impact there, buckling it. They had nearly reached the end of the wall. Scott took the lead, striding out slightly ahead of Annie and Victor, motioning that they should stay behind him. At the end of the wall, just before the vast greenhouse turned a corner, he put out his hand: stop. 'Let's see who's about,' he said, 'If anyone asks, we're foraging for food.'

Annie nodded. Victor bent over, leaning on his knees to catch his breath.

There was the sudden rush of running feet and a group of men rounded the corner of the building and stopped before them. Annie intercepted the look which passed between Scott and Victor; she tensed, ready to run. There was menace in the silence, in the way the men stood still before them. The men looked wild and scruffy, unshaven and unwashed. An animal smell hung in the air. No one spoke. Despite Annie's growing urge to turn and flee, Scott and Victor stood their ground, and Scott raised his eyebrows a fraction – in challenge, it seemed to Annie. It might have been that which prompted one of the men to say, 'And where do you think you're going?' Without waiting for an answer he reached behind him, pulling a cricket bat from his belt. The others drew out lengths of wood, chains, a piece of rusted metal guttering. The group fanned out, blocking their escape, trapping them against the wall of the greenhouse.

73

A bee's greatest defence is to hide its hive or nest in a secret place. The hollow of an empty tree trunk or branch, a cleft in a rock, a roof space or a wall cavity or old rubbish bins.

Some bee species will build their nests underground. Ground-nesting, or miner, bees build their nests in dry soil, and sometimes the only clue, apart from the occasional insect arriving or leaving the nest, will be a small mound of earth at the entrance of the nest.

Some bee species will try to warn an intruder, such as a human being, by bumping into them as they approach the nest and increasing the noise of their buzzing to a warning – the volume will rise; the pitch will change. If you are paying attention you will know if you have roused them.

Bees will form a ball around a smaller intruder – such as a hornet – to their nest or hive. They vibrate their bodies, raising their internal body temperatures, and then forming a living ball around the intruder. They continue to vibrate, raising the body temperature of the intruder so high that it dies, literally cooked alive in its own juices.

J.C. Ravensworth, *Waggle Dance: A Bee Celebration* (Associated University Press, 2010)

74

'Follow us,' said the man. 'And don't try anything,' he added. 'You're not the first, and no one's ever got away with it before.' Annie felt the push of something at her back as the man behind her nudged her forward.

Scott moved off first, and the group of men closed in to surround them, herding them like sheep. Annie sidled closer to Victor until she could feel the warmth of his arm against her own. She was faint with fear and the heat. It beat on the top of her head; it radiated from the glass walls. There was no shade, and she didn't dare to reach round to take her water bottle from her rucksack. When they reached a dilapidated building labelled Reception Office, they stopped. Wordlessly, the group split, four of the men leading Scott and Victor towards the door, the other two taking hold of Annie round the tops of her bare arms, their fingernails digging into her skin.

'Stay strong, Annie,' shouted Scott. 'We'll come find you.' One of the men drew back his arm and struck Scott on the side of his head with the rough piece of wood he carried. Scott staggered but did not fall. Annie didn't make a sound. The men opened the door and drove Victor and Scott inside – the last Annie saw of Scott was his face as he turned, perhaps to reassure her. His eye was half-closed. Blood ran down the side of his face from the blow. The door was firmly closed behind them.

'Come on,' said the man holding Annie's right arm. Together they half-dragged her farther along the track by the glass wall which ran perpendicular to the road. Close-to, the smell of them was acid and sour. In a quiet voice Annie asked where she was being taken. She asked why she had been separated from her friends. She told the men that they'd only been looking for food growing wild. She was ignored. The man on Annie's right side let go of her arm in order to pull the rucksack from her back. His mate tightened his grip on her other side; she was beginning to lose feeling there. The man with her bag was dark-haired, dark-eyed. He was deeply tanned and his face was lined. He found Annie's phone and stuck it into his back pocket. He flipped through her notebook and took that too. Reaching into the bottom of the bag he found her half-full bottle of water and, watching her, unscrewed it and drank deeply. Then he poured the rest out onto the ground and dropped it, empty, back into the rucksack. Annie bit back words. She began to pay attention to where they were taking her. They passed a patch of waste ground to her right where weeds and scrubby grass grew through cracks in the tarmac, and there were the remains of burned-out fires and strewn empty food cans, jagged and rusting. Beyond the far end of the greenhouse Annie thought she could see the glittering line of the sea.

There was an access door in the glass wall. Barely noticeable from a distance, but now Annie was able to see a panel which hinged along one side. There was no door handle on the outside, but as they neared the far corner of the building the door swung open.

The men stopped at the open door and pushed Annie inside, stepping through after her. They were in a sort of airlock, very similar to the ones she'd installed in the simfields. The door closed. The men stood too close to her – she could feel their breath in her hair. She clenched her hands into fists at her sides. The whir of air jets began around them. Annie closed her eyes and put her hands to her face – the dirt was stuck there. Her fingers trembled on her skin. She had to stay calm, find out where the drones were hidden. She had to get back to Scott and Victor as soon as she could. Annie tried not to think about why they had split her off from the others.

The air stopped and the doors in front of her opened. Annie stepped through into the greenhouse, blinking. The air was flooded with sunshine, suffused with brightness. Every surface of the vast space amplified the light which came through the roof and walls. As Annie's eyes became used to the dazzle she saw long beds full of plants. Gravel paths ran between them. Small clouds rose and fell like dust motes above the vegetation.

She looked more closely, recognising certain shapes, certain patterns of movement, pops of bright colour. Closer still and she could identify them: the dance of a peacock butterfly, the sunshine wings of a brimstone. A tentative cloud of tiny hoverflies. Rising and falling in the sunlit space. She hadn't seen some of these species for years – and in such numbers. She stared in wonder.

People knelt amongst the beds, tending the plants, their heads bent close to the foliage. Annie watched as a young woman slipped her hands between the leaves and drew out a glossy red pepper, perfectly ripe. She placed it carefully in the basket at her side. Annie found she was holding her breath.

There were tomato plants growing in the bed next to Annie. She had brushed past the leaves, releasing their scent. She put out her hand to touch them, the soft hairs under the leaves and their velvety smoothness on top. She breathed in the smell. Beyond the tomato plants, cucumbers grew. Squash and carrots. Strawberries, raspberries and melons. Much further back were young trees: apples, pears and plums. Rows and rows of potatoes to her other side, the soil heaped up in mounds around the plants. Straight lines. The wooden edges of the beds, the struts between the glass panes, the pipework along the ceiling. From overhead, the sound of fans taking away the excess heat. The trickle of water along irrigation tubes. And the murmur of bees, flying drowsily, almost drunkenly, amongst the flowers.

'Let's go.' The men at her side took hold of her again, ready to move her on. The skin at the tops of her arms felt raw.

'Wait.' A voice from the other side of the greenhouse, from behind the wall of plants. A young woman came running towards them, crunching through the gravel. She stopped before them, her slight figure dwarfed by a shapeless canvas pinafore. Her hair was wispy and pale. 'He says he'll see her now. He says give her back her notebook. He says there's no need to hold on to her like that.'

They released her then, though the dark-eyed man

did so unwillingly, his fingers tightening into one final excruciating pinch before he let her go. He reached into his back pocket and took out her notebook, handing it back reluctantly.

'Come with me,' said the young woman. She gave both men a nod; they slunk away. 'I'm Rae.'

75

At the end of the greenhouse a series of rooms had been built within the structure, reached by another airlock. Rae took Annie through into a room with a long white dining table and chairs, making sure that Annie was seated comfortably with a glass of water before she took her place on a chair by the wall.

The room was clean and airy. Annie looked down at her grubby T-shirt and jeans. The door opened again, and an elderly man came in. He looked different to the others. He was white-haired and clean-shaven; he wore a white shirt, top button undone. His trousers were a crumpled beige cotton. He took a seat opposite her. Annie pushed her hair away from her face, wincing at the bruising along her arms.

'I am sorry for the way you were treated earlier,' said the man. 'It was a misunderstanding. We have some visitors who are not... friendly.' He had pale papery skin, watery-blue eyes. 'Welcome to Hive,' said the man.

A flicker of something flared in Annie, a memory that she couldn't quite catch.

'We… adopted the buildings after the original occupants left,' said the man. He gazed around him. 'The facilities are marvellously suited to our needs. Once we had restored the structures – there had been deliberate damage, you know – we were able to start the breeding programmes.'

Annie squinted at him. That flicker again – of recognition, and yet she couldn't place him. His thick, luxuriant hair. The lines on his face and around his eyes, the deep tones of his voice.

He tipped his head to one side, studying her. 'Something is troubling you, I think.'

Something clicked then, inside of her, a memory of school days, sitting on the carpet waiting for her teacher to pull the television trolley from its cupboard. Her classmates fidgeting around her while she sat quietly with her chin cupped in her hands, waiting for the video to begin. The familiar music as the titles came up on her favourite programme. The presenter as he stepped into shot: always outside, always covered in protective clothing – veiled beekeepers' hat, overalls, gloves and boots. His voice as he began to speak was commanding yet gentle.

Annie sat up straighter in her chair. 'My God,' she said. 'It's you.'

A smile twitched at the corners of his mouth.

'You're J.C. Ravensworth.'

He nodded, inclined his head. 'Guilty, as charged.' Apart from the change in hair colour he looked just the same. 'Please. Call me John.'

'You're the reason I went into entomology, Dr Ravensworth.' The words were out of her mouth before she could stop them. His eyes gleamed. She'd made herself

284

vulnerable, showing such enthusiasm. She changed tack. 'What is this place?'

'You of all people should know,' he said. 'Dr Abrams.' His smile reached his eyes. 'Oh yes. I know who you are.'

Annie couldn't stop the blush which crept up her neck.

'We're building up insect numbers,' said Ravensworth. 'We nurture young colonies then sell them on when they're ready. And, here in the greenhouses we are also growing and pollinating crops. As you will understand, the growing season is extended well beyond the natural cycle.'

'Where are my friends?'

'Dr Abrams,' said Ravensworth. 'May I call you Dr Abrams?'

She nodded, unable to help the thrill of hearing Ravensworth address her using her title.

'Please do not worry about them. I have asked Dr Edwards to help us with a problem we are having with our heating system, and he has kindly obliged. Victor has agreed to assist him.'

Again, despite herself, Annie nodded, once more the awestruck schoolgirl. Perhaps this might be the best way to play it: the lifelong fan, the sycophant. 'Who is this food for?' asked Annie, thinking of a plate of mashed potatoes with forkfuls of butter melting over it.

'We distribute any surplus to the locals,' said Ravensworth. 'Once the staff have been fed.' He turned to her. 'I hope you will join me later for dinner, and sample some of our excellent produce?' He stood up to go. 'My assistant will take care of you.' He turned and left the room.

Rae led Annie through the narrow corridors separating the rooms within the greenhouse. Offices, perhaps, or storerooms? She opened the door to a small space just big enough to house a narrow single bed with storage drawers beneath, a tiny washbasin with a shelf above it. 'This is one of our guest rooms,' said Rae.

'What will happen to my friends?' said Annie.

'They will be given food and shelter, like you,' said Rae. 'Please don't worry.' Her face was smooth and untroubled. Her eyes seemed warm. 'An evening meal is served at seven and John will host you in the meeting room. It can be difficult to navigate these corridors; I will come to collect you at five minutes to seven. There is a toilet and shower in the room next door to this one.'

Annie nodded, anxious for Rae to leave, so that she could explore her surroundings.

'Please do not try to leave the accommodation area,' said Rae. 'There are security cameras throughout the complex and guards on all the doors.'

At exactly five minutes to seven there was a knock at Annie's door. She opened it. Rae gave her a brief smile. 'I hope you have been able to rest?'

Annie had not. She had taken a shower and tried to shake out the dust from her clothes. It felt wonderful to be clean again, but… why had she been separated from Scott and Victor? She had no reason not to believe Ravensworth, but why was she not able to see them? After her shower Annie had lain on the bed, staring up through the translucent plexiglass panels which formed the ceiling of her room. Rae hurried back along the corridor in front of her, taking a left turn, then a right – Annie was not able to remember the number of turns, or the route back to her room.

'Here we are.' Rae opened the door which looked identical to all the others and pushed it open so that Annie could walk in ahead of her. Ravensworth was already there, seated at the table which was covered with dishes of food. The scent of freshly cooked new potatoes with butter and mint, sliced tomatoes, cucumbers, and fruit juice was almost too much for her to take in. It had been so long since she'd seen so much food in one place. Annie could only stare.

'Please take a seat, Dr Abrams. Rae, thank you, that will be all.' Rae dipped her head and left the room. Annie pulled out the chair opposite Ravensworth. She was hungry, despite everything, and all she could think about was the food. 'Help yourself,' said Ravensworth, passing the bowl of potatoes. She piled her plate, glad that he did not seem to require her to speak. Instead, while she devoured forkfuls of food, he talked.

The old greenhouses had been abandoned, he told her, when the food growers accepted that it would be far more cost-effective to move their operation closer to the cities. Not to mention safer. On the coast they were vulnerable to passing gangs from the sea as well as the land, and it was not something the growers were prepared for. They had left in a hurry. There had been a night when the greenhouses were attacked. A needless act of vandalism, said Ravensworth, spearing a potato on his fork and popping it into his mouth. The greenhouses were in need of some repair, and at present they did not have the means to make it perfect, but it was at least weatherproof and sufficiently airtight that the artificial atmosphere could be maintained. The people who had followed him there shared his interests, his passions. Like him, they wanted to create a utopia from the chaos, he said. To do more than just survive. People who were not afraid to leave everything they had for a chance to embrace a new way of life. It was a settlement, a true community, he said, slicing into a tomato. They worked the greenhouses, cooked, cleaned, made repairs, oversaw childcare. He had a dedicated tech team who maintained the heating, lighting, security and irrigation systems. Annie thought of Scott and Victor. 'Your friends, yes,' said Ravensworth, perhaps noticing a change in Annie's expression. 'Please do not trouble yourself. As you have probably worked out, the computer systems are housed in a different building. It makes no sense to expose our delicate machines to the humidity we experience in the greenhouses. The accommodation for our technicians is in the other building.'

Annie sat back in her chair. Of course.

Not everyone was so understanding, said Ravensworth. She would be surprised at how many people were unhappy with the setup at Hive: protesting about their lifestyle, objecting to the size of the camp. But it was only because those people did not, could not, understand. In fact, the whole operation was self-sustaining – their solar panels provided them with more power than they could use; they were able to sell the spare to the national grid – they were helping, if people only cared to look. They did not require mains water; it all came from their reservoir on site, or the rainwater collected from guttering around the building, or from the condensation inside the greenhouses. The hostility demonstrated by the outsiders was the reason why so many of his workers were involved in the security side of the operation, said Ravensworth, running a finger around the edge of his plate to catch the last of the melted butter.

His followers were assiduous in turning people away. They were a little heavy-handed sometimes, and he was sorry for that. But they were protecting something important, and ground-breaking, and vital to the future. 'If only people could see it, Dr Abrams.'

Annie thought she could see it. She was drowsy and confused. She wanted to sleep. The dishes were empty and her stomach was distended. She had gorged herself. Gulping, swallowing, eating without pausing. She felt ashamed.

76

After a night of broken sleep Annie drifted into fitful dreams of the before times. She was in a garden. There were flowers and butterflies and music, and a marquee with a long table covered with bowls of salads, cold meats and baskets of bread. Waiters, passing with bottles of white wine. She held out her empty glass and the waiter began to pour – she could feel the chill of the glass as it filled. She awoke feeling strangely peaceful, opening her eyes to her strange little cell-like room. The panel above her let the sunlight through. The day had begun. Where were Scott and Victor? She had to find them, to see for herself that they were okay.

A bell rang from somewhere outside, and moments later there was a knock at her door. 'Dr Abrams? Time for breakfast.' It was Rae.

'Just coming.' Annie sat up and swung her legs over the side of the bed. Her eyes were tired and sore, her body ached from walking, her upper arms were mottled with bruises. She unhooked her jeans from the back of the door and stepped into them, slipping her T-shirt over her head, pushing her feet into her trainers. She splashed her face with water then dragged her fingers through her hair.

Rae walked with Annie along the labyrinth of sunlit corridors and through a door which led outside. It was a relief to feel the fresh air on her skin. Across the short stretch of scrubby ground lay the next greenhouse. The door opened onto a space filled with rows of trestle tables and benches. A queue of people snaked back from the counter which separated a kitchen from the eating area. The people were near-silent, standing slope-shouldered and patient, watching with baleful stares as Rae strode to the front of the queue with Annie trailing behind. The man behind the serving counter gave Annie a mug of artificial coffee and plate of scrambled eggs and slices of melon. Rae took nothing. She showed Annie to a place at the end of one of the tables next to a group of people who ate quickly and said nothing. Once they were finished they took their empty dishes to the far end of the counter, and more workers took their place on the benches. Despite her earlier hunger, Annie found it difficult to eat.

Rae checked her watch and clicked her tongue in irritation. 'I have to go,' she said. 'When you've finished, John has asked to see you.'

Annie forced herself to swallow a mouthful of half-chewed melon. 'Of course.'

'His office isn't far,' said Rae. 'Just ask anyone for directions.' She hurried away.

As soon as Rae had gone the workers began to stare openly. Annie finished her food as quickly as she could and left the cafeteria. Nobody tried to stop her as she slipped through the outside door and walked away from the buildings.

Behind the farthest greenhouse was a sort of camp made up of shipping containers, tents, and shacks built of old sheds and tarpaulins. The shacks were set up in the lee of the containers, out of the wind which blew in off the sea. A young woman squatted over the remains of a campfire, holding back her long hair in one hand, resting her other hand on the ground, blowing gently into the embers. A young man stood nearby brushing his teeth, standing with his bare feet firmly planted in the grass, ragged-bottomed jeans, a bare torso which he scratched at with his free hand. When he breathed in, his ribcage showed underneath his skin.

Two men and a woman sat with their backs to one of the shipping containers. They faced out towards the sea, the wind blowing their hair loosely around their faces. The woman had one leg bent, her knee tipped out to one side. She was bending forward, inspecting the sole of her foot. One of the men sat cross-legged, rolling a cigarette, his slender fingers tightening the paper around the sparse leaves, bending his head to flick his tongue along its length, fastening it down. He passed it to the other man who lit up and inhaled deeply before passing it to the woman. She leaned her head back and closed her eyes then expelled the smoke in a long, thin stream.

From one of the tents came the sound of a baby crying: a meagre noise which fell away on the wind. The gusts came up from below the cliffs and snapped at the sides of the tents and made the washing dance on the line.

An older man sat cross-legged outside an open shipping container, hand-washing clothes in a plastic bowl. The water was brown and scummy, with only a small residue of bubbles. An older woman stood nearby and when the man pulled the fabric out of the bowl she stretched out her hand. She took it, wringing it out onto the ground, the water splashing her sandaled feet. She shook it out then and took two clothes pegs from her skirt pocket. There was a rope strung between the door of the shipping container and a tent nearby. She fastened one corner of the pale-blue shirt next to the T-shirts and a dress which already hung there. The shirt was patched with different-coloured pieces of material under the arms and at the elbows. Threads hung from the ends of the sleeves and the hems. The woman finished pegging it out and dropped her hands to her sides. She noticed Annie watching and briefly turned back to say something to the man who had started washing something else. He lifted his head. They stared at Annie, expressionless.

'Dr Abrams.' It was one of the men who had captured Annie and the others the previous day. 'Dr Ravensworth is waiting for you.' He took a step towards her.

'It's okay.' Annie held up her hands. 'I'm coming.'

77

'I trust you slept well?' Ravensworth motioned for Annie to sit down opposite him.

She nodded. She would play along with him for the moment.

'Dr Abrams.' Ravensworth adjusted the cuffs on his long-sleeved shirt. 'I require your help. Your know-how. I have concerns about several of our captive bee species.' His eyes flicked to the protective hat and veil which hung on the back of the door. 'While the vast majority of our pollinators are succeeding in the artificial environments here, some of the bees are failing to thrive. I wonder if I might impose on you to cast your expert eye over our operation here and share your thoughts.' He leaned back in his chair with a sliver of a smile.

If she complied, if she did so willingly and didn't make any trouble, perhaps they might take their eyes off her just long enough for her to find Scott and Victor. Assuming they really were being housed in the tech building away from the humid atmosphere of the greenhouses, perhaps they would be close to the drones. 'Of course,' she said. 'Do you have any data I could take a look at?'

'Thank you, Dr Abrams.' Ravensworth inclined his head. 'I will have Rae show you the numbers. The greenhouses are at your disposal. If you need anything, just ask Rae.'

And there she was at the door as though she'd been summoned. 'Come with me, please, Dr Abrams.'

'Call me Annie, please.'

The office door was open; the meeting was over. Annie got up to follow Rae. She took Annie back to the main greenhouse. 'This is as good a place to start as any,' said Rae. 'Take a good look around, familiarise yourself with the planting and the spread of species. I can go and fetch you a list of the pollinators in each greenhouse along with their estimated weekly numbers.' She hurried away along the path.

Annie wandered through the tropical heat. The humidity was made worse by frequent blasts of spray from somewhere in the roof space. She took refuge under an orange tree and watched clouds of insects dancing in the water droplets. Ravensworth's staff worked through the showers: kneeling in the beds, weeding, staking up tender young plants, thinning out seedlings. Annie watched as two of them working alongside each other became increasingly animated in their conversation, raising their voices, gesticulating to one another. One of them, a tanned young man with a shock of blond hair, got to his feet and began shouting at the other, an older man wearing dark glasses. 'You don't know what you're talking about, mate,' shouted the young man. 'We need more protests. More action, not less. No one takes anything seriously unless you show them you mean business.'

'Violence isn't the way,' said the other man, getting unsteadily to his feet.

The blond man pushed him with enough force to send him staggering backwards into the plants. The other workers stopped what they were doing. 'Leave it,' said one of them to the young man. 'He 'ent worth it.' The blond shook his friend off and went stomping away, out of the beds, leaving others to help the older man up from the dirt. There was a sudden flurry of nudges and lowered voices as they saw Rae approaching. They picked up their tools and slunk back to work so that by the time Rae was close enough to acknowledge them there was nothing for her to see. She handed Annie a stack of papers, a notebook and some pens, looked at her watch, began to turn away to leave.

'I'm not sure how much help I can be,' said Annie. 'What exactly does Dr Ravensworth want?'

'He's a complicated man,' said Rae. 'And he's spent his whole life searching for the answer to a very simple problem. He wants to mend the world. He's wanted to fix things for as long as I've known him.' She dipped her head, as though apologising. 'But the solution has always eluded him. Up until now, anyway.' She smiled. 'And he wants you to be part of it.'

78

A bee's last form of defence is attack: the sting. When bees attack, they are often on a suicide mission – although bees with barbed stingers can often sting other insects without harming themselves. Bees with smoother stingers, such as bumblebees, queen honeybees and other solitary bees can often sting mammals more than once.

But when a bee with a barbed stinger – such as a honeybee – stings a victim with a sufficiently thick skin (e.g. a mammal), the stinger is so barbed that it will lodge in the animal's skin. This tears it loose from the bee's body and the bee will die within minutes.

The sting releases alarm pheromones – even more so if the bee is fatally injured.

It is only the female bee that can sting.

A sting is usually a defence mechanism and only used as a last resort (for example if a lone bee is roughly handled or stepped on).

But if a hive is threatened with attack, the pheromones will alert the other bees to the danger, summoning them to the location of the perceived attacker.

Bee venom gives a painful but relatively harmless sting, unless the victim has an insect sting allergy. In such cases, stings can trigger anaphylactic reactions which can be deadly unless quickly treated.

There is much documented evidence of bee attacks by the Africanised honeybee, or killer bee (a cross between the Western and African honeybees). This bee variety was first introduced to Brazil as a way to increase production of honey. Swarms have since escaped and spread to South and then North America. They have very highly developed defence mechanisms and can react very rapidly to disturbances, on many occasions pursuing, attacking and killing humans, horses and other mammals. Aggressive swarms which have attacked and killed humans are often sought out and destroyed before they can attack again.

J.C. Ravensworth, *Waggle Dance: A Bee Celebration*

(Associated University Press, 2010)

79

Three things Annie knew. One: Dr Ravensworth and Rae were always busy between nine and ten in the morning. Two: she was a familiar face around the site now and people had stopped looking at her. Three: if challenged she simply told them she was doing research for Dr Ravensworth, and nobody questioned her. So after breakfast, as the rest of the workers went to their stations to begin their tasks, Annie took her notebook and pen, and began a tour of the greenhouses, taking notes, pretending to be immersed in thought. But it was when she walked between the greenhouses that she was paying the most attention. Leaving the main greenhouse by the small side door she had a clear view of the building where Scott and Victor had been taken across the scrubby ground blasted by the sun, where weeds grew up through the cracked ground. Two of Ravensworth's men were patrolling the area; Annie stood still against the wall, hoping they would not notice her. They were deep in conversation; their makeshift weapons hung loose in their hands. One of the men had a grubby bandage wrapped around his shin from ankle almost to knee. They passed by, rounding the corner of the building, out of sight.

Now.

Annie sprinted across the open ground, her footfall loud against the dry soil, her shoes throwing up clouds of dust. She didn't have much time – she estimated two or three minutes before the men rounded the other side of the building and started back towards the greenhouse. She was aiming for the corner of the building where the men had disappeared; that way she would be hidden when they reappeared on the other side. Sweat ran down the sides of her face and her breathing became ragged, lungs straining, her chest tight. Not much farther now and she would be in the shade of the building. Don't stop. She crossed the last remaining metres and flattened herself against the wall, wiping her face with the back of her arm, trying to control her breath which came in gasps. There. She could see them, coming back round, heading away from her now. 'He'd better not fucking try it,' she heard. 'I'm not going to just sit there and let him…' The voices faded away. She waited, counting to one hundred, letting the distance open up between them. Then she turned and cautiously approached the first window in the building. If she stood on tiptoe she could just see over the ledge. The blinds were down at the first window, and the second. She inched her way past the door towards the windows on the other side. The top section of the window was open wide. Please, please let the blinds be open, even just a little, so that she could see inside. Safely on the other side of the door she craned her neck to see – there was a small gap. On the other side of the window, boxes were stacked high, almost blocking the view of the room.

Then, movement. Somebody's arm, a shoulder. Somebody coming to the window. She ducked back down. 'What's he going to do about Kai and his mates?' said a man's voice. 'Someone's going to get hurt.'

'Or worse,' said another voice. 'He don't care. Long as his precious bees are okay.' Laughter. Annie continued on round the building. Perhaps Scott and Victor were working on the other side. If she could only see them, it would give her some peace of mind. As she rounded the corner the sun hit her – not even half past nine and already it was softening the tarmac around the base of the building; Annie felt it give under her feet. All of the blinds on this side of the building were pulled across and the windows were tight shut. Annie swore under her breath and, looking back towards the greenhouse, squinting into the light, she saw that the patrol was crossing back towards her. Shit. Shit. She darted back around the building but it was too late. She heard their shouts and their feet running.

'Sorry.' She held up her hands. 'I was looking for the reservoir.'

'You 'ent lost, love. That's guilty behaviour, that is.' The men marched her back to the main building. 'Sit there.' They left her on a chair in the corridor outside Ravensworth's office, like a naughty child waiting to be called in by the headteacher.

As soon as they'd disappeared Annie got up and hurried away down the corridor, back to her room where she could wash and change out of her sweaty clothes. She would go back to the greenhouse and get on with her work, and pretend nothing had happened.

80

When Jed Shull arrived in Hattenden he didn't know where to find Victor. He rode his horse along the high street and stopped when he saw a couple kneeling in their front garden, weeding around their plants. The old man heaved himself to his feet and pressed his hands into the small of his back. 'Just follow the road to the end,' he told Jed, pointing with a grubby finger. 'You won't miss it.'

His wife had risen from the old pillow she used as a kneeler. She stroked the horse's velvety nose and told her how beautiful she was. 'Can she have a carrot?'

Jed nodded. Of course.

She bent carefully to the row of frondy carrot tops and pulled one from the soil, dusting off the excess on her skirt, presenting it to the horse, who took it from her gently.

Maria and Sophie saw a horse coming up the road towards them. They squealed and ran to the arched gateway to watch it pass. But the rider stopped and asked for Victor.

'He's not here,' said Iris, stepping in front of her girls,

sheltering them with her arms.

'I'm a friend,' said Jed, dismounting, holding his horse by the reigns, telling Iris his name.

'He's still not here,' Iris told him. 'Sorry.'

'Mr Shull.' Emily came running from the direction of the simfields. 'You look exhausted. Let me help you.'

It all came out in a tumble of words while Maria and Sophie fetched water for the horse. Iris got a drink for Jed, and Emily tried to make him comfortable on one of the chairs in the overgrown garden.

'I'm sorry, Jed,' Emily told him. 'You're going too fast. I don't understand. Tell me again?'

Jed reached into his pocket and pulled out a piece of paper – a printout from an online news site. He passed it to Emily.

'"A Kent farmer has been found dead in suspicious circumstances,"' read Emily.

Jed passed his sleeve over his forehead. He nodded for her to continue.

'"Mrs Walker's body was discovered in her kitchen. It is believed that her body may have been there for some time before it was found."' Emily put her hand to her mouth. 'My God.' She read on, her voice wavering. '"Mrs Walker had one gunshot wound to her left temple. Her hands had been tied behind her and she had been made to kneel in the stress position."' She let out a sob. Iris, coming out to the garden with a tray of drinks, set it on the table and put her hand on Emily's shoulder. Emily took a deep breath and continued, '"The police have ruled out suicide, believing that she had been forced to confess to something or that her killers wanted to extract some information. Police are appealing for information about this incident. Please contact this number if you can help with their enquiries." Emily turned to Iris, tears running unchecked down her face.

'Caitlin?' asked Iris.

Emily nodded.

Iris sank into one of the chairs. 'No,' she said. It was not possible. She looked over at her daughters, who were both adoring the horse. 'What can I tell my girls?'

Emily put her hand gently on Iris's arm. She stared at the dates in the article. If they were correct then Caitlin's death had come only days after they'd completed pollination at her farm.

Then... what if Caitlin's death had something to do with the drones? If that was the case, the others were walking into danger. She stood up. 'I'm sorry, Jed. I have to go. Iris will look after you.' She looked at Iris, nodding, and Iris nodded back in agreement.

'You're welcome to stay and rest as long as you'd like,' Iris told him. 'Emily?'

'They're in danger,' she said. 'I have to find them.' She started in the direction of the Land Rover.

Iris grabbed Emily's wrist. 'Don't you dare go alone,' she said. 'Drive to Attica's. She'll know what to do. I'll phone ahead, tell her you're on your way.'

81

Annie prepared to leave the greenhouse for the day. She was in the wild greenhouse and had spent the afternoon underneath a spreading fig tree, the sunlight filtering down through the leaves, watching a variety of bee species visiting a patch of clover. She preferred it here, away from the workers who still would not speak to her. The air temperature was adjusted to keep it constant – it would be much warmer outside. Mayflies hovered in clouds around her. Annie waved her hand lazily in front of her face to stop them from landing. She packed her notebooks and pens into her rucksack and drained the last of her water, replacing the lid of her bottle, stowing it all away. A gentle breeze came from the fans high above in the roof space. She tipped her head back and let the motion of the air take her hair from her face. It was so natural – she would have to ask Ravensworth if she could find about more about their systems. She rose, slinging her bag over one shoulder and walking back towards the doors, trailing her hands over the tops of the plants, allowing her fingers to drift through the silky tassels of the wild grasses.

She stood for a moment in the airlock as the air jets did their work, preventing the spread of contaminants between the greenhouses. Then she hit the button to release the outer doors and hurried out into the covered corridor which joined the wild greenhouse to its neighbour, eager to get back to her room for a quick wash before going to the canteen for dinner. She stepped through the doors and collided with Rae as she barrelled past with a stack of paperwork. She dropped everything. Both women knelt on the floor to collect the papers.

'I'm so sorry,' said Annie. 'Totally my fault.'

'Doesn't matter,' said Rae. 'Only, I'm late already.' She scrabbled to pick up the papers.

She must be on her way to see Ravensworth, thought Annie. Only that would cause her to look so anxious. 'Tell him it was my mistake,' said Annie. 'I don't want to get you into trouble.' She pushed her hair back off her face and came away with a strand of grass in her fingers. 'Guess the vacuums missed that one,' she said. She gathered up as many sheets as she could and handed them back to Rae.

'Have you just come from the fields?' said Rae.

Annie nodded.

'Shit.' Rae pushed herself back to her feet. 'You'll be covered in pollen. Those airlocks are worse than useless. I'll have to reprint all these.' Her mouth tightened.

'What's the matter?' asked Annie.

'I can't take the risk of exposing him to—' Rae stopped, suddenly. 'He has allergies.' She changed the subject abruptly. 'He hates it when I'm late. Thanks for your help, Dr Abrams.

See you soon.' She hurried off down the corridor without looking back. Annie picked up her bag and walked in the other direction, back towards her room, wondering what else Rae had been about to say.

82

Emily didn't have to say anything about Caitlin. Attica already knew. The death had taken place in her district. As soon as the police investigation was over, she would be involved with the funeral arrangements. If no family members came forward, most likely she would have to take charge.

'Please,' said Emily. 'Let me help. Annie and Iris, Victor, Scott – they'll want to be a part of it too.'

'I'm so very sorry,' said Attica. 'I should have told you before.'

'I've got an idea about who might have done it,' said Emily, her heart racing. 'The others have gone already – we have to hurry.'

Attica grabbed her car keys. 'Let's go.'

Emily drove the old Toyota pickup. Next to her Attica phoned all of the people on her contacts list, telling them to find each other, to share lifts, to get themselves to the coast as soon as they could. 'We'll meet at the old communications masts,' she told them. 'Go now.'

83

During the lunch break Annie found a table in the cafeteria that was as far away as possible from the men who patrolled the complex. They sat surrounded by their friends, all hunched over their trays of vegetables and protein burgers. The man with the dirty leg bandage had a cut on his head as well and bruising around his eyes. He turned to sneak a glance at the group sitting on the next table. His lips moved. He went back to his food. One of the men on the next table half-rose from the bench. The woman sitting next to him put her hand on his arm and he sat back down. The rest of the cafeteria went very quiet and the people in the queue for food turned to watch. There was silence for a long moment and then, at some unseen signal, both men stood up suddenly and launched themselves across the tables at each other. The cafeteria exploded into noise. Men and women shouting encouragements, warnings, begging them to stop, banging on the tables, whooping. The sound bounced off the plexiglass walls. Some people climbed on to the benches and tables to get a better view, and smaller fights broke out in the crowd. Annie got up and moved away as the other people on her table joined in with the mayhem. She edged around the tables, trying to get to the door, along with some of the others who were leaving, their eyes wide with alarm. They hurried away without speaking to Annie, out of the door, back to the camp. Annie walked round to the smaller greenhouse and sat under one of the cherry trees. Even so far away from the fighting she could still hear it – or she thought she could hear it – over the whirr of the fans in the roof space, over the hum of the insects.

84

The old masts pierced the low clouds at the top of Ripple Hill. Some of the red warning lights were just visible through the mist. Even with so few aircraft flying they were still switched on, providing an unmissable landmark for miles around.

'Word has it you can see these from France,' said Attica, sitting in the passenger seat, peering into the murk for the other vehicles. It was almost dark now, and the chilly sea fret which had blown in would provide some welcome cover for them when they set out for the greenhouses.

'Do they all know where to come?' asked Emily.

'Patience,' said Attica.

Along the coast, on the next rise, a sickly yellow-green glow was cast in the sky.

'That's the greenhouses,' said Attica. 'Think of the energy they must be using.'

'I hope to God we're not too late,' said Emily, leaning forward over the wheel, squinting into the fog. At last – she could just make out a line of lights, snaking its way up the slope towards them.

85

Annie liked to go round the greenhouses in the late evening when everybody else had stopped work. It was cooler then, and she disliked sitting in her claustrophobic little room.

She walked to the end of the wild greenhouse; it was the smallest, and her favourite. There were a couple of benches on the pathway opposite some of the hives. She sat down. 'Help me,' she whispered to the sleeping bees.

The glow of the emergency lighting would be just enough for her to go over the data she'd managed to collect – she had brought her notebook with her – but for the moment she didn't open it. She laid it on her lap and let her eyes rest where they would, enjoying the quiet and the space. The fans provided their usual white noise, blanking out any other sounds, dulling her senses. She slumped further down on the bench, fighting feelings of sleep.

'Dr Abrams, my goodness.' From nowhere, Ravensworth had appeared.

Annie sat upright, gasping.

'What brings you here at this time?' Ravensworth slid

along the bench, emerging out of the gloom. He was dressed in full bee-keeping garb: a hat and thick protective veil, long trousers and long-sleeved shirt, heavy gloves. 'Forgive my outfit, please.'

'I couldn't sleep,' said Annie. She tried to smile.

'Likewise,' said Ravensworth. 'I often come here at night. To think, to reflect on my work, to plan for the future… How funny, that we have not run across each other before.' He stretched out his legs, crossing them at the ankles. 'When I was in the public eye, very often I would long for quiet moments such as these,' he said. 'But now that I have nothing but quiet moments I often find myself… quite bored. Be careful what you wish for, as I believe the saying goes.'

'Your public work was vitally important,' said Annie.

Ravensworth sighed. 'How very gratifying that is to hear,' he said. 'Though ultimately it changed nothing. You know, the reason I decided to have my little career change was that, however much I tried to tell people, tried to warn them, when I spoke of the terrible plight we would experience when the pollinators were gone I believe nobody truly understood the consequences. My whole career was spent in research, writing articles for journals, books and documentaries. Nobody could say that I did not try everything within my power to help people to see the errors of their ways.' He spoke as though he was addressing an auditorium. He spoke as though Annie wasn't there at all. 'It all came down to greed. Corporate greed, the race to develop more resilient crop varieties, to grow food out of season – disrupting the natural laws. And always, *always*, suppliers and consumers demanding lower prices and unblemished, uniform produce. The fertilisers, the pesticides. Increased crop yields. They are killing the world, Dr Abrams.

'People paid lip service to my work, of course. A few bills were raised in the House of Commons; there was a campaign or two which caught the public imagination for a year or so. But it was not enough.' He looked at Annie through the veil with pale, watery eyes. 'People don't want to hear that they need to stop doing the things they love in order to save the planet. The only things people are interested in are personal comfort and making money. Even now, Dr Abrams, with the flames licking around our feet.

'I heard someone say once that the only person you can save is yourself,' he continued. 'And so I disappeared from the stage. I found this place and furnished it with people who wanted to help me. I have taken great strides, Dr Abrams. Here at Hive we can build up insect numbers – and once the tired, sick earth has recovered from the chemicals we have subjected it to, we can repopulate it again. We can be better curators of our world. We can make it beautiful again.

'It is my dream – it is my great wish – that one day we will all live together in harmony on this beautiful planet, Dr Abrams. All plants, all animals. At peace, with us as their guardians. It is childish perhaps, like a fairy story. But I believe it is possible. And so I have dedicated my life.'

Annie chose her words carefully. 'Won't you consider releasing the nanodrones?' she asked. 'People are dying of hunger. If you won't allow us to pollinate the crops in this way, more might starve.'

'If I release the nanodrones, what need will there be for insects? It's an easy fix, Dr Abrams, and I cannot allow it.' He looked at her sadly. 'Mother Nature permits that the world is full of death as well as life, Dr Abrams. We are, I think, too squeamish in this regard. Do you remember? I spoke of the greed of corporations. I believe this greed is the only thing which might spoil my plans. We must work together. We must. Work. Together. Take the events at the Food Summit, Dr Abrams. The leaders at the Paris meetings were not there to help us. They were there to stuff their own pockets with good things, to feed themselves before they considered others. They would never have set aside their own differences in order to work together. They sought to build up food stocks but had no sustainable strategy. They were the ones who killed the Earth in the first place, Dr Abrams. But, do you see, at Hive the ethos is different. I am not doing this for myself, nor for a particular group. I have no allegiance; I am driven only by my duty to do what is best for the whole planet – for every living thing.' He sat back in his chair. Was he imagining applause as the whole auditorium rose to its feet?

Ravensworth watched her like a beneficent uncle. 'You are very dedicated, Dr Abrams. You love your work, I think.'

'It's the most important thing I'll ever do,' she told him. 'I wouldn't do anything to jeopardise it.'

'Hmm.' He peered at her more closely. 'It is an admirable statement, Dr Abrams. Very… worthy. But, even the best of people have their limits, wouldn't you agree? A breaking point.'

She did not raise her eyes.

'For example, you observe your bees, day after day, watching their little lives, making a careful note of each tiny movement. It is for the greater good, and yet, just like me, you wonder if your own small life is really making a difference. You have begun to question it.'

A memory of Matt came, unbidden. The weight of him, his head in her lap as he lay dying. She thought of Scott, turning to her to let her know he would come to rescue her while the blood ran down his face. Stay calm, she told herself. Breathe. 'I believe that if we all try to make a difference, even in our own small way, there is still hope for the world.' It sounded weak.

Ravensworth looked at her differently, then. A spider watching the fly who has landed on its web, checking to see its reactions, gauging the moment to strike.

86

'It was my understanding that you wished to help us, Dr Abrams. And yet it seems I can't trust you. You had no reason to be so far away from the greenhouse complex.'

Annie looked up with the same blank expression she had tried with the patrol. 'I was lost.'

The shadow of a smile. 'Come now, Dr Abrams. Let's not pretend. I have seen the video footage.'

Annie hung her head. 'I'm sorry.'

'I'm very disappointed,' he told her. 'What do you think, Dr Abrams? Wouldn't you agree that colleagues who threaten to endanger such an important project must be made an example of?' Ravensworth slipped his hand into his trouser pocket and languidly drew out a gun. He rested it against his leg, holding it loosely.

Annie had never seen a firearm close up before. It looked heavy. There was a dull sheen to it. She couldn't take her eyes away. 'I can see why you would be very upset,' she said. 'I know how much you value loyalty.'

'If only other people were as astute as you, Dr Abrams.

It's such a shame.' Ravensworth looked wistfully at the hives, allowing himself a few more seconds of reflection before he became suddenly business-like. 'But, what is the point in dwelling on the past, eh? Dr Abrams, surely you agree. We can look to the future; that is what keeps us alive in our spirits – to dream, to allow ourselves to think of happier times. But – and the bees know this…' he gestured towards the hives with his gun, 'all we really have is the present.' He turned back to Annie. 'And now here we both are, Dr Abrams. So, tell me. Is there anything you would like to share with me in this moment? Anything pressing which you feel you need to unburden yourself of? Please, do not be faint-hearted.'

Annie would not allow her voice to falter. She sat up very straight. 'I believe my work is important to you and to the project. When the environment is suitably recovered and we can send the bees back out into the wild, I know I can be of even more assistance to you.' She swallowed. Her throat was dry. 'If there is some way in which I can improve, tell me. I'm willing to learn from my mistakes.'

'Perhaps,' said Ravensworth, his hand beginning to tighten around the gun, 'your mistake is that you cannot admit to your weaknesses. Perhaps you think you are better than everyone else.'

'Oh, no,' said Annie. 'I would never presume to—'

'Then tell me,' said Ravensworth, not taking his eyes off hers, keeping her caught in a cobra's gaze. 'What were you doing earlier?'

'Such a lot has happened today,' said Annie, stalling for time.

She pushed herself away from him along the bench, her heart racing.

Without warning, alarms sounded, blaring into life over their heads, filling the air, making it impossible to think. Annie could hear them sounding throughout the complex.

Ravensworth pointed the gun straight at her. 'Get moving,' he said. 'Now.'

She stood up and walked to the end of the pathway where it split into two – one path leading back to the rest of the greenhouses, the other towards the insect breeding area, small rooms containing nurseries for new colonies. 'Which way?' she asked Ravensworth. There was the sound of breaking glass from one of the other greenhouses. Screams and shouting. 'Which way?' she repeated.

'Be quiet.' Ravensworth motioned with his gun. 'Go.' He pointed in the direction of the nurseries, away from the accommodation block and the camp. His phone rang and he put it to his ear. 'What's happening?' A pause. 'Well, who then? Go – go,' he said to Annie, waving the gun to urge her on. She walked in front of him, up the dark path. A door at the end led to a corridor with doors leading off along either side. 'Keep going,' Ravensworth told her. They were rapidly approaching the end of the corridor. 'See them off,' he shouted into his phone. 'Get them out of here. Do whatever you have to do.' He opened the last door on the left. 'In here,' he told Annie. 'And stay quiet.' He kicked the door closed and turned on the lights.

Annie flinched at the sudden brightness.

The room was divided into two by a floor-to-ceiling glass panel. On one side, Annie and Ravensworth, a desk, two chairs, a computer and a video camera on a tripod facing the glass. On the other side, the interior of a beehive like a cutaway diagram with the glass panel acting as the back wall of the hive.

When the light went on the bees began to stir, reacting to it like a sudden sunrise, moving around amongst the waxy cells, drowsily shifting and shuffling.

'It is a shame to disturb the bees,' said Ravensworth, as a crash from overhead made them both start in alarm. There was a collective flinch from the bees as they felt the vibration. Ravensworth pulled out one of the chairs from underneath the desk and sat down. He was trembling. His face under the veil was ashen. He rested the gun on the table for a moment and Annie tried to assess her chances. 'Dr Abrams, you may sit down if you wish.' She shook her head – if she stood where she was, between him and the door, there was a chance she could get out. She would not sit down. She thought again of Matt, of the bleeding which would not stop. She hoped there would not be too much blood.

'You are remembering your friend,' said Ravensworth, as though she'd spoken out loud. 'Dr Abrams, try not to trouble yourself. It is a shame. I did not want her to die.'

Annie stared at his mouth as it moved. I did not want *her* to die? Who was he talking about? He spoke of a crumbling farm in the valley, of orchards of apple trees, of an old woman alone in a shabby living room and a regrettable misunderstanding. Caitlin. It could only be Caitlin. Annie stood silently: too stunned to move, too terrified to react. But there was something else building inside her now, stronger than her fear – a rolling, seething anger. Behind the plate glass screen the wall of bees heaved and shifted, like the surface of a pan of water nearing the boil. The insects crawled over each other, as though trying to find their right place, but not settling. There was an audible low hum through the glass.

Ravensworth talked on, about the failings of people, about his great disappointment. The gun was on the table now. He moved his hands away as he warmed to his theme, motioning with his gloved hands as he spoke.

Now. Annie dived for the table; the gap was not far – she threw herself across it, hands out to grab for the gun. Ravensworth was slower to react. He reached towards the gun – too slow. The impact of Annie's body pushed the table back and the gun skidded, coming to rest on the far edge of the table top. It was just out of Ravensworth's grasp now, and he pushed himself to stretch a little further. Annie got there before him – not quite close enough to take hold of the butt; she knocked it off the table and it hit the tiled floor with a clatter. Ravensworth groped his way round to the other side of the table to get it and Annie, guessing at his intention, shoved the table into him. It caught him hard in the belly and he staggered for a moment then recovered himself quickly, leaning forward again – she stepped forward and hooked the gun with her shoe, kicking it back and away from Ravensworth; the gun skittered across the shiny floor and disappeared under a computer console. Annie ran after it, throwing herself onto the floor, pushing her left hand through the narrow gap – the gun was wedged deep underneath; she could just touch it. She would need time to wiggle it free – and Ravensworth was only a step or two behind her. He grabbed her right arm and twisted it back so hard that she thought she heard it snap. White-hot pain seared through her. She kicked out hard with her feet, connecting with his legs; he staggered backwards with a howl, giving her enough time to push herself to her feet with her one good arm. Get out, leave the gun – she crossed the room to the door and was almost there, reaching out towards the handle when she felt Ravensworth's gloved hand on the shoulder he'd just wrenched back. He snatched at her with his other hand – she swung round and pushed him away, and he grabbed at her again. It was almost impossible to catch hold of Ravensworth through the loose clothing he wore, the gloves, the veil on his hat. He seized her around the top of each arm; the pain in her right arm blinded her, his gloved fingers digging into her, connecting with the bruises from the first day. Ravensworth dragged her closer. 'I am disappointed in you, Dr Abrams.' He thrust her backwards into the glass panelling behind which the bees moved in waves. There was a crack as her body hit the glass; it forced the breath from her body, leaving her gasping.

From elsewhere in the greenhouse came shouting and the drum of running feet.

Ravensworth reached for her again, looming, his body shapeless under the overalls as he gathered himself again to attack. She was certain now that he meant to kill her if he could – and in the same instant she knew she would not let him win. At the thought of escape and the world outside a rush of strength surged through her. She swept her arms up between his, breaking his grip, grabbing his shoulders in an echo of the way he'd been holding her. He was unprepared; she took full advantage of it – in the same movement she swung him round against the panel and shoved him hard against it, his body juddering against the glass. Again – a crack as the glass took the impact and when he pulled away she saw fractures in the panel. Again – she pushed him back. His body was still tensed in her grip but he offered little resistance – she must get the upper hand and soon before he could recover himself. She threw him back with a roar. The fracture split – lengthening, widening. The bees behind the glass were taking flight now, visibly distressed. Ravensworth's eyes widened. 'No,' he said, his voice barely louder than a whisper. He raised his arms to grab for her and Annie gave one more desperate push with all the strength she had left in her body. The whole panel seemed to shiver, and suddenly it was riddled with tiny fissures – it splintered, falling to the floor in a sheet, then there was nothing between them and the bees, who rose from the shattered hive and began to drift out into the room, bumping against Annie and Ravensworth in warning.

He laughed beneath his hat and veil. 'Oh dear, Dr Abrams. It seems you are in for a rather uncomfortable time.' The bees continued to butt up against them. 'Any minute now you'll feel the first sting.' Even as he spoke she felt it – a white heat piercing her forearm where the skin was exposed. The little insect tried to wriggle free of her and as it did so its sting broke off in her skin and the bee flew away. She pinched out the sting with her finger and thumb. It lay on her finger: a tiny dark curl. 'Fatally wounded,' said Ravensworth. 'Nature can be terribly cruel.' He sounded almost gleeful. Annie felt another barb pierce the skin on her collarbone. And then, another sting on her arm, from inside her shirt, as they crept up inside her clothes. Bees clouded the air in the room, landing drowsily on the walls, pausing on the desk and the floor.

Ravensworth turned to her. 'And now, I wonder what might happen if...' He walked forward and stepped, deliberately, on two bees just in front of him, crushing them, leaving their small bodies smeared on the tiles. 'This should excite the others into action,' he said, almost to himself. He turned slowly, looking down at the floor, raising his foot again, the bees swarming around his body, colliding with him, crawling on his clothing. Fresh rage surged through Annie. Before he could tread on any more of the bees she threw herself at him, taking him by surprise, knocking him to the floor. She tugged at his protective gloves; they came away easily and she cast them over her shoulder. She turned to Ravensworth's hat and veil while he fought against her – catching hold of it in both hands and wrenching it to one side. His bare hands pulled down on the veil, attempting to keep it in place, but the loss of his gloves had thrown him and she was able to throw the hat to one side, exposing his face. He seemed small under the veil; his face was pallid and sweating. She thought she saw fear in his eyes. But – only for an instant – his expression changed to one of grim determination and he lunged back at her with a wild cry, bringing her to the ground, his hands on her shoulders, weighing her down, pinning her to the floor. His hands around her neck, tightening, tightening. Pushing her face to one side, pressing her skin into the broken glass. And then – his expression changed again as the first bee stung him above his left eye, in the delicate skin around the socket. He didn't let go of Annie's throat. Nor when the second sting came, nor the third. But when the bees began their concerted attack he released her, getting to his feet, shouting, hands flailing, trying to cover himself again with the veil but it was crawling inside and out with bees. 'Help me,' he implored her. 'For God's sake.' The bees swarmed over his body. 'I was never going to kill you, stupid girl.' The bees were in his mouth. More and more, when he opened it to scream, and in his hair, and in between his fingers. His skin began to blotch and swell. Annie pushed herself into a sitting position and backed across the floor until she was as far away from him as she could get, cradling her injured arm, leaning against the far wall, watching as the tiny little insects brought him to his knees and, when he could no longer kneel, he lay on the ground and watched her through the swollen skin around his eyes, his face and neck an angry red, his mouth open, gasping, gurgling, drooling.

87

There was crash at the door of the hive room. The walls shuddered but the door did not give way. A pause and then another crash, then another. The door began to bulge and break, wooden splinters appearing at the point of impact. Annie watched dully from her place on the floor.

One last slam and they were through: Emily, her face and hair wild. She stood for a moment in the doorway in the cloud of disorientated bees. Attica appeared beside her, holding an axe. 'There,' said Emily, pointing at Ravensworth, while she picked her way through the bees on the floor and knelt next to Annie. 'Can you walk?'

Attica squatted next to Ravensworth, pressed her fingers to the swollen skin on his neck, bent her face close to his. She raised up, shaking her head. 'He's gone.'

'Let's go.' Emily helped Annie to her feet. They left the room amongst the haze of bees who were drifting out into the corridor. They hurried through the darkened greenhouses, where some of the workers were picking what was ripe, stuffing it into pockets and bags. Out into the cool night air. There were no clouds. A three-quarter moon cast its light onto the sea and Annie could hear the waves far below. Tents had been trampled and torn; one of the shacks was on fire. A young couple hurried away dragging a child's wagon; a small girl lay inside in a nest of blankets: her knees drawn up to her chin, her eyes squeezed shut. The elderly couple sat in the open doorway of their container; he held the cowering woman in the sheltering crook of his arm. People streamed away from the campsite carrying bundles and bags; in the light from the moon and the fires they trailed down the hill away from the buildings.

One figure stood alone by the door to the main greenhouse. Rae, wearing a too-big jacket which hung loosely from her shoulders, the sleeves falling down past her hands. 'Did you see him?' she asked Annie, her chin trembling.

'I'm sorry,' said Annie.

Rae nodded. Perhaps she'd already known. She pulled the sides of the jacket around herself.

The sky began to lighten. Annie sat on an upturned crate, watching as the insects streamed away through the broken greenhouse windows. She should take some of the nursery hives back to Hattenden back with her. She would ask Emily to help her as soon as she came back. Where was she? Annie looked around, searching through the chaos on the ground. Somebody was calling her name. She turned to see Emily with Scott and Victor, making their way through the strewn possessions and broken glass. Scott opened his arms to embrace her and she pushed him away. 'Everything hurts,' she said. Her throat was raw with pain. It hurt to swallow. The stings on her body throbbed; her shoulder and arm burned where Ravensworth had wrenched them back. The injury on Scott's face looked blotchy and infected. 'Are you okay?'

His eyes glittered in the early dawn light. 'We've got the drones,' he said.

It was over.

88

One week later

After Caitlin's funeral, Annie wandered from the church back towards the college hand in hand with Maria and Sophie. The rest of the villagers meandered after them. The Dining Hall was transformed. The boards had been taken off the windows to let in the golden sunlight, the floor was swept clean and the long wooden tables gleamed. Along the centre of the table, small posies of wildflowers were arranged in jam jars. Annie sat with Maria to one side of her and Sophie to the other. The bee stings were no longer painful and her bruises were fading. Her arms and shoulders would need more time, and the others had made sure she had nothing to do except rest. She looked over to the main doors where Victor and Iris were welcoming the villagers. Everyone carried a dish or a plate, vegetables fresh from their plots, pies – the pastry made from saved rations. Glass bowls of berries, sliced tomatoes dressed with garden herbs. Fresh eggs, cheese. And from somewhere the smell of sausages and bacon. It wouldn't be a very productive harvest – they had all known it and prepared themselves – but in sharing their small offerings the table was full. People gathered round the table to greet Annie, telling her how glad they were to have her back home safe and sound. Their voices were warm, their faces were concerned. Annie felt herself undeserving of their kindness.

They drank a toast to Annie, and Emily, and Victor and Iris. They drank to Maria and Sophie too (both girls smiled and Sophie dropped a bashful curtsey). Then Annie rose. 'To Matt,' she said. They raised their glasses. 'To Matt,' they chorused, and Annie lifted her glass in Emily's direction. They both blinked back tears. 'We all owe Matt a huge debt of gratitude,' said Annie. 'Because of his hard work and dedication our simfields were always a great success. Because of his ingenuity we have the promise of new bee colonies and hope for a future of good harvests,' said Annie. 'And we are forever grateful.' She thought again of what she'd found, hidden deep in the overgrown college grounds.

On Annie's return to Hattenden she had rested, and when she was not resting she had walked. In the simfields, during the few days they'd been away, the few vegetables which were managing to grow seemed to have doubled in size. She watched as Victor and Emily installed the hives they'd rescued from Ravensworth's greenhouses; they would use them to start new colonies. Scott assessed the state of the nanodrones; there seemed to be minimal damage, he said, hopeful that he could get them to work just as well as they had before. One afternoon he set the drones up in the college gardens and they all gathered: Victor with his arm around Iris, their daughters close by, fizzing with excitement. Annie crossed her fingers at her sides. Emily checked that the nanodrones were on standby. She gave Scott a thumbs-up and took a step back. Annie held her breath. The lead drone took off and, after a long pause, the rest of the swarm rose into the air. Sophie whooped and ran below the cloud, calling for Maria to join her. They followed the drones as Scott guided the lead to the rose arch and set it down on an upturned yellow flower, its petals fully open. The rest of the drones followed the lead and only then did Scott allow himself to sigh with relief. Annie watched him, turned to watch all of them. This little group to whom she owed everything, their faces suffused with the light of the late afternoon, delighted by the mechanical bees on the rambling roses. Technology and nature, together. It was an imperfect solution. But, for the moment, it would do. She turned and walked to the edge of the lawns, to where the garden had been left to grow wild. An overgrown path led between a grove of birch trees to a small wildflower meadow. When they were ready to start a new hive this would be an ideal place to put it, she thought, tucking the idea away to share with Emily later. She walked through the meadow, trailing her fingers over the long grasses and flowers, imagining it filled with hoverflies, butterflies and bees. Beyond the meadow she could see the silhouettes of outbuildings overgrown with ivy and bindweed. She had never come this way before. The path invited her farther in. The three lumpish buildings were greenhouses. Abandoned. She parted the delicate leaves of the bindweed to look inside the first one – the windowpane was cracked, part of it missing. Inside the greenhouse was crowded with plants. They grew in profusion, chaotically. At a certain point, at the beginning, they would have been seedlings, set in rows, but now they grew together, over and around each other, twisting and clambering, reaching towards the light. Leaves unfurled into every available space. Wild tendrils, wandering stems. There was such energy in the small space, it was almost tangible, a kind of electricity which kept the plants surging upwards. As she peered at the plants a bee flew in past her head, and she looked closer, waiting. Another bee flew in past her and then another flew out. *Apis mellifera.* The shape that was so familiar to her. She could hear them, in the heart of the greenhouse – it was alive with the thrum of bees.

We should keep some of the hives back, as insurance. Matt. She saw him again – half mischievous, half serious – as they'd waited for Emily to come back in the Land Rover. And she'd said no, because Attica would be taking them all. *Not if she can't find them all.*

Matt. He had done this. And… the bees had thrived. Maybe there were more. She would check the other greenhouses, and beyond, to see whether some of the new queens had set out to establish their own hives in this forgotten place.

89

Five years later

Annie lay on her back under an open sky. The breezes on her cheek were real. Long grasses brushed her bare arms; buttercups danced in her peripheral vision. Under the apple trees in Caitlin's favourite field, Scott and Emily were laying out the food for their daughter Daisy's third birthday party. Rations were gradually being relaxed, and from somewhere the ingredients had been found for a cake.

Victor and his family lived at Caitlin's farm now, and Victor was using the first generation of nanodrones to pollinate the crops along his old route.

Scott's patented drone design was in use all over the world to pollinate crops while the surviving insect species were monitored. He'd travelled back to Hattenden from London that morning after a meeting with various backers to discuss improvements to the design.

Alongside Annie's research in the simfields and out in the woodlands and farms around Hattenden, she had nearly finished writing her book. She hoped her data would support what she suspected – local insect populations were in recovery. She listened to Daisy's liquid laugh and Scott's deep chuckles as they played together.

Maria and Sophie were teenagers now. They sat together on a low tree branch, deep in conversation, their honey-gold hair gleaming in the sun. Sophie was still delicate – perhaps she always would be, but she was over the worst. She was out of danger. She caught Annie's eye and beckoned her over.

Annie would join them soon. But for just a moment longer she lay still, overwhelmed by it all: the sunshine and flowers and the buzz, the hum, the life of the bees.

Acknowledgements

Thank you to all the people who have helped me with this book. To the BFs, who have tirelessly supported me and cheered me on through the highs and lows. To Tricia Wastvedt and Emma Darwin for their feedback and expert guidance during the editing process. To Su and Marjorie, trusted readers of early drafts.

Above all, grateful thanks to those who are with me every step of the way: Mike, the first and most patient reader. And Ed and Harry, my lovely boys.